COLD POWDER VENGEANCE

BLACK POWDER BURNS HOT. REVENGE DOESN'T.

COLD POWDER VENGEANCE

BLACK POWDER BURNS HOT. REVENGE DOESN'T.

STONE JUSTICE BOOK ONE

D.N. SAMPLE

HAT CREEK

HAT CREEK

an imprint of
Roan & Weatherford Publishing Associates, LLC
Bentonville, Arkansas
www.roanweatherford.com

Library of Congress Cataloging-in-Publication Data
Names: Sample, D.N., author
Title: Cold Powder Vengeance/D.N. Sample | Stone Justice #1
Description: First Edition | Bentonville: Hat Creek, 2025.
Identifiers: LCCN: 2025943393 | IBSN: 979-8-89299-067-7 (trade paperback) | ISBN: 979-8-89299-068-4 (eBook)
Subjects: FICTION/Westerns | FICTION/Action & Adventure | FICTION/Historical
LC record available at: https://lccn.loc.gov.2025943393

Hat Creek trade paperback edition November, 2025

Editing by Anthony Wood & Don Money
Cover by Casey W. Cowan
Interior Design by John Bredesen

For Gerald and Leo:
My heroes.
The toughest men I've ever known. They dedicated their lives to
the women they loved and their families.

For Andrew:
I'm proud of the man you've become.

And always, for Sheryl:
My rock. My heart is forever yours.

ACKNOWLEDGEMENTS

THERE ARE SO many people to thank for their assistance with this project that I'm sure to miss some. For that I apologize right off the bat.

My many critique partners from both South Carolina and St Louis have spent countless hours helping me develop my style and voice as well as working out the kinks in both my writing and the story.

My team at Roan and Weatherford, who have made this project so much better than it was. Casey, who believed in me from the moment we met and hauled me out of a deep pit of despair more than once. Bob, may he rest in peace, for sharing his knowledge. Anthony for his kind words, encouragement, thoughtful suggestions, sound advice, and giving of himself as both friend and editor. Don for fixing my grammar—I never did meet a comma I didn't like. Dennis for making me look deeper for historical accuracy. Amy and her team who worked their tails off behind the scenes to make this the best book it could be.

There are many others who have offered encouragement, understanding, and support. St. Louis Anthony, my many clients who inquire regularly about my progress, Sally Ann from Michigan, to name just a few. I especially want to thank my boss, Anna, who's given me time off when necessary to pursue this dream.

My son Andrew—Oz to his friends—who put his blackbelt training to good use helping me choreograph the big fight scene.

Lastly, my Rock, my Love, Sheryl. You've believed in me every step of our forty plus years and without your tears of joy after reading the first draft—though you had me scared for a second, LOL—support, sometimes not so gentle prodding, and loving encouragement, I would never have completed this book.

CHAPTER 1

HAMMERING LOCOMOTIVE PISTONS threatened to burst through Stone's skull. Boots pounded—running. A familiar popping pressed through the murk of his consciousness. He should know the sound. But what? Something… from long ago.

He lay still, fighting to open his eyes. The forces demanding the return to unconsciousness battled against his will to regain awareness. Stone won. Slits at first. Light stabbed white-hot pokers deep into his head. His lips threatened to call out. Instead, he clenched his jaw tighter—bit back whatever curses came to his lips. Sally hated it when he cursed.

Sally! Where was she? He should remember this.

That popping again. And again. Muffled, as if heard from underwater. Bees buzzed in his ears. His head throbbed. Had to think. Stone tried. Where was he?

Home?

Eyes again squeezed tight. He gnashed his teeth. Think damn it.

Yes—home. Stone shook his head to clear the cobwebs. Lightning exploded behind his eyes and the tang of copper coated his tongue. His hand grazed the knot at his temple. Wet. Sticky.

Blood.

A tentative prod at his nose drew a wince.

A hole burned through the haze like a single, focused ray of morning sunlight drilling a solitary opening in the early mists. Stone's eyes snapped open. "Sally!" Rapid breaths came in ragged gulps. "Where?" The snarl ripped from his throat. Stone rolled, lunged to his feet, eyes seeking her.

His head swam. The insistent buzz swelled in his ears.

A crumpled heap sprawled in pooled blood. So much blood. Blinking did little to clear his eyes.

No!

His legs buckled, dumping him back to the floor. Bile burned his throat.

On hands and knees, he clawed toward Sally. Pain knifed up his arm. It collapsed under him—face and shoulders smashed into the plank floor. Agony screamed and his mind threatened to retreat back to the darkness.

Not again. Not this time. He shifted—supported his weight with just his left arm. Blood trickled down the other arm.

He dragged himself forward. A hard swallow battled the tide rising in this throat.

The familiar noise again. Closer.

Memory nudged forward but at the edge of remembrance. Just out of reach.

More pounding—boots on wood. Every footfall a gong reverberating through his skull. Spurs jingled. Close.

And that sound again. Staccato pops.

The fog evaporated into a flood from a different lifetime. Memories launched themselves at him like demons attacking a lost soul. Stone's head snapped up, eyes wide.

The door to the house crashed open, and a bullet whined past his ear. He dove aside. A toppled chair offered scant cover, but it was there—it would have to do... for now.

"Stone. Get down. Get down you damned fool." Howard Willis

slammed the door shut behind him. His large, powerful body contorted to fit under the nearby window as a fusillade of rifle fire smashed into the door and frame where he had been only a moment before. Breathing heavily, Howard flipped open the loading gate of his Colt Peacemaker and worked the ejector rod. Five empty shell cases dropped to the floor—individual pings toned as each struck the wood planks in quick succession. The big man plucked fresh shells from the gun belt buckled around his waist.

As he thumbed them into the cylinder, he turned and looked at Stone. "You okay? Look like hell." The sixth shell slipped into place—no empty chamber this time. A glance, no more than a quick half-rise, and he ducked back behind the wall. This time he gave Stone a longer look. "You're bleeding." He pointed to his own temple, then his arm. "Looks bad. Gonna need Doc Brady—if we get out of this alive." He turned back to the window and lifted himself enough to glance through it.

From behind the chair, Stone stared at the young man.

Bracing himself, Stone gingerly touched his head again. He refused to wince. Let the pain confirm he was still alive. The goose egg had grown more in the moments since the last check. Blood dripped into his eye.

"What's happening?" Stone's sharp tone forced Howard to make eye contact. Other questions came to mind, like "Where'd you come from?" or "Who's shooting at us?"—but "what's happening" was the only one he could focus on.

Howard's large brown eyes seemed to want to hold Stone's stare but instead turned away. Only nineteen and big as a prize bull, yet he lacked the steel that life and hardship forged in a man.

"I was just out riding. Left my horse yonder when I heard a gunshot." A thick finger pointed vaguely past Stone toward the south side of the house. "About then, three strangers come tearing off your porch. Started shooting as soon as they saw me. I shot back, but they were too far away. Left my rifle with the horse." He looked past the homesteader and nodded toward....

Stone refused to think about what—who—Howard indicated.

"Is she...?" Howard dropped his eyes toward the floor at his feet.

Stone ignored the question. Half stumbling, half crawling, he took position behind Howard. Careful to expose as little as possible, he eased his head up enough to peek out the window. Three men on horseback were just topping the rise beyond the barn. Seven hundred yards to the ridgeline—too far for his Henry hung by the front door.

Distance blended most of the details into indistinction, but one stood out—the man riding one of the roans appeared noticeably shorter than his companions.

The crack of a single shot echoed across the open hillside.

Howard and Stone ducked behind the window frame. They waited a few seconds. When no more gunfire followed, they rose again. The strangers were gone.

"I didn't see who fired that last shot. You?"

Stone ignored the question and moved toward the door. "There's someone on the ridge covering their retreat." He pulled the Henry from brackets he'd built to hold it. Big letters—"U.S."—were still faintly visible on the well-worn stock.

"That old thing even loaded?"

Stone looked at him. "Gun that ain't loaded ain't much use." With a jerk, he threw open the door, banging it hard against the wall. In a low crouch, he rushed through the open doorway onto the porch and took a position behind a thick support post. Standing sideways, he swept his practiced gaze over the ridge, long forgotten habits wrenched by need to the fore as if from just yesterday.

One minute passed. Howard came to stand behind another post. He opened his mouth as if to speak, but a glare from Stone discouraged the thought. Two more minutes. Nothing stirred on the ridgeline. Stone remained still. Watching. Waiting. The ugly scar along his left jawline itched—a memento of another time, another place. Luck had favored him that day. Taught him the virtue of patience. The scar itched whenever he needed reminding.

Howard shifted his weight, but another glance from Stone stilled him.

Minutes passed. Five. Ten. At last, he was confident they were gone. Stone turned back to the house. Hesitated.

"I'm going back to town to fetch Doc Brady and the sheriff. You okay alone?"

Stone nodded once but said nothing. Howard descended the stairs and disappeared around a corner of the house.

When he heard the rapid beat of hooves on hard earth, Stone hurried back to.... He forced himself to think it. To Sally. He inched nearer.

She was dead. He knew it—had known it the moment he first saw her, when he had stepped through the doorway coming in from the barn. His past held too many battlefields, too many dead. He knew.

He knelt beside her and reached out. With the awkward tenderness of a man more familiar with rough work, Stone drew her body to him and cradled her in his arms. Her best summer dress—now soaked in blood. She'd been waiting for him. They were to go to town that afternoon. Should have already been gone, except he'd decided to plow a few more rows.

He'd been so sure he'd get the rough side of her tongue for taking so long putting up the team. Not that she ever really scolded him. She was too sweet, too forgiving. Moisture gathered in his eyes. "I'm sorry, Sally. So sorry. Should a come in earlier."

The dam burst and sobs racked his body.

For how long, he didn't know. Tears that wouldn't stop soaked his shirt front until the sobs grew to howls, followed by quiet weeps, until there were no more tears. He held Sally until he passed out.

CHAPTER 2

VICTOR "FRANKIE" FRANKIEWICZ stopped pacing to roll another cigarette. He stood by his chestnut mare while he dug the makings from his vest pocket. Three butts littered the ground around the horse. With the quick flick of his fingers, he sent the match flying.

Frankie resumed his pacing, following the path he'd already worn in the ankle-high prairie grass. His left leg dragged along the ground—a mining accident in his youth left him with a permanent limp and kept him out of the army during the war. As he swung around, his bad leg caught in some low scrub brush and wrenched his knee. "Ouch. God durned, that hurt. Damned leg." His face contorted into a series of squints and grimaces as if the right expression would ease the pain. When the ache subsided, he resumed pacing.

One of the pack mules brayed and swished its tail at a congregation of flies gnawing its flanks.

Sweat dripped from Frankie's nose, and he swiped at it with his kerchief. "What's taking those coffee boilers so long?" Neither the glance, nor his muttering did anything to make his companions appear from over the ridge. "Probably met some coyote-faced granger's wife and started jawin' with her like she was some bar maid."

He rolled another cigarette and lit it.

A few minutes later yet another smoke followed the first four.

Stooping low, he looked straight at one of the mules. "How long's it take to git di-rections?"

Large, sad brown eyes returned the stare, and the mule flicked an ear, but said nothing.

"Ouch." The cigarette, burned to a nub, dropped and Frankie shook his fingers. The makings in his pocket were almost gone, so he returned to his mare. As he reached into his saddlebag, a volley of gunfire broke the silence.

"Tarnation, what've them boys got into?" Frankie touched the saddle scabbard, paused, and blinked before grabbing his Winchester—the new repeater '73 some shopkeeper in Pittsburgh had talked him into. The lump growing deep in his throat refused to be swallowed. He was no coward—Lord knew it took courage to crawl around in dark coal mines miles underground—but this was different. He'd never been shot at or even fired a gun. A vision of himself bleeding out flashed across his mind as he limped up the slope as fast as he could drag his bum leg behind him.

Frankie's heart pounded through his chest. As he neared the crest, his toe struck a rock, sending him into a headfirst tumble—an awkward parody of a dive. He landed hard and the wind blew from lungs already taxed by the rush up the hill. Frankie couldn't breathe. Seconds felt like minutes while he fought to regain his breath.

More gunfire.

As if shocked by the shooting, his lungs opened, and he gasped air—fresh, wonderful, air.

Using his elbows, Frankie dragged himself the final few feet to peer over the edge.

Both hands grasped his rifle, one on the barrel grip and one under the breach, index finger on the trigger. Ten knuckles turned white. His entire body shook. How did this gun work?

Sweat stung his eyes, blinding him. The back of his hand wiped his brow, clearing his vision—wishing he hadn't, even as his eyes were still widening.

Rifles held low to their sides, ready for use, his three companions charged fast toward the ridge as if the Devil himself gave chase—and right at him. Frankie's brows rose. Hooves flashed right in front of him, and he buried his face in the ground. Clods of earth pelted him. When Frankie lifted his head, Shorty's roan mare was less than five feet from him bearing down hard on him. Frankie's eyes stretched to their limit.

The roan leaped. Frankie ducked his head again and rolled to his left. Slashing hooves tugged at his hair, missing his head by mere inches.

However, one of the roan's rear hooves clipped the rifle as the horse passed over Frankie. The Winchester, Frankie's finger still jammed against the trigger, was ripped from his death-like grip.

The rifle went off.

Cutting a deep crease across the stubbled flesh of Curly's chin, the bullet whizzed past him. Meanwhile, the weapon rose into the air, spinning in lopsided arcs. Frankie watched it descend. The stock crashed into the rocky ground with a splintering crack that elicited a wince from him, the pain as real as if he had been shot himself.

Blood poured through the fingers Curly had pressed to his chin. "You danged fool. Didn't anyone ever teach you how to hold a gun? You darn near got me killed, and your—"

"Never mind that." Shorty glanced over his shoulder toward the house they'd just left, then turned back to his companions. "We need to skedaddle." He shot another look behind them. "Fast." Shorty's nasal tone grew more pronounced with each word. "They's sure to be ridin' after us."

"What happened?" Frankie asked. "What did you three go and do?"

Shorty's eyes narrowed. His chin rose and jaw thrust forward, long bushy beard lifting off his puffed chest, the tip of his bent nose pointed off to his right. "We ain't done nothin'."

Frankie avoided Shorty's glare. His heart was still pounding hard, and he couldn't think straight. *What did they do? People don't just start shooting for no reason, do they? What do I really know about these men? What've I got myself into?*

CHAPTER 3

STONE AWOKE TO a low buzzing. Ringing still filled his ears, but this was different. Voices. He forced his eyes open. Doc Brady and Marshal Burke had arrived.

"He's lost a fair bit of blood, probably has a concussion, and that hole in his arm needs stitches—fortunately the bullet went through cleanly. Just missed the brachial artery—could have been much worse. Take him to my place. I'll watch him for the next few days."

Stone cringed inside his mind. Doc Brady was a tough old veteran of a couple wars and expected to be obeyed. He'd demand Stone stay abed until told otherwise.

Marshal Clement Burke rubbed a hand from above his eyes to the back of his head, seeming to push back hair that no longer existed. In fact, the only hair he still possessed was a thin reddish-brown band stretching from ear to ear around the back of his head. "Fine, Doc. Howard's gittin' Stone's wagon hitched up so he and a couple of the boys can take him in."

Burke had once been an adequate lawman despite the yellow streak running down his spine—Stockman hadn't been the kind of place to attract a bad element. At least until gold fever had brought all manner of men to the Dakota Territory. Stockman sat right on the road dreamers took to get to the newly discovered gold in Deadwood.

"Know how Sally died, yet?" The marshal's casual tone, like query-ing as to the weather, instead of the first murder in Stockman's histo-ry—and of a woman at that—failed to hide its slight tremble.

"I won't know for sure until I get her on my table, but at first glance it looks like she was strangled." Doc Brady's voice was thick, and he paused to clear his throat. After an accident five years earlier resulted in a miscarriage, dashing any hopes of children of her own, Sally had begun assisting Doc Brady with childbirths and other pro-cedures. They'd grown close—she was like the daughter the old wid-ower never had. "Whoever it was, looks like they intended to molest her, but from the scuffs and bruises on her knuckles, seems she fought back. Struck her pretty hard—you can see the bruise on her jaw—her head hit the chair and tore open her scalp, accounting for most of the blood, but it didn't kill her. You can see the marks where big, strong hands crushed her larynx. She likely died slow, unable to breathe."

Stone closed his eyes, not making a sound, absorbing the con-versation. Anger surged in him. Sally had been so beautiful and hap-py. All she ever wanted in life was a family and a home. She sure as hell didn't deserve this. He suppressed the snarl that rose unbidden. The killer didn't know it yet, but he'd dug his grave the moment he laid hands on Sally—Stone would make sure of that—no matter who tried to stop him.

"Well, guess I better git back to town and wire the U.S. mar-shal. He'll have to form a posse, I reckon. When Stone wakes, I need to talk to him."

"Might be a while—"

Stone tried to stand. "I'm awake." By the time he made it to his feet, his legs trembled like a newborn colt's. He fell back against the table, grabbed at it, but missed, instead dropping to the floor.

The old physician hurried to him. Hunched back and stooped shoulders gave him a shuffling gait. A muted smile touched his eyes in spite of the obvious pain walking caused him. "Rest easy there, Judiah.

Stay down." He was the only one who used his given name. Sally had called him Judd, but he was just Stone to everyone else.

Doc Brady stretched his arms out, hands palms down, as if to keep Stone on the ground. "The boys'll be around soon—they'll load you into the wagon and take you to my office." A creased and mottled hand settled on Stone's shoulder, adding emphasis to his words.

From his spot on the floor, Stone gazed at the weathered old man and hoped the doctor read the gratitude he felt but wouldn't take the time to express. Instead, he turned to Burke—he couldn't bring himself to think of the man as Marshal Burke. "They're getting away. Could take the U.S. marshal a week or more to get here. We can't wait that long."

"I know how you feel—"

Stone glowered at the lawman. "You know how I feel? Was your wife just murdered?" He clenched his jaw to bite back another angry retort.

"Look here. Price's gotta handle this. I ain't got the authority to take a posse out. 'Sides, we know where they're headin'."

"I'm not waiting." Stone's voice grew colder than a Dakota winter. "With you or without you, Burke."

"Judiah, you need—"

"Now see here. You—"

Doc Brady turned to Burke with a glare that would melt an icy lake. Burke tried to meet it, but after a brief stare-down, he lowered his gaze and used one foot to toe dirt on the floor. Doc softened his expression as he returned his attention to Stone.

"Son, you need rest. I'll stitch you up, but it'll take weeks to heal, assuming the wound stays free of infection. Let the law handle Sally's murderers. Marshal Price is a man to ride the river with—he'll find them and bring them in."

Stone stared pensively at the physician. Left arm against the table leg behind him, he once again struggled to push himself up. Neither watcher interfered. After what seemed like several minutes but was likely only ten seconds, he managed to stand. His head swam and legs shook like an old man's hand, threatening to dump him back on the floor. He touched the table lightly and gritted his teeth, willing obedience from his rebel body.

Raised eyebrows greeted his dubious success. He wasn't fooling either man or himself. But he'd be off as soon as he could stand. Come hell or high water, he wasn't waiting for Price or his damned posse.

"Marshal—"

"Now jess you see here, Stone." Burke cut him off, one thick thumb stuck through a suspender strap, while a pudgy index finger poked the air to emphasize his point. "I'll not have you goin' out playin' vigilante. You leave this here alone and let the U.S. marshal handle it."

"Clem—"

"I'll arrest you if you don't do as I say, farmer." The lawman hitched his pants up over a paunch that spoke of too many years behind a desk. "Now, set down till the wagon gits here. You ain't goin' after 'em. Period."

Stone tensed, his nostrils flared and his eyes hardened. Burke was a lazy, bumbling fool who'd rather drink beer or sit behind his desk than do his job. He had no right to command anyone, let alone a former major in the Army of the Potomac. Still, Stone couldn't hunt from behind bars. One deep breath followed another.

"Fine, Marshal." Disgust dripped from the words and Stone sucked in another long draw of air and forced himself to release it slowly. "I'll go with Doc and wait for Price to blow in."

Burke harrumphed as he stomped out the door. "Durn right he'll wait. I told him to, didn't—" The slam of the door closing cut off whatever else the marshal was muttering about.

Doc Brady gave Stone a speculative look. He remained quiet, but his steady gaze and crinkled forehead opened his thoughts as clearly as the headline of an advertising bill.

"Son... Judiah." The physician shot a furtive glance at the door, as if it might open any second. After a few moments, he returned his attention to Stone. "After two wars and forty years in practice, I'm adept at reading people. Men like you, most times peace-loving, but tough as old shoe leather when forced to fight, do what needs doing just because it needs doing." He paused and offered another glance at the door.

"I can't keep you from going after Sally's killers, and personally, I'm not sure I want to." He paused to give Stone a hard stare. "Promise me this. Promise you'll allow me to patch you up before leaving. At least wait until tomorrow. A night's rest will do you a world of good, and you'll want to see to Sally's burial too. Perhaps by then we'll have news of Marshal Price's arrival."

Stone stood silent for a long time. Thoughts of Sally, the life they'd made for themselves out of the low hills and hard soil of the eastern Dakota Territory, filled his mind. He glanced at her body. A white sheet covered her now, drying, congealed blood visible at the edges. Doc Brady would have thought of that. Burke was a waste of good breathing air. Howard had been in too much of a hurry to fetch the doctor and marshal to cover her. Mentally shaking himself out of his reverie, he caught the doc's eye and nodded his assent.

"You promise?" Doc's eyebrows accentuated the question. "I can always get Burke to lock you up. In your current state you couldn't do much about it."

"All right. I promise." He grimaced. Doc had forced him to do it. He was too honorable to break his word, but damn it, he'd made a promise to Sally too. "One day."

———

STONE'S EYES NARROWED as he watched Burke dismount from his borrowed mare and tie her to the granite hitching post in front of Doc Brady's house. The iron-frame bed Stone lay in afforded him a view of the street through the tall front window of Doc Brady's modest two-story Greek revival home. Like most frontier doctors, the office and patient bedroom were in the front of the house.

Burke bent slightly at the waist, gripping his lower back. He swung open the white picket gate that matched the doctor's perfect white picket fence. Without closing it behind him, he entered the flower-lined path from the street that crossed the small, well-manicured lawn, ending at the deep porch. At the single granite step, Burke paused for a second before gripping the handrail and hauling himself to the porch. His groan was loud enough that Stone could hear it through the open window.

Moments later the front door squeaked open without so much as a courtesy knock. Boots clomped on the wood floor and Marshal Burke appeared at the doorway to the patient bedroom Stone occupied.

Burke hobbled through the door and plopped into the oak rocker in the corner of the room. The chair creaked and strained to contain the lawman. "Heard back from Marshal Price. Be here four days from now."

Stone stared at him. "Four days?"

"What he said. In the meantime, says for you to jess set still and rest—wants to talk to you when he gits here."

"And you're not going to form a posse yourself?" The thick layer of annoyance in his own voice should have bothered Stone, but he just couldn't bring himself to care about Burke's feelings.

"No. I already—"

"Burke, you know Larson would go. So would Emmitt Jackson—he fought in one of the negro units. A dozen men would accompany you. Good men. But they need you to lead them. Damn it, you can't just wait for Price."

"I've been over this with you. Ain't got the authority to arrest anyone outside of town. Besides, my lumbago's actin' up. It's killin' me jess from ridin' out to your place earlier today."

Stone closed his eyes and took a deep breath. He blew it out to a silent ten count. It did nothing to relieve the tension in his shoulders, but it settled his anger to a simmer. Burke wasn't fooling him. While what the lawman said was technically true, no court would challenge his right to hunt down murderers and bring them back to face justice. No, the real truth was that Burke was both lazy and a coward. Had Charles Willis, Howard's father, been in this situation, a posse would already be assembled and on the road. Short of that, no one could make him stick his neck out.

"Fine, Burke." Bitterness like burnt coffee was thick in his voice. "Reverend Goodman is going to bury Sally tomorrow afternoon out at my homestead. Doc said with a little rest tonight I should be fine in the morning, except for my arm."

Burke glanced around. "Where is Doc?"

"Wouldn't let me go down to the saloon to get supper. Said he meant for me to lie still until morning, so he's bringing it to me. Be back in a few minutes if you need to see him."

"Nope. Jess stopped to pass along Price's message. See ya tomorrow." Burke heaved himself out of the chair with a loud moan. Stone almost swore the chair echoed the sentiment.

Stone shook his head as he watched out the window while the marshal limped down the path toward his mare. "If Burke thinks I'm going to lie around and wait for United States Marshal Zebulon Price, he's addle-headed. I promised Doc one day, and I'll keep my promise. But as soon as the preacher has Sally buried, I'm going after the bastards."

Stone's lip curled into a snarl. "And God help them when I find them."

CHAPTER 4

A LOUSY PAIR of fives. Quince Martin, oblivious to the others at his table, held his cards in front of his eyes, so close to his face that his cheroot threatened to singe their bottom edges. The teamster was losing and in a sour mood, though his ill-temper had nothing to do with the game—he was used to bad cards and losing. A chip dangled from his gnarled fingers and then dropped. It clinked against those already in the center pot.

A cheer carried from the bar. *Damn kids.* Quince scrubbed the thick stubble on his chin.

Stinky Ames banged out a raucous ditty on a beat-up Webber upright. Wrong notes abounded and the song was as unrecognizable as his stepmother's stew—either the instrument was out of tune or Stinky couldn't play. Quince wasn't sure which. No one ever seemed to care.

Laughs and shouts rose from the bar behind him, but Quince ignored the disruption. "Come on, Em. Bets to you." He clenched the mauled end of his cigar between stained teeth. A cloud of blue smoke rose from the stogie to join the thick haze floating below the pressed tin ceiling of the Wagon Wheel Saloon.

He got no response.

Quince lowered his hand. Four neat piles of cards lay face down. His companions contemplated the revelry across the room.

A dozen young men, all from Stockman or the surrounding farms, gathered in a tight bunch at the bar. Laughter and back slaps came from the group. A single head protruded from the center like a copula.

Quince strained to hear what the youths were saying.

"What was—"

"You saved his li—"

"Are you riding with the—"

Howard Willis towered over the crowd around him. He turned his back to the bar to face his venerators. A smile cracked his serious facade, and he thrust a mug of beer above his head.

"Damn straight I'm going with the posse. Gotta finish what I started today. Wish I had brought my rifle—I'd a bagged me one or two this afternoon. But we'll bring Sally's killers back, I can promise you that. Dad's even putting up a reward. Five hundred dollars apiece." He turned to his left and rang the spittoon with a direct hit. "Dead or alive."

The announcement elicited more cheers.

Quince stared from the corner. *Fool kids. Ever-one knowed about the re-ward, a'ready. Charles jest announced it an hour 'go. Seemed like the entire town turned out to hear that flannel mouth.*

The teamster growled. "Let's play."

The others around the table ignored him.

The crowd of young men bought rounds and listened as Howard recounted the events and his heroic efforts to drive off the murderers and protect the Stones. They all seemed to listen to the giant in rapt attention—likely none of them had ever been in a gunfight. Cheers interrupted his dramatic narrative at the appropriate points.

Quince puffed furiously on his cigar—smoke billowed like the dark clouds from a locomotive.

"Back to the game. Howard's done told that story three times in the last hour."

"Raise." Emmitt Jackson tossed a pair of chips into the center. He was lean and wiry, but with the powerful shoulders and massive arms of those in his trade. Black men had drifted west after the war with hopes of better lives. Emmitt was no different. He'd brought his wife and infant son along with the blacksmithing skills honed on a plantation somewhere and found a small town that needed them—the farther north the better. He cast a quick glance at the group at the bar and then spoke softly. "What's up with Howard? Ain't like him to do for someone else. Especially Stone 'n Sally. The Willises never held no truck with them before."

"Does make a body wonder, don't it?" Angus Hoeckerman, tall and wiry, owned the dry goods store in town. He folded his cards and dropped the stack on the table.

The comment drew a single nod from Quince. "Ol' man Muehler's powerful worried. Word around the freighting company is the railroad's a coming through all the way to Fort Pierre." *An' I'll be out of a job.*

Hiram Thorpe picked his head up from his hand and added a couple chips to the growing pile. Sawdust from his lumber mill dusted his thinning brown hair. "Call." Ash from his cigarette also dropped on the chips. "Might explain why Willis is buying land. Bought out Ahlgren and Niequist two weeks back, and I hear he's talking to Flater about his."

Emmitt squinted at Hiram. "Flater's spread's the next place past Stone's, ain't it?"

Hiram's eyebrows rose as he nodded. "Yup. Shore is. Share homestead markers on the north side of Stone's."

"You don't think Willis has anything to do with these miners murdering Sally, do you?" Isaac Metterman scratched his gray-brown beard—the only hair on his head. Every Thursday for the last three years his wife had manned their mercantile alone so he could join this game. "I can't see it, my own self."

"Nawww. Howard wouldn't a stopped 'em if his pa was involved." Quince flipped a chip into the middle. "Call."

"Pair a threes." Hiram showed his hand.

Quince fanned his cards out face up on the table. "Fives. Ace high."

A frown creased Emmitt's face. "Twos."

Quince smiled for the first time that night. "'Bout time my luck turned." His arm snaked around the pot, only to be stopped by a scarred black hand settling on his wrist. The look he shot Emmitt would've blistered tar paper. Emmitt, face a blank mask, flipped his cards. Four deuces stared at Quince. "Damn."

Emmitt offered him a wide, yellow-toothed smile.

While at the bar the celebration went on.

———————

A COOL HAND pressed against his forehead. Stone forced his eyes open. Doc Brady leaned over him, the oil lamp's glow revealing the concern etched in his wrinkled face.

"Go back to sleep, Son."

"I wasn't sleeping. Thinking."

"You have a funny way of thinking then. Your snores had the house shaking like it'd been thundering outside." The old man offered a grin at his own joke, but no mirth reflected in his piercing greyish blue eyes—eyes that seemed to penetrate the emotional wall that Sally had spent a decade trying to pull down brick by brick. Her murder had rebuilt it in an instant, higher, thicker, stronger than before. Yet Doc's gaze bared his most intimate secrets as surely as if Stone proclaimed them on parade day through a speaking trumpet.

Stone smiled. Forced the smile, really. And only for a second. There was no room for joy in a soul gorging on anger and bitterness. Why? Sally hadn't deserved to die. Had done nothing to anyone except be kind and caring. Yet, someone had broken into the home they shared and stole her life from her.

And from him.

Stone hammered his leg with his fist. Once, twice, more until he lost count. Doc Brady laid a hand on his wrist. Despite the gentleness of the touch, the firm grip held the fist in place against his thigh despite Stone's efforts to wrench it away.

When he gave up, Stone took a pair of long deep breaths. Calm returned, at least for the moment. He turned his face away from Doc as moisture formed in his eyes.

Doc Brady said nothing but released his grip and patted Stone's hand, before touching his stethoscope to Stone's chest. The metallic iciness elicited no response. No shiver. No gooseflesh. No sudden inhalation. His body may as well have been as dead as he felt.

The stillness of the moment, while Doc listened for whatever it was physicians listened for, grew oppressive, yet silence seemed preferable.

After moving the stethoscope to numerous places about the patient's chest, poking and prodding for lord only knew what, he spoke, his voice low but resolute. "You'll heal just fine, but you need rest." A pause lingered. There was that penetrating gaze again. "Lots of rest."

The obvious implication drew no response from Stone. His mind went elsewhere. Strong fingers dug into the bed sheet and dragged the edge from under the mattress and gathered it into his tightening fist. Through a clenched jaw he said, "What can you tell me about Sally's death? Was she... you know?"

Doc Brady shook his head and patted Stone's shoulder. "No. Not violated." He swallowed and his expression changed. Grew pensive, as if considering how much to say.

Stone's death grip on the fabric loosened, though he continued to hold it bunched in his curled fist. At least she'd not been forced to endure that. "How *did* she die, then?"

Doc offered a sympathetic look. "Sure you want to know?" A single emphatic nod answered the question and urged him forward. His tone changed, grew cold, void of emotion—clinical. This couldn't be easy for him either. "She lost a lot of blood from hitting her head on the table, but that isn't what killed her. Someone strangled her."

"Strangled? Heard you say that at the house, but I was just waking up. Thought maybe I'd misunderstood."

"No misunderstanding."

"Why would they need to strangle her? Sally was a strong woman, but she couldn't have fought off three men."

"Looked like maybe she'd been pushed or wrenched herself away from an attacker, lost her balance and fell, striking the corner of the table. She'd have started bleeding heavily almost immediately. Probably lost consciousness too. Maybe the man got angry or scared. Hard to say what goes through someone's mind at a moment like that." Doc shrugged. "What I do know is whoever did it had big, strong hands. The marks on her neck were clear."

Stone's thoughts turned to those moments. He imagined three men grabbing at her, pushing her from one to another. She fought and twisted away from one of the men but tripped with the effort. Did she call out for Stone as she fell? A lump grew in his throat.

"It wasn't your fault."

"If I'd come in from plowing when I'd told her I would, instead of having to get just two more rows done, she'd still be alive."

"Maybe. Or more likely you'd both be dead."

"Or maybe we'd have been gone when they came by."

"You can't blame yourself. The only person to blame is the one, or ones, who murdered her." Doc pointed a gnarled finger at him. "You were lucky, you know."

Stone turned his gaze away from Doc Brady and stared at the ceiling.

"Not that you feel lucky. I understand. But you could've died today too. That slug went clean through. One inch." Doc lifted his hand, thumb and index fingers held an inch apart. He paused until Stone turned his head to look at him again. "One inch higher the bone is broken, likely shattered. How many soldiers did you know whose arms were broken by a bullet, never to work right again?" Doc Brady's brows lifted enough to emphasize his point, but he didn't wait for an answer that Stone wasn't inclined to offer anyway. "One inch lower—the artery is severed, and you'd have bled out in less than two minutes."

Doc dropped his hand and took a deep breath. "As it is, a few weeks, and you'll be healing nicely. A month should see you good as new."

Stone snarled. "Maybe once those bastards are dead it'll be different, but right now I don't feel it." Stone locked eyes with the old man, the anger still tasted bitter in his mouth. The silence hung for a few seconds. His glare dared the old man to challenge him.

Gentle, loving eyes matched his stare, refusing to turn away. At last, Stone lifted his good arm and touched the knot on his head, now covered by bandages. When he spoke, his voice was thick. "One of them clocked me good. Maybe the same one shot me. How'd he miss? That close and all he does is shoot me in the arm? Don't make sense. Had to be trying to kill me. Why not finish the job? Why stop with one shot? Maybe in some way, Howard saved me. Heard him coming and just ran?"

"Doesn't make sense to me either. It wasn't a large hole. Small caliber. Maybe a single shot weapon."

"But all three were carrying repeating rifles. What'd Howard say? You remember?"

"I wasn't paying attention to him out at your place. Him or Burke, either one. When I took supper dishes back down to the Wagon Wheel, he was there talking about it, but he and his friends were already all liquored up."

Doc opened his mouth as if to say more, but then shook his head and turned for the lamp. "Rest now. Holler if you need anything. I'll be in the next room." He blew out the lamp and left Stone alone in the dark with his thoughts.

CHAPTER 5

MOTHER NATURE MOURNED with Stone. Charcoal gray clouds hung heavy across the sky. No buzz of hummingbird wings. No cicada chirps. No flutter of sparrows darting about. No crow caws or meadowlark's song.

A pair of local men turned the final shovelfuls of dirt onto Sally's grave. They bent to replace the squares of grass. On the ground lay the whitewashed wooden cross another member of the community had built, the long end sharpened. Eventually Stone would replace it with a granite marker, but it would do for now.

The last of the carriages disappeared over the ridge on their way back to Stockman. There had been the obligatory handshakes—awkward for more than just the use of off hands—and mumbled regrets from the men. They had tried to hide behind the masks of warmth and sincerity, but beneath their condolences both relief and self-loathing were evident. Salved that it had been his Sally instead of their own wives or daughters—mortified for thinking such thoughts.

The women had touched him gently on his good shoulder and whispered heartfelt sympathies or offered him a small hug. None seemed able to bring themselves to make eye contact. Black lace veils could not hide the fear on their faces. It could have happened to any one of them. It still could. This was the frontier.

One by one they had approached and one by one they had left to return to their farms, their homes, and their businesses—back to their everyday lives. Only Doc Brady remained. He stood to one side. Silent. Watching. Waiting.

The white cross finally in place, Stone approached the burial crew and pressed a gold half-eagle into each man's hand. He remained at the head of the grave while they retreated. He had chosen a knoll that overlooked the creek that ran near their house. The water bubbled over a series of rocks for a hundred feet before it tumbled over a shelf no higher than a man's waist. It pooled at the bottom where a narrow grove of cottonwoods along the edge stretched their limbs over the basin to shade it during the heat of the day. Sally had loved this spot. Stone hoped the peacefulness of the location would comfort her spirit.

After several minutes, Stone finally walked toward the hoary physician.

"Doc, I...." Stone stopped and rubbed the back of his neck.

Both men stood, eyes downcast, for a long time. At last, Doc broke the silence.

"Son, take an old man's advice. Wait for Marshal Price." He reached his wrinkled hand to touch Stone's shoulder. The gentle contact spoke volumes to Stone. "Even if you catch them, you're in no shape to take on these murderers."

"Doc—"

"No, listen to me. Your body needs time to heal."

"Nothing's holding me back. I can still ride."

"How will you confront at least three men, maybe four or more? Have you thought about that?"

"I'll worry about that when the time comes." Stone grimaced and swept his gaze across the sky. "Look at those clouds rolling in. This storm'll wash out their sign. I can't—won't—lose their trail." Determination tinged with anger hardened his voice. "I'm one man—even injured I can move faster. A week, maybe less to catch up."

He turned back to Doc Brady. "But only if I leave today. Now. I'm not waiting for any posse."

Doc sighed. His grayish blue eyes glazed over and seemed to look past Stone, at something far away or long ago. Seconds passed, then minutes.

Stone waited.

At last, Doc spoke. "I've known many men like you in my life—men of action, full of grit and determination—tough, honest men, driven by principle—fighting for right regardless of the odds. That spirit will eventually tame this wild frontier." He turned his face up and locked eyes with Stone. "But it won't civilize it. Only one thing can do that." He paused. Took a breath as he cocked his head as if contemplating what he would say next. "I want to ask you a favor before you leave."

Stone's stomach clenched. He knew what was coming. Every muscle stiff, every breath labored and rapid, he stood for fifteen seconds that seemed fifteen minutes.

Doc said nothing.

The night had been a restless one for Stone, but it had been neither the pain in his arm, the ache in his head, nor even the constant buzz in his ear that made it such.

Doc continued to stare at Stone but said nothing.

Stone forced himself to meet the old man's steady gaze. His voice was thick as he answered. "Ask."

"When you find them, bring them back for trial. Don't take the law into your own hands. If not for me, do it for Sally. You know it's what she believed was right." His pause was followed by a quiet whisper. "Do it for yourself."

Stone turned away and stared at the western horizon—in the direction the men had ridden just yesterday. Images came to mind. Sally in the pool of blood. Those men escaping over the crest—escaping justice.

Winter in the Dakota Territory was frigid and brutal. On cold winter nights, debate or conversation was the only entertainment. He and Sally had debated this issue many times. As he had laid the previous evening, tossing and turning as much as his injured arm would allow, those many conversations replayed themselves unbidden and unwelcome. She believed in the rule-of-law, period, as the only way to bring civilization to the frontier. He countered that when the nearest legal authority could be days away, swift vigilante justice served the same purpose. Sally grew up listening to the stories of her Irish great grandparents, murdered by a mob in 1777 for daring to support the Revolution in a town of Tories. To her, vigilante meant nothing more than murder—not justice.

Whirling on his heel to face Doc Brady, Stone spoke through clenched teeth, his voice little more than a harsh whisper. "They don't deserve it." He paused again. Paced a short distance away and back several times before stopping in front of Doc again. "Damn it. I'll promise you something. The only promise I can make." His whisper turned to a snarl. "Those bastards will face justice—either the law's—or mine."

Doc nodded, sorrow bleeding onto his face from some pool deep within. He stretched out his arm and patted Stone on the back. "Then let's trust it'll be the law's."

Stone stared but said nothing.

When he turned back, Doc Brady shuffled toward his horse and buggy for the long ride back to Stockman. The road from town passed behind Stone's house, past Flater's spread and the few homesteads beyond before it melted into the prairie. It wasn't much of a road—more just parallel ruts worn into the hardened earth with a grassy ridge between. Like most such, it came to be because folks naturally took the easiest way between places. Over time a path was worn, which became a trail, and eventually a road.

Doc wheeled his chaise around the home. On the south side, he reappeared, his horse moving at a practiced clip down the rough road.

In less than a minute, he crested the low rolling hill and was swallowed by the valley beyond. Minutes later, he reappeared on the far
slope and then dropped over the next ridge and into the valley beyond.

Watching Doc ride away, Stone sensed the house he'd shared with
Sally all these years—felt it looming over him, a specter of their life
together. In every way that house represented who *they* were. They'd
labored and scrimped and saved and sweated to be able to build it. Just
the two of them—raised cash crops on land that demanded their blood
and toil before producing the first few meager morsels. Stone looked
at his hands, ran thumbs over rough calluses, more proof of his manhood than the scars of the too numerous battles fought, regardless of
the nobleness of the cause. The calluses represented the labor. The
house represented the fruit.

A gentle breeze touched his neck and reminded him of Sally,
whose hands, too, possessed the proof of their hardscrabble life together. But they'd been happy.

His sigh caught in his throat, and he daubed moisture from his
cheek while turning toward the house—their home. He'd not been
back inside since being carried out the day before. Arriving early for
the funeral, he'd instead opted to care for his animals, despite arrang-
ing for their care with the Flaters while he was gone—and making
arrangements in case he didn't make it back.

But now there was no other option. It was time to find
these bastards.

Stone searched the yard in front of his house, but all the activity
since the shoot-out had destroyed any sign left by the murderers. As
he turned back to the porch, a sickly-sweet odor assaulted him. He
squinted and crinkled his nose, even as his stomach threatened to re-
ject the morning's breakfast. Following his nose, he soon discovered
the source next to the porch steps—a half-dried pile of vomit.

He didn't remember being sick, but so much of the previous day's
events remained shrouded in fog.

His boots made the only sound as he climbed the stairs—a hollow thump on each wooden step. At the top, wounds to the siding from yesterday drew him. With his Bowie, he dug several slugs from the wood. He rolled the smashed projectiles around in his palm, unsure what he expected to find. He shook his head—just a distraction—a distraction from what he knew he must do. Anything to avoid walking inside. Somehow, until he went inside none of this was real. The body in the casket they'd just buried could have been anyone. He hadn't seen the body, had only the undertaker's word regarding the who. But once he confirmed she wasn't home, all hope died.

"Do it now. Or you might not ever do it." There was no one to hear except himself, but Stone needed the verbal encouragement, even if he had to provide it himself. Slipping the mutilated lumps of lead into his pocket, he quickly pushed open the front door, took a deep breath, and stepped through.

A fleeting thought tugged at the back of his brain as he crossed the threshold. It spun him around as if it had been a physical phenomenon. He wobbled—the door casing caught his weight, preventing his collapse. Outside, a dust devil swirled along the empty hitching rail where just an hour before so many horses had stomped and pawed. A crease formed in his brow while he tried to pry the thought loose from his subconscious.

Yesterday, just before discovering Sally, he'd been in the barn putting the team away and preparing the wagon for the trip to Stockman. Finished, he was almost to the barn door but hesitated while still in the shadows. A pause to examine the yard—almost as if he knew something had been amiss.

But why? What triggered it?

And what tickled at his brain now?

He stared at nothing. Seconds passed, then minutes. It niggled at him but would not come to mind. Stone pounded the doorframe with his good hand. He kicked the door, and it slammed shut. Stone's body quivered, his hands curled into fists, his chest heaved, his eyes clenched shut.

Deep breath after deep breath finally burned out the wave of rage, leaving him drenched in sweat, but also ready to face their home.

It was nothing large or fancy—a kitchen area to the left with a loft bedroom above, fireplace and sitting area to the right. Over the fireplace hung a long mantle, home to their entire collection of books.

Stone owned an even dozen—a large library by local standards— among them Plato's *The Republic*, *The Wealth of Nations* by Adam Smith, and a French language version of Sun Tzu's *The Art of War*. The latter reminded him of his mother every time he picked it up. The granddaughter of French farmers who left their native country following Napoleon's abdication, she had insisted her children learn to read, write, and speak French.

Nestled against the back wall was the dinner table and chairs where Stone had discovered Sally's body. Details, unnoticed yesterday, leapt at him—chairs strewn, shattered dishes from the shelf over the table, a tuft of blonde hair that still clung to the table corner where Sally's head struck. The fireplace shovel lay in the middle of the floor, its crumpled blade stained with dried and crusted blood.

His blood. Without thinking he fingered the bump on his head.

Near the fireplace a bloody boot print miraculously survived yesterday's commotion intact and still crisp. The heel was cut across its width at an unusual angle. Did it belong to Sally's murderer, or one of the men who'd helped him into Doc's buggy? He burned that detail into his memory, just in case. Blood stained the pine planks where he'd fallen after someone used his head to reshape the shovel. Once again, he used the Bowie to dig lead, this time, out of the floor. He hefted the metal in his hand. Not much to it. Mangled as it was, he learned little about the weapon used to shoot him other than it was probably a small caliber— maybe a Derringer or some other pocket gun. That confirmed what Doc Brady had said. The metal joined the other pieces in his pocket.

Minutes passed as he searched for more clues—anything that might help him piece it together. The constant buzz in his head made thinking difficult. Answers seemed ephemeral, floating within easy reach only to flit away and escape every attempt to grasp them. Worrying on them would not bring them any faster. Like the niggling earlier, they would come when they were ready.

Instead, Stone gathered his supplies. The Henry repeater still hung where it belonged, replaced by him or someone yesterday. Officer's field glasses from a lifetime ago joined dried goods, spare ammunition, and other supplies he'd need. Saddlebags, blanket roll, slicker, and packs formed a pile by the door.

The small kitchen area held a Ben Franklin stove and a cabinet he'd built from scrap lumber. In first one drawer, then the next, he looked for a little-used item he thought might come in handy. In the far back of the third drawer, he found the hunting knife his father had given him. Growing up near one of the Senaca Nation reservations in the western part of New York, hunting had been an important means of keeping a family fed, and he'd been taught from a young age to handle guns. More importantly, three of his closest friends had been members of the Senaca tribe and when they weren't wrestling or playing games, the boys had taught each other their traditional hunting and fishing methods.

The razor-sharp five-inch blade designed for gutting and skinning had a handle made from the antler of the first buck he'd taken. The memory brought a grim smile to his face. Less than a year later his father was dead, and the family moved to Erie to live with Ma's brother and sister-in-law.

At last, he turned to the stairs. Fourteen. Fourteen steps from floor to loft. Waiting at the top were the most intimate reminders in the most intimate place they'd shared. He swallowed hard, gripped the railing, and took the first step. Knowing what to expect at the top made the climb that much harder.

Warm air grew closer as he neared the loft. At the top the heat was stifling. Every breath seared his nostrils. Not in the literal sense, but the figurative. Memories of her. Signs of Sally filled the space. Atop the bed lay the quilt she'd spent all last summer sewing. Draped over it was her gray everyday dress. She'd have laid it out to change into when they returned from town yesterday.

In the corner, by the window, her most prized possession—a Singer treadle sewing machine. A wedding gift from his aunt and uncle, she had earned enough cash money with it over the years that last summer's locust swarm hadn't destroyed them as it had many other families. Most dirt farmers survived season to season on seed loans made by the local banks, their homesteads pledged against the paper. When the harvest came in, the proceeds paid off the loan and left enough to purchase the supplies the farmer couldn't raise or make himself. Year after year that cycle repeated itself, until the summer of '74 had brought the winged terrors. In a matter of hours, entire fields of cash crops were eaten to nothing, leaving dust in their wake. With their crops destroyed, many locals had been forced to forfeit their lands to Charles Willis. But thanks to Sally's sewing, they hadn't needed seed loans and were even able to plant a late crop after the swarm moved on.

Stone set his jaw, pushed aside thoughts of Sally, and knelt beside the bed they'd shared for a decade. From under the bed, he hauled a long-forgotten trunk. Little more than a crude, lidded box constructed of rough boards, it held the remnants of a life he wished he could forget. He released the leather strap and buckles and threw open the lid. Folded neatly on top, creased crisp and tight, was his Union officer's uniform. He tossed it aside where it landed in a disheveled heap. Under it was the one item Stone sought—his Colt Army Model revolver, still nestled in the holster he'd worn so long ago.

After the war, he'd packed it away and never expected to need it again. Easterners believed every western man wore a handgun of some sort, but that was the stuff of dime novels. In towns it wasn't unusual for a family to not own a firearm of any kind. If they did, a rifle was the most common choice, but even they were rare among townsmen.

Gun ownership on the surrounding farms was a different matter. Every family had rifles and shotguns enough for every male and many also had rifles for the women. They were essential tools needed for hunting, protection against wolves and other predators, or to defend against attacks by native tribes. However, few owned revolvers.

Stone removed the weapon from the holster and turned it over and over in his hands. Many times over the years he'd considered selling the Colt. It had served no purpose packed away in the trunk and the cash money welcome. Still, he'd always decided against it.

Now, he was glad he hadn't.

Military life had taught him to be neat and orderly even in dire circumstances, so he determined to repack the trunk, even if his mind was screaming to get moving. As he replaced the first items, he realized the Colt had been lying atop his zouave jacket. An ever so slight smile cracked his façade. Then moisture formed in his eye.

CHAPTER 6

THE WAR HAD ended more than three months ago, but it took until early July for Stone to fully muster out. Parades in Washington, then accounting for weapons and other gear that belonged to Uncle Sam. Finally, the V Corps disbanded. The 83rd Pennsylvania Volunteers traveled to Harrisburg to collect their final paychecks and sign endless paperwork to complete the mustering out process. With the ink drying on the last signature of the last form, it was time to go home.

Stone sighed. Like every soldier ever, he missed his family—Mom, brother Theodore, baby sister Rachael, Aunt Elizabeth, Uncle Stanton. He touched the ticket in his jacket pocket. Harrisburg to Pittsburgh to Erie. By this time tomorrow he'd be home.

But Stone wasn't ready to go home.

The men of the 83rd milled about the rail station in Harrisburg—men he'd served with. He scanned their faces. Too few of those who'd volunteered with him back in '61 remained. Had it really been only four years ago? It seemed an eternity. The faces of those buried on battlefields—Bull Run, Richmond, Antietam, Fredericksburg, Chancellorsville, Gettysburg, some nameless wilderness, Spotsylvania, Cold Harbor, Petersburg, Appomattox, other places—passed through his mind. Men he had known from his childhood. He wasn't ready to answer their families' questions—so many dead—dead because time after time they had followed him into the storm of enemy fire. That they fought for a noble cause meant nothing to those left behind.

He couldn't face them—the mothers. Widows. Children.

Stone had to go elsewhere. Where was immaterial. Anyplace would do, so long as the ghosts weren't there.

So, he took the first available train. To Buffalo.

Billy Yanks crowded the streets of the bustling port city. Many killed the hours between connecting trains to wherever home was. Others, like him, reluctant to return to families or homes forever changed by the war, or with no family to return to, wandered the city in search of work, peace, or something else they couldn't identify. Most had the hollow eyes of men who'd seen things that couldn't be unseen.

The afternoon was spent finding a place to stay. Boarding houses and inns were packed with the returning soldiers. After three hours of looking, he climbed the steps to the Fedick Boarding House.

The price had been more than planned and included a catch—he'd have to share a room with another man. The proprietress, Mrs. Fedick, a tall, sturdy, middle-aged woman with twinkling brown eyes and grey-streaked brown hair twisted into a bun, fussed over Stone as if he were her own son. She showed him to his room and introduced him to Homer O'Shea, a veteran of the 63rd New York.

The morning of his second day in the city, Stone rose early. As he finished his morning ablution, and threw on his uniform, a besotted Homer staggered through the door from a night experience the Irishman would likely struggle to remember. Not Stone. He intended to see everything and be able to tell his children about it.

The docks drew him.

Mrs. Fedick giggled and shooed Stone as he pilfered several biscuits fresh from her oven. The first rays of dawn draped golden yellows and hints of pink over the dark silhouette of the city as he walked. At the docks, a crate outside one of dozens of warehouses offered the perfect perch to enjoy the flakey delights. A passing businessman hunched in his coat and leaned on a cane. Thin brown wisps poked from beneath his black bowler. He might once have been tall, but the crook of his back and shoulders made it impossible to know. He paused and turned to face Stone, his small nose scrunched tight, narrow lips parted.

"Please excuse my manners." Regardless of his appearance, the man's voice was strong and authoritative—the voice of a man used to being listened to. "How, ever, can you eat with such a stench in the air?"

Stone stared at the man. The docks here had the same sickly-sweet scent of rotting fish guts and the accumulated excrement of the local birds that he remembered from Erie. Some found the pong repulsive. Others were so used to it that they hardly noticed. Stone fell into neither category.

He shrugged. "Smell of home. Spent eight years working the docks."

"Why, you're several years shy of thirty, and by the looks have spent some years fighting Johnny Reb."

Stone nodded. "Turned twenty-four a few months ago. I was twelve when my father was killed in a farming accident. Ma was forced to move us in with Uncle Stanton. I was the oldest." He shrugged, as if he did what anyone would have. Another bite, broken from the biscuit's edge, disappeared into his mouth. "Uncle owned a shipping company, so I worked the docks." He paused for another bite. A humorless smile cracked his façade. "Besides, after four years of battlefield odors, this seems like a field of daisies."

The man chuckled as he walked away. Overhead, gulls screamed as they circled, searching for breakfast. Small bites he tossed to the wharf were quickly snatched by those birds brave enough to venture near him. Across a narrow channel the Great West, a three-masted schooner, unloaded at the Watson elevator. Her mooring ropes creaked, and waves splashed against her wooden hull. The thick brogue of the mostly Irish stevedores drifted across the water.

Breakfast finished, Stone left the docks behind him and explored the city itself, wandering from one block to the next. He was no stranger to cities. Many times during the war he patrolled or paraded the streets of one city or another. Not even the nation's capital was immune from the ruin of war. But here—here was a city untouched, nearly pristine in its virginal innocence. Here, no cannonades scarred the edifices of civilization. Here no bullets pockmarked homes of poor or elite. Here no crops had been destroyed—no daughters of the city drawn and emaciated. Only mourning's black offered any indication of the war's burden, but even that had lifted to be replaced by the celebrations of returning sons and fathers.

Prosperity surrounded him. Along a short stretch of city blocks, he passed a pair of haberdasheries, four mercantile, a butcher, several jewelers, three banks, and a host of other shops. He found a streetside café for lunch and then wandered the afternoon away until it was at last time to return to his room where he'd meet Homer for supper, followed by a night in the saloons.

Folks hurried for home or dinner appointments. The street in front of the boarding house was busy with buggy and horse traffic. Waiting for a break to cross, he glanced around. The window display of a nearby seamstress shop caught his eye, and he approached for a better view—maybe he'd ship a pretty dress to Ma. Wire forms dressed in satin and lace ballroom gowns reminded him of tin types some of the Rebs carried as reminders of home. More out of boredom than anything, Stone glanced through the glass to the interior, expecting only dresses and old hags. Instead, taking the measurements of a matronly patron, stood the most beautiful woman he'd ever seen. The young lady shook her head to flick hair from her face. Sunlight from the window glowed through gossamer strawberry-blonde tresses.

Stone stared into the store. Women had followed the army, some washed and mended clothes, others cooked for their man, while some of the more entrepreneurial performed other services for the men in camp. All of them had the same hollow, sunken eyes and exhausted expressions as the men they cared for. Maybe under all the dirt, under the grime of camp life, some had been beautiful, but he doubted it. In the southern cities, the women with their drawn and haggard expressions wore expensive dresses that had once fit but now hung from thin frames. North of the Mason-Dixon, women appeared less affected by war shortages. There'd been plenty of beautiful young ladies, but the memories of war were still too strong for him to take an interest in them.

Until now. This young lady took his breath away. He had to meet her. But how? It wasn't like he could just walk in and talk to her. She was busy with a customer and would frown on such behavior. Pondering his dilemma, he paced out of sight of the window. An idea slapped him into action.

Headlong into the busy street, he raced across. A black-stockinged sorrel bucked, sending his surprised rider into the dirt. A paint mare, too close behind the sorrel to just stop, reared, threatening to unseat her rider. Another mare, hitched to a gig, screamed, and jerked hard left as the driver, a thin, middle-aged man in a silk suit and top hat, hauled hard on the reins, tipping the small carriage onto one wheel. It balanced precariously on the narrow steel hoop, looking like it might overturn. At the last second, the cursing driver managed to straighten the conveyance. It bounced hard on the street, sideswiped the hitching rail, scarring the black paint of the gig. Men shouted curses and shook fists at the rude young man.

Stone ignored them.

With two bounding leaps he cleared the eight steps leading to the boarding house's front porch. He burst through the front door and pounded up the stairs. The room's door opened, and Stone bowled over wide-eyed Homer.

"Hey. Watch where y're goin', laddie."

Stone pushed past the man he'd only just met the night before without acknowledging him. His valise was stowed away under the bed they were forced to share. It contained his uniform, an extra suit of clothes, his Colt, some letters from home he'd managed to save, and little else. Stone pawed through the items a second time as if he might have missed something, but still nothing. He was about to close the bag when his hand found something buried under his standard blue uniform. At the bottom lay the ill-fitting Zouave uniform he'd been issued. This would do.

Tossing aside the baggy pants and colorful sash, he grabbed the jacket that had always been too restrictive for combat use. Coat in hand, he dashed back down the stairs and out the door. More riders cursed him as he cut in front of them crossing the busy avenue.

Once outside the shop's door, butterflies flittered in his gut. As he reached for the door, his hand shook. "Nervous as a damned drunk in church." He realized he'd muttered the thought aloud when he drew an odd look from a passerby.

Stone once again reached for the door latch. Anxiety frayed nerves pushed the door open too hard, and it banged against the wall. He stepped inside quickly, vowed to get control, and closed the door behind him with an exaggerated gentleness.

An elderly lady stood atop a platform facing a large mirror. The angel knelt beside her, a piece of chalk in one hand. Both women turned to stare at him. A quick chuckle escaped the old woman before she turned back to the mirror. Stone barely noticed. He had eyes only for *her*.

With the garment clutched in both hands, arms extended toward the young seamstress, Stone swallowed hard. "Hi. I need my jacket let out." The words ran together in rapid succession as if only a single word shot from a gatling gun.

The angel's forest-green eyes seemed to scold him. "I'll be with you as soon as I finish." A hint of mirth tinged her voice. "Why don't you take a seat over there?" She pointed to a chair in the corner of the tiny shop. When he only stared in response, she arched her brows and tilted her head. "Go on. Right over there. I'll only be a few more minutes."

Stone tried to straighten the inane expression he expected was plastered to his face as he backed to the chair. His eyes remained fixated on her. The edge of the chair against the back of his legs stopped him. His gaze never leaving her, he dropped into the chair.

Except he had misjudged and caught only its edge. The chair tipped and Stone sprawled on the floor. Both women laughed openly. Heat flashed up his neck and warmed his cheeks. "Excuse me." Dusting the floor dust and his dignity from his pants, Stone righted the chair and sat on it.

CHAPTER 7

DUST SWIRLED ABOUT the street, kicked up by the strong, chilly breeze that smelled of an approaching spring gale. Marshal Clement Burke glanced at the dark, heavy clouds and thought that in a few hours the street would be a muddy mess. He stood stooped over on the boardwalk, one hand gripped the wooden hitching rail while the other clutched at his sore back. Despite the coolness of the air, sweat dripped from his bald head and his stained linen shirt clung to his skin.

Nearly three dozen men crowded the narrow street. After Sally's funeral, these men had gathered at the Wagon Wheel for drinks. Clem was just finishing his third beer when they entered the saloon. Talk naturally turned to forming a posse and when the conversation grew heated, Burke stalked out. The mob followed, led by Sven Larson and Emmitt Jackson, two of the most respected men in town.

"Marshal. Vhy you not put together a posse?" Sven Larson turned to the crowd behind him. "Ve need to be after dese men."

"You know ever' one of us would ride with you. We all fought in the war." Emmitt Jackson stepped away from the relative safety of the gathered men to move closer to Burke. "To a man, we all know how to use long guns."

Before Emmitt finished, a man in back yelled. "Posse." In seconds, others took up the cry. "Let's go, Marshal."

"Coward."

"Yella' belly."

Burke's face reddened and his lips formed a snarl. "Now see here. Who said that?" He straightened to get a better view of the men in the rear. Grimacing, he knuckled his back—jeers erupted from the throng.

"I ain't afeared, and no man can say...." His eye caught Charles Willis across the street, standing in the doorway of the saloon.

Willis was tall and strong, but pudgy in the way men unaccustomed to physical labor grew. Nonetheless, he maintained a commanding presence. He had founded Stockman, as well as many other frontier towns in the Dakota Territory. Shrewd land speculation had made him one of the wealthiest men in the territory. As was true for most of the property owners in and around town, Willis carried the mortgage on Clement's hovel on the edge of town.

The two men locked eyes over the crowd for the briefest of moments. Even at this distance, Willis's stare bored into Burke like an auger bit. An almost imperceptible tilt to the wealthy man's head and single lifted brow seemed to ask a silent question.

"I've already told y'all that I don't have the authority to arrest anyone outside the town limits."

Larson squinted one eye and pointed an accusatory finger at Burke. "You arrested dat man dat stole a horse last summer."

"'Course the horse belonged to Willis." Jackson slapped his thigh and laughed at his own joke, joined by everyone—except the marshal.

"That was different, and you knows it. 'Sides, the U.S. marshal has ordered me to wait."

"Well, he ain't ordered us to wait. Deputize us an' we'll go without you," someone shouted.

Again, Marshal Burke looked across the street to Willis. A steady stare was all the answer he received. Willis had been in the marshal's office when his son, Howard, tore into town with news of the attack on Sally. After the initial shock had worn off, but before Burke rode to the Stone homestead, Willis had been clear that no posse was to leave Stockman until the U.S. marshal arrived. He'd pointed out that technically Burke had no authority outside town limits, stressing the importance of rule-of-law. "These lawless murderers must not get off on a technicality," he'd said. Willis made it equally clear that Burke's job depended on his following orders.

The town marshal scanned the crowd. Howard was missing. As he thought about it, Burke realized Willis's son hadn't been in the crowd at all. He strained to remember if Howard had been in the saloon after the funeral, but the place had been crowded.

"I won't deputize any one a you. Price will have to do that when he arrives. That means you'll jess be a vigilante lynch mob if you go on your own. And—" Groans and jeers from the gathered men cut him off. Burke shouted to be heard over them. "If I have to arrest all of you to keep you in town, I will. Don't think I won't." More sweat gushed down his neck. He couldn't risk these men forming their own posse. "Now, jess go 'bout your own business and leave this alone till Price gits here."

Marshal Burke stood glowering at the crowd, one pudgy thumb stuck through a suspender strap. Tough men stared back.

Posse duty was dangerous—could get a man killed. If they were so anxious to get dead he ought a let 'em. Fools. Burke knew they weren't really fools. To a man they were men to ride the river with, brave men, more afraid of idle time in jail away from their livelihoods than the prospects of facing Injuns and murderers.

He swallowed at the lump in his throat. Why was he so afraid? He sneaked a furtive glance at Willis, whose hard eyes still bore holes in him. Instinctively, he knuckled the pain in his back. It wasn't his imagination—it really did hurt.

"Well, git on with you. Go 'bout your business. Now."

One by one, the town's men left for their homes or places of business. As the last of them turned away, Burke realized he'd been holding his breath. He sighed and looked up in time to catch Willis's eye again. The businessman spun on his heel and strode into the Wagon Wheel.

A single shiver crawled up Burke's spine.

STONE SECURED THE last of the supplies on the pack horse. When he was sure the knot was tight enough, he walked to his own mount, stepped into the stirrup, and swung his leg over the saddle. Sally's murderers had a full day's head start. It would take some hard riding to catch up. Threatening clouds hung heavy in the darkening mid-afternoon sky. He needed to pick up their trail before the storm washed away any sign of their passing.

Cordelia, his coal-black mare, pranced her excitement, sensing a hunt. She'd been a foal in 1865 when Sally made her Stone's wedding gift. Cordelia loved the hunt. She and Stone had ridden many trails together, some near, some far, but always tracking game for the table. This was still a hunting trail, but the difference was not lost on Stone.

He looped the pack horse's leads around the pommel and nudged Cordelia with his knees. The trail led west, over the rise beyond the barn. Cresting the hill, the first sign appeared, clear as a painting. A cracked and splintered walnut rifle stock lay at the ridge. The wood had not begun weathering and Stone wondered what had happened to the weapon.

Farther down the slope, four horses and an equal number of heavily laden pack mules had ridden in from the southeast—Yankton most likely, though it mattered little enough that he'd not ride their back trail to be sure. Tracks of a trio of horses broke off and disappeared over the top, heading toward the Stone homestead. These would be the three men who killed Sally and put a bullet in him. He clenched and unclenched his fists.

The fourth had remained with the pack animals. The butt ends of several cigarettes lay scattered along a worn path such as one might make by pacing back and forth. The man who had covered the escape from the ridge. Had he been worried? Bored? Something else? Stone could form no conclusions with so little to work with, so he quickly moved on. Hard packed earth didn't take much by way of prints, but near where the mules had been picketed a single impression showed the fellow's feet, or at least his boots, were unusually long and narrow. A series of arced furrows, each about the length of a man's pace, followed both sides of the line of trampled grass. Stone pondered it for a minute, trying to imagine the cause. Nothing. But it'd be easy enough to recognize if he saw it again.

He climbed back into the saddle. "Let's ride, girl."

Cordelia snorted and shook her head as if she understood. The trail turned west with a northern drift. Stone nodded. He'd regularly tracked game over an area seventy-five miles in any direction. Occasionally farther. Tracking humans was little different than tracking animals—more about getting into the mind of the quarry than reading the sign. Think like them.

Where were they headed? Howard claimed they had been miners. What else could they have been? It seemed that every traveler of late was headed for the Black Hills—in particular Deadwood Gulch.

Results from Custer's excursion into the Black Hills were supposed to have remained secret, but keeping secrets about gold was like holding water in a sluice. The discovery had appeared in every eastern paper almost before the expedition exited the lands ceded to the Sioux as part of the treaty ending Red Cloud's War. Stone shook his head. He doubted the military had really wanted the secret kept—they had a way of discouraging loose lips when it mattered to them.

Deadwood.

That's where these woman-murdering snakes would head. Stone intended to dog their trail until every man jack of them paid for what they did.

MILES OF UNDULATING hills lay behind. Broken plants, a partial boot print in a muddy spring, droppings left by the horses and mules—the trail read like an open book. Either the men didn't know how to hide their sign or didn't believe anyone would follow. Not that it mattered, the trail was like a straight line drawn between their homestead—a forlorn moment touched his soul with grief, and he shook his head. Just his homestead, now—and Deadwood.

Stone pressed forward, riding hard.

Afternoon waned to evening. His vision blurred and his eyes closed, his chin drooped. He started awake with a jerk, just in time to catch himself from falling. The black paused, but with a fierce slap to his own face Stone touched his knee to her flank, nudging her onward at a fast cantor. A mile later he almost nodded off again.

He finally stopped for a brief rest. Cordelia blew hard, a frothy white lather stood out against her obsidian coat. Stone slumped in his saddle, chin buried in his broad chest. His gunshot arm hung like dead weight. Somewhere was the sling the doc had given him, but that would have to wait. He hunched his shoulders to ease the pain. Dried and crusted blood clogged his nostrils and forced him to suck ragged breaths through cracked lips. He scrubbed a hand across his face. It came away sticky and crimson smeared. A mixture of blood and sweat dripped from his chin where he'd accidentally ripped away scabs from yesterday. Sometime during the afternoon's hard ride, the wound in his arm had re-opened, and blood dribbled down his elbow.

With his left knuckles, he kneaded his eyes. He'd not slept well at Doc's.

A cold gust slapped his face. The air temperature had dropped from the early afternoon's spring-time briskness and now hovered near freezing. An icy raindrop struck Stone's forehead. He blinked and his eyes widened.

To the west a thick charcoal drapery of clouds, edges tinged green, surged forward in relentless waves. Cold winds carried the front forward at a ruthless pace. His black duster whipped about, catching briefly behind his Colt Army before unfurling again in the glacial wind.

Pounding rain shattered like icicles against the mask of scabs, bruises, and reopened wounds covering his face. He forced himself to sit tall in the saddle and lifted the old field glasses that hung by a leather thong about his neck.

Shelter—he needed shelter or none of them would survive the night.

He nudged Cordelia to the crest of the next hill. "Come on, Girl."

At the top, another polar gale caught him. He shivered as he lifted the glasses to his eyes and swept the landscape before him.

Nothing. Only endless prairie.

Lightning on the horizon danced closer. Streaks jumped across the sky, illuminating the ominous clouds behind each flash. Cordelia shivered in the wake of another frigid blast. The paint pack horse pranced and whinnied.

Stone resumed his sweep, combing the plain for some sign of shelter. Something. Anything. He swallowed the lump that formed in his throat.

He lengthened his search, deeper into the prairie. Scant trees bent by the force of the wind, short buffalo grass swaying, a black blotch against a rolling hill, prairie sunflowers quivering.

Still nothing.

Wait. He swung the glasses back toward the black shape. Indistinct, but out of place. He adjusted the glasses. Could it be a building of some sort?

A long ride. He glanced at Cordelia—twisted to evaluate the paint. Did the mounts have enough left for one more arduous dash tonight?

Did he?

Survival demanded it.

"We got one last run before we rest. You can do this, Girl." Reaching down he patted the mare's neck and whispered encouragement. Behind him, the gelding snorted. Stone turned and offered as much encouraging smile as he had in him.

His heart thumped in his chest. Had to try. Had to make it.

"Yah!" Stone touched heels to coal black flanks as he shouted. The three rushed across the grassland into the storm's growing intensity. Heavy drops of freezing rain stung like a swarm of bees. He shouted over the wind. "Come on, Cord, run."

The dark outline of a barn took shape. Hope surged through Stone. The mare blew hard, her flanks heaved with exertion. On they pressed, closing the distance at a snail's pace as lightning flashed in rapid bursts that reminded Stone of rolling artillery barrages.

Each burst illuminated the barn—momentary glimpses of too distant salvation—before darkening just in time for the next, like a slow turning stroboscope. The roof sagged like a swayback nag. Cracked and missing boards left walls pockmarked as if riddled by grapeshot.

This was their salvation? Damn!

The mare was slowing. She stumbled and caught herself. The barn was still a distance away. Would they make it before Cordelia died underneath him, leaving Stone to die alongside her? Stone tried, but his shouts of encouragement were lost in the howling wind. He leaned low one more time, pressing his cheek to her neck. "You're doing great. Not much farther."

Lightning struck close. The air crackled with electricity. Waves of rain driven by the force of the gale hammered at them, and Stone closed his eyes against the pelting slaps. Both horses and the lone rider bent into the teeth of the wind, struggling to make headway.

The barn had to be close. Stone sagged, his remaining strength ebbed. Had they missed it? Ridden past their only hope? They'd never make it. In the next moment, a flash of lightning revealed the barn—right in front of them.

Stone fell more than stepped from the saddle—wet, mushy grass and thick mud cushioned his impact. With the last reserves of strength, he pulled the door open against the gale. A heavy gust caught the door, threatening to rip it from its hinges. It banged against his useless arm, and he winced, gritting his teeth against the pain.

The horses needed no encouragement to race inside. Stone followed and the savage wind slammed the door closed, rattling the entire barn. Soaked, freezing, and played out, Stone slumped to the floor.

SOMETHING COLD AND moist nudged his face. "We made it, Cord." He groaned. "Thank you." He reached to pat her snout. "How long was I out?" Cordelia's only answer was a snort. Not long—the tempest still rattled the rafters. Lightning flashes showed through the numerous gaps in the wall boards. Rain pelted the old barn and water drizzling through holes in the roof maintained a steady humming trickle just audible over the wind whistling through the gaps.

Another prod encouraged him to roll to his side. Pain lanced through his arm, and he winced as he struggled to an upright position. Shrugging off the dripping duster brought another surge of agony, but he gritted his teeth and allowed it to slip off his shoulders to the barn floor.

Cordelia stepped to him and dug her snout into him again, more insistent.

"I know. I'm sorry. Let me get up and get you two taken care of." His voice sounded tired and weak even to his own ears. Standing took more energy than normal, and once on his feet, he wobbled. His head swam, and he grabbed the black for support. Flashes from the storm grew less frequent but offered enough erratic light for him to strip the saddle and packs from both horses—tasks made difficult with only one arm. Oats from one of the bags kept both mounts contented while he rubbed them down. Leaden arm dragged each stroke. His chin dropped to his chest, and he awoke with a start, the brush pressed to Cordelia's flank, unmoving.

"Sorry, girl. How long? Don't even remember falling asleep."

Sleep beckoned twice more before the task was finished. At last, he stumbled to the driest piece of floor he could find, his legs wobbling like a new-born calf's. Instead of easing Stone to the floor, they dumped him like so much compost. Rolling to his back, mind screaming for the release of sleep, he contemplated ignoring the last thing he needed to do before seeking blessed sleep. Sitting upright, simple and easy enough always before, proved far more of a struggle tonight. With a tight grip on his pants just above the knee, and an accompanying loud grunt that might have been a groan, he heaved and hauled himself into a sitting position.

Legs stretched straight out in front, he managed to unwrap the bandages covering the wound. Another lightning flash allowed him to see the damage—the first time since Doc stitched him up. He had been lucky. A weave of black thread knitted the arm together. Some of the stitches had broken, however, allowing the flesh to separate. The bleeding hadn't yet stopped.

During the war, he'd seen sepsis rob many good men of limbs. And too often, their lives, as well. He wasn't prepared for either. A yawn escaped as he reached for the medical supplies Doc sent him with. Before he finished the second yawn, he was asleep.

DAKOTA TERRITORY, SATURDAY, MAY 1ST, 1875

STONE SNAPPED HIS eyes open, bandages and ointments still clutched in his hand. Ephemeral bars of light streamed through gaps in the wall that just last night offered windows to the lightning storm. Swirling clouds of dust and hay seeds rode the rays of penetrating light. Meadowlarks welcomed the new day with joyous songs—the previous night's storm long forgotten.

The pain from sitting up drew a wince. Dried blood trailed from the wound, down his arm, to the floor where a rusty colored stain the size of a saucer offered evidence of how much he'd bled after passing out. With the back of his hand, he scrubbed sand and crusted blood from his eyes. From a long-sitting position, he worked his shoulders in circles and twisted his trunk to loosen sore, tight muscles. Slowly the knots worked out of his body.

Doc had given him specific instructions which Stone followed to the letter. The wound was in an awkward position, but he managed to apply the salves and ointments. With the assistance of his teeth, he tied off the last bandage just as his stomach rumbled. Cordelia and Ulysses echoed their own interest in food. Noon the previous day had been his last meal. He'd had every intention of eating when he stopped, but exhaustion turned out to be the greater need. At least the mounts ate last night. Maybe they were just anxious to pick up the trail.

The image of Sally, broken and bloody, flashed unbidden across his mind. He knew that soon he'd need to channel this memory to do what needed doing, but for now he preferred to remember her another way.

CHAPTER 8

"**H**OW CAN I help you?" While Stone sat red-faced, the angel had finished taking measurements, then escorted the older lady from the shop after first assisting her to step off the platform she'd been standing on. When the door closed behind the woman, the angel turned to him.

Stone stared into her green eyes that drew him into their depths. She was as beautiful a woman as he'd seen, maybe ever. Smooth cheeks and full, red lips surrounded by a halo of long, curling, strawberry-blonde locks. After years of war, formerly beautiful things turned ugly. Wilderness which Stone had loved as a child was scarred by the ravages of endless battles, turning the landscape into some mockery of hell. Even marching through cities, women would come out to watch. They looked gaunt from lack of nourishment and drawn from exhaustion and the constant drone of war. The only way Stone knew they had once been elegant and beautiful was the pride with which they carried themselves—erect, chin high, shoulders back.

"Sir? How can I help you?"

Stone shook his head. "I'm sorry. Um. What did you just say?"

"I asked how I could help you. Do you need that jacket let out?"

"Uh, yes." Stone paused to glance at the hand that held the Zouave uniform. What was that? Then it came to him. "Yes. Yes, this needs to be let out." He held it out to the angel.

She reached for it, saying nothing. Instead, she examined him head to toe, her expression skeptical. Then she directed her stare to his eyes, boring deep into his heart as if she could strip bare his soul and know everything about him—including things he didn't know about himself.

After what seemed an eternity, she smiled, revealing perfect teeth, a sparkle in her eye, and a glowing aura about her. "Well, then you've brought it to the right place." She held the jacket at arm's length by the epaulets. The examination seemed as thorough as the one she'd put his soul through just moments prior.

Before Stone could move, she stepped close to him and shoved the uniform shoulders to within an inch of his. "Turn around."

Stone blinked. "Oh, oh." He snapped to. "Yes, s...." He bit his tongue hard. What a fool he'd made of himself. As if it wasn't enough that he'd fallen to the floor earlier, now he almost called her "sir." He spun with the drilled precision of a soldier. Behind him a stifled giggle burned his ears. Warmth spread up his neck.

This time she raised the jacket to him, her fingers pressing into his shoulders. His breath caught, and a shiver ran down his back, and he was sure, even through his regular uniform, that her hands were hot as a campfire. This was a new sensation, and he didn't know what to do about it. Had she felt it too? When was the last time he'd reacted to a woman's touch? Hell, for that matter, when was the last time a woman who wasn't his mother, sister, or aunt had touched him?

Stone had never indulged himself with any of the many camp followers who sold their bodies. For one, he was an officer and such behavior was unacceptable. But more than that, he hadn't the interest in such recreation. It wasn't like he'd never kissed a girl. Before the war there'd been a couple of young ladies who interested him. After mustering in, he'd never written, and neither had they. That was different. Their touch never really excited him. This angel's rocked him to his toes.

"Okay. Step up onto the platform. I need to take some measurements." Her firm, professional tone hid something else, something far different.

Stone moved to comply, this time not verbalizing any response to avoid yet another embarrassment. Once on the dais, she worked quickly and efficiently taking down numbers as she worked.

"Did that jacket use to fit you?"

"Truthfully, no. My unit won these uniforms before marching off to our first battle. They're French foreign legion. This was the biggest size they had. "I... I've always been some bigger than my friends." That had been the problem with the Zouave's. Many of the men in the unit couldn't get one big enough. Apparently, the French didn't grow their soldiers as big as the farm boys of the 83rd Pennsylvania.

"Well, I don't have this material in the shop. It'll need to be ordered, but I think I can get it quickly. I do have other work ahead of yours, but I should be able to have this done in a week. Is that okay?"

"Sure." He felt her touch still lingering on his shoulders, though she had moved to stand in front of him. Emerald eyes met his and his knees weakened. He rushed to clarify. "I mean, yes. Yes, that'll be fine."

"That'll be thirty-five dollars."

"Okay."

The angel held her hand out. "Before I start work."

"What. Oh. Sure." Stone felt a fool. Again. He jammed a hand deep into his pocket and pulled out a wad of bills, which he handed her without looking. "Here you go, ma'am."

Ma'am. He still didn't know her name. A smirk crossed her face as she counted the bills. "The war must have made you wealthy. Or are you just always this careless with money."

"What?"

She reached a small stack of bills in his direction. "Are you always so careless with money? You have change coming back. You gave me nearly two hundred dollars."

"Oh." He accepted the bills and crammed them back into his pocket.

"What name do I put on the order? You know, just in case I'm not here when you come pick it up."

"I'll be sure to come back when you're here."

"Still, I need a name."

"Stone. Major Stone. Judiah." Why had he said that? "But no one calls me that. It's just Stone."

"Well Major Judiah Stone. I'll see you in a week."

Stone backed out of the shop, eyes only for the seamstress. He reached behind him, opened the door, and stepped backward—right into a group of a dozen soldiers. Three of the men fell to the board-walk with loud thumps.

"Hey, watch where you're going." The shout came at once from several of the men.

"Look. An officer."

"In a dress shop."

Derisive laughter erupted among the men.

As if stepping from the store released him from its enchantment, Stone was once again the battle-hardened Union officer. He spun on the men, most of whom appeared to be much younger. Late recruits who'd seen little of the war. He glared at them, a voiceless challenge that silenced them. "You forgotten how to salute, soldier?" Any soft-ness that may have been in his voice in the shop, had turned to gravel.

"No... no, sir." The men stiffened, backs rigid, and snapped crisp salutes before they hurried away.

CHAPTER 9

STONE STOOD ALONG a meandering stream, gnawing on jerked buffalo. Hidden in the deep shadows of a cottonwood grove, he watched a vixen hunt her next meal. Merigold and yam coat blended with the lush earthy tones of the prairie grasses around her. Her kits' faint yips rode the gentle breeze brushing past him to be lost in the vast expanse of emptiness.

Cordelia bent to lap at the tepid water, while the pack horse munched on a patch of clover on the far bank. Both beasts seemed contented. They'd worked hard all morning—Stone kept them moving as fast as he dared.

This was the third day out. He was alone and moving fast. The previous night he rode as deep into the darkness as he dared, using moonlight to travel by. After a short rest, he rose before the sun and started back on the trail soon after. His gut said he was closing in on Sally's murderers. They were four plus numerous pack animals loaded with supplies. They could only travel so fast, even knowing a posse followed behind—and only fools would murder a woman and think the law wouldn't be after them. Despite the lack of sign since the storm, he was confident they were close.

Deep in thought, Stone absentmindedly bent over, slipped a hand inside his boot, and pulled out the small hunting knife from his father that he kept there. With a practiced hand he used the razor-sharp tip of the clipped blade to dig a strand of jerk stuck between his front teeth.

Before the storm their trail pointed northwest, arrow-straight, toward Fort Pierre. Originally the base camp of a French fur trading company, the town now served as the transition point for men traveling to the Black Hills from the east. Upon arrival at the hamlet of Pierre, travelers caught the ferry across to the converted trading post and then headed overland toward the gold fields.

So long as he continued pushing as he had the day before, there was time to catch them at the trading post, but hopefully before. If he hadn't caught them before reaching Fort Pierre, he would make inquiries to confirm they'd passed through. If necessary, he'd criss-cross the prairie west of the old fort until he picked up their trail. Vengeance was not far off.

Stone gathered his horses and mounted. As he nudged Cordelia, the vixen caught his attention again. Momma fox halted, her ears pricked forward, bushy tail straight behind her as she crouched, intent on a rodent or other small creature in the grass ahead of her. She took two rapid steps forward and leapt high into the air. At the apex, the huntress arched her back and dove headfirst into a grass clump. Even before booted forepaws touched down, her snout rooted for her prey. Would she kill the unlucky creature herself, or take it to her kits alive, but maimed, to let them make the kill?

Dead or alive?

"DON'T THIS PRAIRIE never end?" Shorty, shoulders slumped and head hanging, reached to rub his lower back. More used to walking or crawling through mines, he'd never ridden this much, and he ached all over from the constant jostling.

A dilapidated old barn they'd passed a few hours after the shootout had been the last sign of civilization. Since then, they'd seen little but endless undulating plain. An occasional antelope or flock of pheasants stirred, disturbed by their passage. Once they'd spotted a dozen buffalo in the distance. The beasts, tails swishing, watched the riders for a few seconds before dipping their heads to continue grazing. Birds sang by day—wolves, coyotes, and insects by night. For all the miles they'd traveled, not one human sign, as if the four men were the only people in the territory.

"I just wish the durned sun would go away." A lifelong coal miner, Frankie had no tolerance for bright light or the sun's burning rays. Despite the floppy hat, brim folded back to attach to the crown in front, and the long sleeve shirts he wore, much of his face and neck remained exposed and had burned soon after leaving Yankton. None of his companions fared better.

"Shut up you two. I'm tired of your complaining." Curly snatched the hat off his head and swiped his hand across his temple. "And keep your eyes open. Just 'cause we ain't seen an Injun don't mean there ain't none."

Frankie hung his head and turned away from the others. Fidgeting with one side of his handlebar moustache, rolling and twisting it between two digits, his thoughts turned to the shooting incident. For the twentieth time that morning, he turned to glance along the trail behind them, half expecting a posse to come charging over the crest of the last hillock. Nothing stirred. Still, it gnawed at his belly. What had his companions done to get into a shootout?

"What was that gun play about the other day? What happened down there?" This wasn't the first time Frankie had asked. Every inquiry led to the inevitable answer. Nothing to talk about. Even Curly, who never failed to grow serious whenever the topic was broached, refused to discuss it.

"Don't know. Weren't doin' nothing. Some dude just opened up on us." Shorty's lip curled into a snarl.

"Well, what were *you* doing when he started shooting?"

Shorty stopped his mare. He turned in his saddle and shot a glare at Frankie. "What're you s'jestin', mister?"

Frankie met his companion's stare as he nudged his mare closer. He pulled up next to him and loomed over Shorty, forcing the smaller man to stare straight up to keep eye contact. "Nothin'. Ain't suggestin' nothin'. But I surely have a right to know what happened."

"And I done told ya." Shorty broke eye contact and snapped his reins to catch up with Curly and Erik who had continued riding and were now fifty yards ahead.

Frankie watched him go. The response was always the same. It didn't add up. Why would someone just shoot at them for no reason? Did Shorty start trouble? Why wouldn't Curly or Erik discuss it? They walked away whenever he mentioned anything about it. Shaking his head, he tugged to get the string of pack mules moving. "Don't make sense. Not sure if I'm more scared of Injuns or whoever might be following us?"

Only the beasts of burden heard him.

———————————

STONE ALMOST MISSED the tracks.

It was early afternoon, and he'd stopped by a clear brook. As he knelt with his canteen submerged in the water, his gaze fell on a single impression in front of him. Little more than a line in the sand just under the surface, he at first thought an antelope had made it, maybe while drinking. He glanced about. Seeing nothing, he bent closer. The tracks of several riders suddenly stood out like words in a book. Dread gripped him, and he fought to swallow the lump in his throat. These weren't the hoof prints he was looking for.

"Girl, unshod ponies and recent—an hour ago, maybe." He patted the mare's neck as he whispered in her ear. "We best keep our wits about us, or you'll both end up on some brave's string with my scalp on his lance."

The black nickered, her tone suggesting that she both understood the problem and wished to avoid that fate.

He eased the Army Colt at his side, then pulled the Henry from its boot and levered a round into the chamber. One last sweep of the plain with his field glasses revealed empty prairie. Whoever they were, there was no sign of them now.

Henry in hand, he remounted. He turned in the saddle and scanned the prairie behind. Cutting straight through was a path of bent grasses—his path. Awareness slammed into him like a fist to the wind. In his rush to find Sally's murderers, he left a backtrail laid out like a map that even a blind man could follow.

A sense of impending doom filled him. In his mind he pictured Sioux warriors laughing at the fool white man as they rode him down, driving lances through his body already peppered with their arrows.

CHARLES WILLIS TAPPED his foot and set his jaw. The secretary, Mr. Addison, had shown him in, explaining that Mr. Lockhart was attending to other business and would be with Charles shortly.

A massive Chippendale pedestal desk dominated one side of the office. Sunlight from the overhead skylight reflected off the desk's highly polished surface. The only item on the desktop was a mahogany cigar box that rested on one corner, perfectly aligned with the edges. Six tall windows lined the walls of the large open bay behind his desk. Four across plus one on each end aligned perpendicular to the quad grouping, stained glass forming an intricate pattern along the upper edge of each pane. In the bay's corners, rich green brocaded draperies hung, waiting to be drawn.

Mahogany paneling covered the walls of the room and served as a backdrop for a number of railroad themed paintings. Perfectly situated across the room from the desk and under a commanding Albert Bierstadt landscape was a cherry-wood bar cart with a half-dozen decanters filled with amber-colored liquids.

In addition to the desk, a pair of intricately carved mahogany chairs upholstered in a red brocade sat opposite a matching love seat to form an intimate conversation area. Ebony serving tables sat on either end of the loveseat with a third situated between the chairs.

For the fourth time in the last ten minutes, he reached under his jacket into his vest to pull the gold watch from its slit. His thick, un-calloused thumb popped open the engraved cover. Without looking at the watch's face, he snapped it shut and jammed the timepiece back into the pocket. He turned on his heel and marched to the window, his long legs carrying him there in just two strides. The large office once again filled with the rhythmic tap of his foot.

A handful of gardeners worked trimming the hundreds of shrubs that formed an interlocking web of geometric shapes across Lockhart's south lawn. Each shape seemed precise and perfectly aligned such that when taken as a whole, the interlocking web took on the appearance of a locomotive, the letters DMWR forming the coal tender. Clever. Did Lockhart design it himself?

As Charles reached into his vest pocket once again, the door creaked. He spun in time to catch Emerson Lockhart, the elfin vice president of the Dakota and Montana Western Railway, glide into the room. Dark curls, combed back from a single part on the side, and thick sideburns that ended just below his ears, framed a face many times too small for the nose that protruded like the beak of a large predatory bird.

"Mister Willis." Lockhart's voice had a nasal quality to it that both annoyed and grated on Charles. The vice president stepped past Charles and took a seat at his desk. "Sit." With a dismissive gesture he waved his visitor into one of the hard-backed chairs situated for his guests.

A surge of anger welled up and Charles wrestled it under control. Oh, if only he didn't stand to make a fortune via his association with this pompous ass and his corporation. Instead, he tugged a chair away from the edge and lowered himself into it.

"Let's get right to it. You have the deeds?"

"I do. I have secured title to all the properties we discussed." Charles hesitated before he continued and tried to work some moisture into his mouth. "Except for—"

"Except for the Stone place. This *is* what you were going to say, isn't it?"

Charles's jaw tightened. How did he know that? Or only suspect it? What else does he know? He ran his tongue along the inside of one cheek and took a deep breath. Blinking, he unclenched his teeth and forced a calm into his voice. "Yes. That is what I was going t—"

"Not good enough." The railroad executive went scarlet from his neck to his forehead. "I require all those deeds. Now." He slammed his fist down on his desk, the *thump* weak in the sudden stillness of the room.

The large man choked back the laugh that rose in his throat despite the tension of the moment. He coughed. "Emerson, be reasonable. Stone is out hunting his wife's killers, alone, in Indian territory. The Sioux will kill him, if they haven't already. I expect to hear from the posse that they found him staked out on the prairie somewhere, scalped and dead. Then I can just take his land."

The smaller man's eyes opened so wide Charles expected them to pop out of his head. Then they closed into an angry squint. The sound of grinding teeth came from his mouth. His response was tight and clipped. "Governor Brooks gave me until our meeting next month to make good on my part of our, ah… arrangement. If those deeds are not in my possession by then, he'll open discussions with other companies." Lockhart spit the word out like a bad taste, then took a deep breath. "Make no mistake, a railroad will soon connect Yankton to the gold fields of the Black Hills. Land grants worth hundreds of thousands of dollars go to whoever contracts to build it. Already agents of the Central Pacific are sniffing around. The Northern Pacific and Duluth-Milwaukee won't be far behind."

The diminutive man rose from his chair and walked around his desk, curling his fingers into a ball. When he came eye to eye with the seated Charles, he shook the clenched fist in Charles's face. Charles stiffened and fought the urge to lean back in the chair.

"I don't possess the resources of the CP and cannot win a bidding war with them." Lockhart waggled his index finger under Charles's nose. "Don't forget. You have a huge stake in this too. The CP'll follow the river valley route, completely bypassing Stockman." His tone turned cruel. "Stockman will dry up like so much chaff, and you won't be able to give away your holdings."

Charles's cheeks burned. No way he would allow this tiny blowhard to intimidate him. His hands rose from the arms of the chair. Oh, how he wanted to lash out, to crush this—this bug. He scowled but deep inside he also recognized the truth of the railroad man's prophecy. With a Herculean effort, he managed to tamp down his anger. All the land he owned—not just Stockman, but undeveloped town sites from Stockman all the way to Yankton and more west of Stockman. If the DMRW won the day, people would flood to them. Sales of the commercial plots alone could make him richer than even he could imagine, not to mention the commissions on farmland and interest on loans just for starters. The stuff of dreams.

Swallowing hard, Charles moderated the tone of his retort. "Trust me, I haven't forgotten." His voice trembled. "The woman wouldn't even listen to an off—"

"You should have gone to Stone in the first place. Men can be reasoned with. Bought. Or threatened." Lockhart jerked his hands down and grasped them in the small of his back. He stepped behind the desk and paced the length of the bay, head down, brows crinkled.

For two minutes neither man spoke. Without glancing up he paused mid-pace. "When will you know if Stone is dead?"

"Three weeks. Maybe a month."

Lockhart turned and stared at the large man, his eyes icy and hard.

He spoke through gritted teeth. "One week. I need that deed, and I don't care what *else* you have to do to get it."

FROM THE VANTAGE of a window tucked into a front turret, Lockhart watched Willis storm down the stone paver path and turn onto the dirt street toward Yankton's main street. Mr. Addison stood beside him, also watching. The vice president turned to his secretary, a smile creasing his face. "Has there been any word from Cyrus Clinton?"

"No, sir. But we did not expect any until his arrival." Mr. Addison's British accent was clipped and proper. "The last word I had was just before he left Chicago. Nasty business, that, though he seemed quite pleased with his bonus. At that time, he expected it would be two weeks before he arrived. If I might, sir, the man knows his job, and it will be handled. He is the best."

The small man sighed. "No doubt, you're right. Stone will be dead as soon as he shows up in Deadwood. If the Sioux don't get him first."

CHARLES FUMED, HIS body stiff. His shoulders quaked with barely suppressed rage. The sea of people parted for him as walked down the crowded boardwalk. He was dimly aware of the muttered curses that followed in his wake. That little man. He growled. A lady paused to stare at him before she hurried on. His face grew hot—he hadn't realized his growl was audible.

He swung into an alley. Air came in ragged gasps, and he grabbed the corner of the building to steady legs that shook and threatened collapse. His head swam. He had worked too hard. If only Sally'd listened to reason. He'd even offered enough money for them to start over somewhere else and have a nice nest egg to boot.

How to get Stone's deed? He could be anywhere between Stockman and Deadwood Gulch. If only he'd stayed in Stockman like he was ordered. But, no. As stubborn as that bitch he was married to. Damn.

Charles startled himself. He wasn't given to profanity, even in his thoughts—the sign of a weak and uncultured man, and he was neither. He had to get that deed. Stone should've stayed. He stopped. Pondered the idea. "Should have stayed. Hmmm." His eyes widened, and he straightened. He had it. A laugh came like an uninvited but welcome guest. Fifteen minutes passed, Charles deep in thought, working the idea over in his mind.

With a newfound energy, Charles stepped back onto the boardwalk and turned toward the railroad station. On the corner opposite the depot, he turned into the telegraph office. "I need a message sent out immediately."

CHAPTER 10

DAKOTA TERRITORY, MONDAY, MAY 3RD, 1875

THE SKIN ON Frankie's back prickled in the mid-morning sun. He doused himself with a hatful of water from the stream, sputtered, and shook the excess from his face and hair. Rainbows sparkled amongst them as they sprayed Shorty, who stood next to him.

"Hey. Why I ought a...." Shorty chuckled, which drew a guffaw from Frankie. Even the normally cantankerous Shorty was in good cheer—the misery of yesterday's afternoon heat forgotten in the coolness of the late-spring morning.

Rocky stream sides lined either side of the creek while the wide draw's high banks topped with scrub brush and tall grasses blocked out the unending prairie. For a few moments, the monotony of the trip was forgotten in this hidden oasis.

As the two laughed, something crashed through the brush behind Frankie, rolling hard into him. The tumbling fulcrum, whatever it was, kicked his legs from beneath him, sending him flying. Arms flailed as he toppled backward to lay sprawled on the rough ground.

"Hey, what the—" Frankie spat through still dripping strands of hair hanging into his open mouth.

Erik, who'd been on watch, rolled out from under Frankie's feet.

"Kraut, you need to watch—" Erik's pasty face and wild, saucer-like blue eyes stopped Frankie.

Erik held a single, shaking finger in front of his pursed lips. His hard swallow widened his eyes more. "Indians!"

Cold sweat beaded across Frankie's forehead. Sand flew in every direction as he scrambled to his feet. Both Curly and Shorty blanched, their sun-browned skin whiter than the day they walked out of the coal mines. As one, the four men gathered at the edge of the draw, stooped to keep their heads out of sight. They lifted enough to peer over the thick grass lining the edge. Erik pointed north, toward a dust cloud that hung like a bad omen above the horizon.

Squinting against the sun's glare, he identified silhouettes, not much more than dark specks overlaying the advancing brown veil, heading right at them.

Frankie's legs buckled.

MARSHAL PRICE SET down the stack of handbills he'd been studying. He glanced again at the Regulator clock hung on the wall in the Stockman marshal's office. Burke had to be around town somewhere, but it sure wasn't here. Price leaned back in Burke's chair and glanced outside, hoping to spot the sorry excuse for a lawman.

Price's speckled stallion stood tied to the hitching rail. A young boy, maybe seven or eight, stood on the boardwalk outside the jail. He gawked at the horse as if he'd never seen one so large. At eighteen hands, the horse was massive, a trait the marshal had occasionally found useful and once had almost gotten them both killed.

The waif brushed a shock of mouse brown hair from his freckled face. Braces and a hemp rope knotted in front held up homespun pants covered in quilt-like, mismatched patches—near certain proof the boy had several older brothers who'd already outgrown the britches.

The boy took a tentative step toward the horse. "You're a good boy, ain't cha." The lad patted the horse on the nose.

The stallion took a half-step toward him and nickered a soft greeting.

"I wish I had somethin' for ya." He jammed his hands into baggy pockets and shrugged. "I shore don't." The boy hung his head, and the stallion offered a gentle nudge on his shoulder, as if he commiserated with the lad's problem.

The office door stood open, allowing Price to hear the conversation between his horse and the boy. A grin cracked his sour mood. "Hey, son."

Had he been taller the lad's jump might've bumped the overhanging sheriff's office sign. As it was, it drew a guffaw from Price.

"I-I'm sorry, Mister." The boy's body trembled. "I didn't me—"

"You're fine, kid." The wooden swivel chair creaked as Price rose. His boots beat hollow thuds on the plank floor as he strode around the desk. "Would you like to feed him?"

"You bet I would, Mister." The boy's smile spread ear to ear. "Can I?"

Price stepped through the doorway onto the boardwalk.

"You're the U.S. marshal, ain't cha?"

"United States Marshal Zebulon Ezra Price, at your service, young man." At the end he added a mock bow and flourish.

"Oh, boy. Wait'll I tell Pete." He glanced at the boardwalk. A big smile crossed his face, and he lifted his head until he could look the marshal in the eye. "Can I feed your horse, sir? I'd really like that."

"Sure thing. But first I have two questions for you."

A cloud crossed the boy's face. "But what if I ain't got no answer?"

"You can still feed Zeus."

"Okay."

Price knelt on one knee and looked the boy directly in his eye. "What's your name, son?"

"Tommy. Ma calls me Thomas when she's mad."

"Okay, Tommy. Second question. Do you know where Marshal Burke is?"

"Why I shore do. That's easy." He pointed at the building on the other side of the dusty street. "He's at the Wagon Wheel. Ever'one knows if'n he ain't at the jail he's there. B'sides, I seen him go in a bit ago and ain't seen him come out, yet."

"Thank you. Tell you what." Price stepped over to the horse and reached into a saddlebag, producing a foot-long carrot complete with another foot of greens. "You can give this to Zeus now. Then, if you'll do me a favor, I'll give you a sugar cube to feed him plus I'll pay you a nickel."

The boy took the carrot and held it out where the stallion could reach it. "Here you go, Zeus." With a gentle touch, the offering was accepted. "Shore is a funny name for a horse." Tommy chatted while the carrot disappeared in a series of crunches and munches. When it was gone he stretched on his tip toes again and patted the horse on the nose, telling him what a good boy he was. A shake of his head and mane, followed by a soft whinny was the answer.

Tommy screwed up his eyes and leaned his head toward Price. "What favor do you need?" Suspicion was thick in his tone. "When my big sister offers to pay me for a favor, it's somethin' like diggin' a new outhouse." Tommy pinched his nose as if to emphasize his point. "You ain't wantin' me to do somethin' like that are you?"

Price chuckled. "No. Nothing like that. I want you to run over to the Wagon Wheel and tell the marshal I need to see him right away."

Disappointment couldn't have crashed the boy's face any harder if he'd been told to quit playing and take a bath. "My ma, she don't let me go there. Calls it a den of ini—inik—"

"Iniquity?"

"That's it."

"Well, it probably is that. Your momma sounds pretty wise. How about instead if you run over there and tell that man sitting on that bench. He can get the marshal."

"I'll still get a nickel?"

"Deals a deal."

"Gotta share with that man?"

"Doesn't even have to know about our arrangement. Just tell him I sent you over."

"Gosh. Thanks."

"Make sure the man knows to tell Marshal Burke that I want to see him right away. It's important."

Tommy ran off, bare feet kicking up dust in the street. Halfway across, he jumped high, one tiny fist punching at the sky. "A whole nickel."

Price returned to the jailhouse, settled into Burke's chair, and propped his booted feet on the desk. A moment later he took up the thick stack of handbills again.

The boy returned quickly to collect his reward.

"Marshal Burke said he'd be over soon's he drinks his beer."

Price's right eye twitched and the muscles in his cheeks and neck tightened. An instant later he forced himself to offer the boy his best toothy grin and the reward.

———————

STONE RODE ALONG another draw. Water splashed with each hoof-fall. Since yesterday's scare, he'd slowed his pace, taking precautions against leaving an obvious back trail. This close to the Missouri River, ubiquitous feeder creeks and streams offered endless opportunities to confuse anyone following. False trails—a broken branch here, a shirt thread there, and horseshoe scratch on bare rock—laid before exiting creek beds or shallow cuts slowed his progress but also cost pursuers even more time.

Around a meander, splotches of sunlight filtered through a small grove of cottonwood and oak, leaving the sandy beach on one side dappled in shade and sun. The opposite side remained in deep shadow. Fifty feet ahead the bank had collapsed, and soft soil and rock swept across the sand. Stone used the grade to climb out of the draw leaving deep tracks in the loose debris.

He dismounted a hundred feet away within a stand of cotton-woods. Ground-tying the horses he secured a large, dead branch and began sweeping away tracks. The breeze, a regular companion on the prairie, shifted slightly from the north. The subtle change might have gone unnoticed except for new scents. Gone was the sweet bouquet of prairie grasses and flowers, replaced with the crisp tang of a shady river—rotted fish guts, bird leavings, stagnant water algae, moss, and—something else he couldn't identify—something acrid, almost smokey.

Stone jerked straight up. He inhaled and his eyes narrowed. His nostrils flared. He sniffed again. He glanced at the sun. Mid-morning. It smelled like the remnants of a poorly attended campfire. But this late in the day the only trace remaining should be visual.

Around another bend, deep in the shadow of the southeastern bank, he found the source—a still-smoldering campfire. And from the looks, much larger than four men needed to heat water for coffee and ablution, or to cook over.

Damned tenderfoots were gonna draw Yankton or Yanktonai warriors—if they were lucky. If not, it could also be Hunkpapa or some other Lakota tribe. That would not be lucky. Boot tracks dotted the soft sand around the fire, none distinct—the fine grit wouldn't hold an impression.

A faint snake-like trail led him atop the draw's bank. In soft dirt under a cottonwood was a single pair of fresh prints. Someone had stood in a single spot long enough to compress the soil. Someone with a long narrow foot, and a bad left leg.

Up to this point it had only been speculation that this was their campsite, but the track confirmed. They had been here, just this morning. Four hours, tops. Stone's breaths came in jagged gulps.

He was close.

"WHAT'RE WE GONNA do?" None of Shorty's usual bluster sounded in the whispered rasp.

Three men turned to Curly, who, having served as a corporal in Lee's army, was the only one of the four with military experience. "Frankie, grab the stock and get them hobbled. See if there ain't a spot farther up the draw that's deep enough to keep them out of sight." He pointed back over his shoulder. "Shorty, he'p him. Erik, keep an eye on the red devils, but stay out a sight. I'll gather our guns and extra ammo and scout for a better spot to defend in case they spot us."

Frankie frowned. "What about me? My gun's all busted up."

"Yeah, 'cause you're a danged fool." Curly paused and closed his eyes. A grimace crossed his face, though Frankie couldn't tell if he was angry, frustrated, praying, thinking, or some of all of them. A few seconds later he opened them and nodded to Frankie. "I got a spare revolver in my pack you can use. Now all a you, get movin'. Them Injuns'll be on us pretty soon."

As Frankie and Shorty walked back to the group from having hidden the animals, Curly hissed at them and waved them forward. He stood bent low at a spot where the draw bulged a dozen feet into the prairie, like a castle turret. Heavy scrub and tall grass lined the top of the bank while a small grove of cottonwoods rose from the sandy soil at the base. The location offered a clear view of the area above the animals, while affording the men good cover as well as wide, intersecting fields of fire.

Curly spaced everyone around the jut, stationing himself at the point, Shorty and Frankie along the south wall and Erik the north. As he positioned Frankie, he also handed him an old handgun. "Remember this ain't no rifle. Won't be accurate past fifty feet, so don't shoot till your target is close."

Frankie felt his face blanch as he swallowed hard. His hand shook. The gun's weight surprised him, and he fumbled with it, nearly dropping the heavy revolver. Rust pocked the long barrel and cylinder edges. "This thing even shoot? Ain't gonna blow me up is it?"

"It's fine. Took it off'n a dead Yank. Never had much use for it after the war. Tested it 'fore I left home." Curly pulled a couple of boxes from his pocket. "Extra loads and caps just in case, though if you need 'em, likely we're all in trouble."

He trotted back to his station, turning to Frankie before taking position. "And don't shoot unless I do. Got it?"

Frankie nodded.

Eyes hard, Curly swept his gaze to Shorty, paused, then continued to Erik. "You two got it? No firing until I say. If we're lucky they'll ride right on past without ever spotting us." He didn't wait for their agreement before returning his attention to the Indians thundering closer.

Frankie marveled at the horsemanship and speed—he couldn't ride at more than a slow cantor. Fierce, savage faces painted bright red, yellow, and black seemed to stare right at him. Dark blotches hung from several lances.

"What's that tied to their lances?" Frankie's whispering voice squeaked.

"Scalps, you danged fool." Curly shot him a glare that would've melted an iceberg. "Now hobble your lips."

Hard swallows had Frankie's Adam's apple bobbing. He was sure Death stood before him, scythe ready to reap its harvest.

"Heard the Indians tie their enemies to stakes with their guts hanging out." Shorty's voice quaked. "Leave 'em alive for the coyotes to eat.

Frankie's throat tightened. Why'd he ever leave Pennsylvania? "Please don't let it hurt." He jumped, not realizing he had whispered aloud.

Soon fewer than a hundred yards stood between him and the Indians. He sneaked a peek over his shoulder at Shorty. A large wet spot was visible on the front of the man's pants. Despite the fear gnawing his own innards, Frankie grinned. Shorty was even more scared than he was.

"Kiyiyiyiyi!" A single piercing whoop sliced the air.

Frankie jerked his attention back to the Indians. His guts twisted and cramped. An act of will was all that kept his breakfast down.

One of the riders raised a fist high and the entire band of charging horsemen halted almost as one. They were close enough to pick out details. Gray streaked the hair of the rider who raised his fist. Heavy wrinkles cut into his weathered features and made him appear much older than the others. With the breeze in his face, Frankie was sure he could smell the savages—almost feel their hot, fetid breath on the wind.

A single warrior galloped in from the south. The new arrival plunged his mount into the center of the halted bunch. Instead of racing past, at the last second, he pulled his pony up and careened to a stop in front of the old man. His speech accompanied with wild gesticulations, the newcomer jabbered at the leader. Through holes in the scrub Frankie peered at them, but couldn't hear what was being said—not that he'd understood if he could.

A flurry of activity broke out among the Indians. The old chief shouted and raised his lance high. His horse reared up, and its front hooves pawed the air. With a wild yell from the chief, the horse dropped back and raced southwest with the others right behind, their screams joining with the chief's.

Frankie's trigger finger had turned white, and he realized his gun wavered in front of him. His throat dried as he fought to suppress a cough. The weapon dropped from his grip into the dirt. Shivers coursed down his body and his legs sagged. Warm wetness flooded his pants.

TWENTY-SEVEN.

Price had counted every single one of the twenty-seven minutes required for Burke to finish his beer and find his way across the street to meet with the United States marshal. Every five minutes or so he swapped where he rested his feet, alternating between Burke's desk and the floor. Price glanced up from the handbill he held as the town's marshal pushed open the door and walked in. When Price returned his attention to the wanted poster, each white-knuckled fist held a crumpled half of the paper—he hadn't heard it tear.

Price found the local lawman's eyes with his steady gaze, but he made no effort to stand, extend a hand, or remove his booted feet from the desk. "Marshal Burke, glad you finally managed to finish that beer." A deep breath and iron will were all that kept his tone even.

"Price." Burke nodded his greeting, his gaze sweeping past Price's eyes to instead find something in the street to stare at.

"You ready to ride out to Stone's place? Need to ask him some questions and invite him to join the posse."

"Do you *really* need me?" The big man knuckled the small of his back. "My back's plum sore still from ridin' out there for Sally's funeral."

"Wasn't that four days ago? You haven't been back since?"

Burke turned toward the U.S. marshal—his glance lingered on the marshal's feet propped on his desk. With a sigh he pulled a wooden chair from beside the wall over to the desk and plopped into it. "'Course not. Why would I?"

A mental satisfaction, the sort that comes from a delicious meal or the completion of a difficult task, at Burke's response—both to the boots on his desk and the refusal to allow Burke use of his own desk chair—filled Price's mind without touching his facial expression. "To check on him. Make sure he stuck around like I told him to. Maybe to see if he was okay. He did just lose his wife."

Anger and defiance fought for dominance in the glare Burke shot Price. "Not my job."

"I see. Any of the town folk been out?"

"Wouldn't know. Don't rightly care."

"Don't care about anyone in town? Or don't care about Stone?" Price gave Burke a moment to answer, but none came. "Well, I went there before coming here. I'd hoped he had waited, but he didn't. By the looks of it, he's been gone several days." In a smooth, easy motion that belied its suddenness, he pulled his feet off Burke's desk, sat up, and leaned toward Burke as far as possible. The weight of his stare pressed Burke deeper into the chair he occupied, holding him there like invisible bonds. "Did you *even* tell him that I said to wait here for me?"

"C... course I did. Ask Doc Brady, he heard me." Burke squirmed in his chair. "Don't surprise me none that he run off on his own, though. Always was a damned stubborn fool."

"But you weren't aware that he'd left?"

"No, I didn't know. Why would I know or care?"

Marshal Price's voice softened to a whisper. "Maybe because the last thing I said in my telegram was for *you* to make sure he didn't chase after the murderers alone."

"Not like I can watch him all the time."

"At the very least you could have kept in touch by sending folks out to check on him. Or did they already know he was going after Sally's killers? Why didn't you know that?"

"Now, see he—"

"No." Price backhanded the stack of wanted posters. They whirled and floated to the floor. Immediately, he moderated his tone, but kept the contempt. "This is your town. Why didn't you know, if they knew? Makes me wonder just how effective you are, Burke."

"That's a bit harsh, now, Marshal." Charles Willis filled the doorway. "Surely you can't blame him if no one reported Stone's departure. Besides, he was busy quelling a near riot, here."

"That's right." Burke, who had slid in his chair, sat up straighter. "And a good thing I was here too. Half the town was up in arms fixin' to form a posse their own selves. Figured they'd have themselves a necktie party."

Charles stepped deeper into the office and stood beside Burke, large meaty hand resting on the marshal's shoulder. "The town has been most upset that you ordered Marshal Burke to wait. Everyone in town loved sweet Sally. Aren't many here that wouldn't do for

Stone either. Despite his surly streak, he helped anyone who needed it. Why, he helped half the Swede's build their soddies. Ask anyone. Stone would help anyone in need."

Marshal Price stared at Charles. "Then let's hope Stone doesn't do anything I'd be forced to arrest him for." He paused but continued to stare at Charles. "I need to interview all the witnesses before I get the posse pulled together. We leave at first light."

PRICE INTERVIEWED BURKE first.

"Mister Willis came in all in a perspiration. Rode back from Yankton that morning and jess got into town. Lots a strangers ridin' up an' was worried about trouble, so he come seen me." Burke paused long enough to jam his thumbs behind his suspender straps. "Kind a' advance warnin', might say."

"Anyway, he and I were discussing what to do about these strangers when his son, Howard, came burstin' in. He blabbered on about miners and Stone being hurt and Sally murdered and a gun fight. Didn't make no sense a'tall. Had to slow him down and drag the whole story out a him. Once I heard it, why I rounded up a couple men and had Howard take us all out to the Stone farm."

"Anything else? You get the doctor?"

"Yup, had one a the fellers run tell Doc Brady. Told him to help the doc hook up his buggy."

"And what about Charles Willis? He go out with you?"

"Nope, shore didn't. Had pressin' business in town. But he did remind me that the Stone place was your jurisdiction, and thus, I didn't have any authority to round up a posse."

HOWARD WILLIS SAT across from Price, tall but loose, arms folded across his thick chest, one leg thrown over the other. Sky-blue eyes looked around the room, occasionally glancing at the marshal, but not making direct eye contact. A crooked smile dimpled cheeks covered with a thin growth of peach fuzz. Light brown curls just brushed the collar of his blue shirt.

Price watched the man-child but said nothing.

Howard shifted the weight on his buttocks in the chair and switched legs.

Price continued to stare but said nothing. What lay underneath the boy-man? Some might mistake the expression—the look in his eye—as mirth. Except it wasn't. It was something else. What? Pondering wasn't answering the question, but he'd figure it out soon enough.

"How'd you happen to be out at the Stone place Thursday?" He leaned in and used the intensity of his gaze to capture Howard's, almost forcing the boy-man to hold his stare.

Howard switched legs again. "I was on my way to do some hunting. I like to go out past the Stone's to the Oak Grove Hill area. Some forest and a meadow there with lots of small game."

"Go out past the Flater place too?"

"Yup. Well, it ain't the Flater's anymore. Dad bought them out last week."

"I'd heard your dad was buying farmers out along the valley, but didn't know he'd bought that far out." Price began drumming his fingers on the desk. "Any idea why?"

Howard squinted like he wasn't sure what the marshal was asking. "You mean why Dad bought out Flater? Couldn't farm worth a lick. Wife was expecting again. Heard he was gonna try his hand at gold mining."

"Heard from your father?"

He shook his head. "Dad hasn't said anything to me about it, except that morning he asked me to check in on the place. You know, make sure Flater had moved out."

"Go on. Tell me what happened as you rode past the Stone's." He held his hand up and rolled his wrist to emphasize his command.

"Yah. So, like I said, I was going hunting. I was just cresting the ridge south of their place when I heard a gunshot. Just a second or two later three men busted out of the house like a grizzly was after them." He uncrossed his legs and planted both feet on the floor in front of him. Leaning forward, his eyes widened. "As they mounted up one of them saw me. Before I knew it, they opened up on me with their rifles while they rode away."

"And where were you, again, when you first spotted them?"

"On the road just coming down the hill south of the house."

"How far would you say?"

"Oh, maybe two hundred yards, give or take a little."

"Within easy rifle range?"

Howard nodded.

"But you didn't return fire at that point?"

"Didn't have my rifle. Just my Colt." He touched the revolver on his hip. Faint pastel shades of pink and blue swirled under the opalescent surface of the grips. The belt was tooled with some fancy design. "Latest from Colt, you know. The .44-.40. Dad bought it for me last year. Had the pearl grips installed special and paid some leatherworker a bundle for the belt. Designed for a quick draw. Slick, huh."

"I'm familiar with the gun." He reached into the open drawer on his right and dropped a matched pair in plain holsters rolled up in a gun belt on the desk. His own had the more practical wooden grips—he'd seen men die because their fancy grips were slick, or the gun hung up in their embellished holsters. Ornate didn't make fast—or accurate. "Thought you said you were going hunting? Without your rifle?"

"I like to practice my fast draw against the rabbits and coyotes."

"Rabbits don't shoot back."

"So?"

Price shook his head. He'd buried a few young men over the years.

Damn dime novels and their wild stories about James Butler Hickock, especially that fight with that Tutt fellow down in Springfield. Fool kids. "Then what happened?"

"Figured the Stone's must be in some kind of trouble, so I rode hard to the porch. The three men turned toward me, so I was forced to shoot my way to the door. Got inside just in time. That's when I found Stone just starting to sit up. Had blood all over his face and shirt, like he was hurt bad. And, Sally was, well, you know."

The marshal made Howard repeat the story twice more, hauling every detail from the man-child. It wasn't much, but it was a start.

———————

STONE EXAMINED THE loam at the edge of the draw. Prints were sown like chicken feed all along a forty-yard length, concentrated in a natural, curving redan jutting into the prairie. Loose soil made most of the prints indistinguishable from any other, but there was enough sign to tell the story. Farther upstream a remuda had been picketed, but here four men had defended this position just this morning. One stood as if he had military training. Among the other three sets of prints to either side, one had long, narrow feet. He was still on the right trail.

Stone's military training convinced him this had been some form of skirmish line, except there was no indication a battle ever took place. He poked at grass clumps, broken twigs, detritus deposited along the stream, but he couldn't find any blood, no shell casings, no fired caps carelessly tossed aside, no broken lances, and no stray arrows.

With his chin cradled in the web of his thumb and forefinger, he scratched at his stubbled jowls, eyes unfocused, trying to see what caused them to take a defensive position. What had happened here?

Stone shook his head as he mounted. He didn't go far before he knew what spooked the miners. Fifty yards into the prairie, the tall grass had been trampled and ground under the unshod hooves of a large herd of horses. Deeper impressions clustered around one spot, as if in discussion. To one side many lighter prints marred the prairie. So, more than half the herd were riderless. Stolen by a raiding party? Or spare mounts for hunting? He'd crossed onto reservation land day before yesterday, so these had to be Sioux.

A black speck on the ground caught his eye, and he nudged his mare closer. He dismounted and knelt to examine it. A feather caught in a soil clod—a crow's feather. Blood stained the quill and coated portions of the vane. The dried blood looked fresh, maybe three or four days old. It must have fallen unnoticed from some brave's lance while they rested here.

The Sioux and Crow tribes had been mortal enemies for a long time. Competing interests in the same hunting grounds brought conflicts. Also, from time to time a party of young braves of either tribe would go raiding to prove their courage. This inevitably led to a retaliatory strike.

This far east on the reservation probably marked this as one of the Dakota Sioux tribes, most likely Yankton or Yanktonai, but Lakota—Oglala or Brule—weren't out of the question. Far better if the former. Regardless, the braves would still be excited from the raid, anxious for more. With any luck they'd keep riding and never know he'd been here.

With his field glasses he scanned the horizon to the north. They'd come from that direction, heading south toward one of several villages that dotted the Missouri River shore. Checking to the south, there was no sign of any riders. He followed the trail of bent and broken tall grass that marked their trail, keeping the glasses trained on it as it swung.

Then the blood drained from his face.

MARSHAL PRICE'S HEAD pounded in time to the tune the brassy

pianist beat out of the ivories. Men stood three deep and shoulder to shoulder at the Wagon Wheel's bar. Many planned to leave with him in the morning—more than half were men who had never ridden with a posse or fired a weapon at another human being. Their nervousness and its engendered bravado added to the stress feeding the marshal's headache.

He was allowing the inexperienced to come against his better judgment—not that he had a choice. The problems started with Howard Willis. He was the only one who saw the attackers and Price needed his identification when they were caught. Even Mr. Willis agreed that his son should go, much to the marshal's surprise.

Unfortunately, though, that also meant that young Howard's friends insisted on going. One young man along was an acceptable risk, but a crew of them begged for trouble. Price tried to leave them home, but Charles Willis disagreed, threatening to involve the territorial governor if necessary. Since the two were friends, the marshal knew if he wanted to remain the U.S. marshal, pressing the issue wasn't the smart play. On the other hand, if he wanted to stay alive, it might be the only way.

It wasn't the murderers they chased that worried him. Troubles with the Sioux had already started. If they encountered a war party and one of these green horns got an itch, the whole posse would be in danger. The last report from the army indicated that Red Cloud and Spotted Tail were still on the reservation. But Sitting Bull of the Hunkpapa, White Bull of the Cheyenne, and others had stepped up their raids.

Maybe there won't be any shooting and everything will be okay. And maybe pigs will fly. Price rubbed his temples. *What am I getting myself into?*

AN ITCH DEVELOPED exactly halfway between Stone's shoulder blades. This itch had no cure. Backing up to a tree or barn door would not relieve it, a wife's scratching would not make it go away. No, this itch came from deep inside the primitive soul buried within every man. Civilization, try as it might, could not smother that part of the spirit, though it could bury it deeper and dull a man's ability to sense it. Stone was different. Years of war followed by frontier living taught him how to stay open to that ancient self. This was the itch of the hunted. The trail of the Sioux turned east. Within an hour, two at the most, they would intersect his trail. As he examined the tracks, his best guess made them three hours old.

Gooseflesh crawled up his spine like a slow-moving snake. Even now they could be following his trail. As a child growing up amongst the Seneca in New York west of the Finger Lakes, his native friends could track better than most experienced white hunters. On the plains, almost all the tribes survived by hunting. Children were taught to read sign. By the time they were adults, they had become experts. He scanned the prairie he'd just crossed again. A copse of cottonwoods attracted his attention. Was a brave even now watching from there, waiting for the opportunity to take his scalp? He wouldn't know. Sioux were masters at using the landscape to hide. A dozen warriors could even now be within fifty feet—one could remain hidden even within ten feet—and he'd never see them.

A trickle of sweat ran down his temple, across his cheek, and disappeared into the forest of stubble it found there.

He'd been careful since realizing he had been leaving a backtrail a novice could follow, so it seemed more likely they would discover the trail he'd been following. But that was little comfort as now he stood between this war party and the men he, too, hunted.

CHAPTER 11

MRS. FEDICK'S FRONT parlor measured exactly six paces across. Stone knew this because over the last hour he had paced from one side to the other enough times to be positive of the count. Since the room was essentially square, he assumed it was also six paces from front to back. The Greek Revival house sported the tall front windows typical of the style. Left open overnight to cool the house's accumulation of heat from the cooking stove and the summer sun drew a breeze from the kitchen which carried the aroma of frying sausage and fresh-baked biscuits, but he barely noticed.

Outside the streetlamps had not yet been extinguished for the day, though the gray blanket of predawn was just beginning to lift.

The week had dragged. The emerald-eyed angel, whose name he still didn't know, was all he could think about. A dozen times a day Stone stopped himself—stopped himself from dropping by the dress shop to see her—stopped himself from staring through the shop window to watch her—stopped himself from keeping vigil on the shop from Mrs. Fedick's front parlor. He couldn't sleep. Ate sparingly. One night, desperate to catch a fleeting glimpse of her leaving the shop, he sat in the parlor waiting for her to close. He abandoned his post after a few minutes for fear someone would appear to escort her to her home. Any time he wanted to dash across the street, he thought about the smirk she flashed when he fumbled over his words. She knew he was there because of her. If he was to have any chance with her, he couldn't keep playing the fool in front of her.

"Breakfast is ready." Mrs. Fedick tugged at his arm. "The others are waiting."

One chair remained empty for him. No one wanted to sit at the head of the table. That spot had always been reserved for Mr. Fedick. He'd been dead for a few years, so now whoever came last sat there, and it became their responsibility to say grace. Stone lowered himself into the chair without saying a word. Around the table heads bowed and eyes closed.

A minute passed. Stone sat mute. The middle-aged businessman who sat on his left opened one eye. He kicked Stone's foot, which had the desired effect. Stone stumbled through a prayer.

Flatware clinked and clattered on everyday china as the boarders attacked the repast with abandon. Except Stone. He pushed eggs around the plate, dredging them through sausage gravy, but he ate nothing.

"Mister Stone. The war may be over, but eggs are still dear. Why don't you eat? The young lady will appreciate it if you don't faint away while calling on her."

"Huh." Stone shook his head. "Did you ask me something, Missus Fedick?"

The nine other men at the table guffawed, two added a knee slap. To her credit, Mrs. Fedick only smiled. "Eat, Mister Stone. You'll need your strength for later, when you call on the young lady."

Stone furled his brows. "What makes you think—"

"Tsk tsk. Come now, I raised four boys. Not to mention that I was a young lady once myself. Mister Fedick was as nervous as a mouse in a house of tabbies when he came calling the first time." A twinkle flashed in one eye, and she chuckled. "Thought surely Daddy would meet him at the door with his musket loaded." She waggled her index finger and fixed him with a motherly stare.

Warmth crawled up Stone's neck straight to his ears.

"Wasted good food on you all week. Now eat. It's going to be whatever it is."

EVEN AFTER THE emerald-eyed angel unlocked the door, Stone forced himself to wait—they didn't open for another half hour, and he didn't want to seem too anxious. He'd wait until mid-morning. As he watched from a wicker chair deep in the parlor, where no one from outside would notice him, a gray-haired woman, medium height, and just on the pleasant side of plump, arrived ten minutes after the angel. As the woman opened the door, her mouth moved as if speaking, but even with the parlor windows open to the cool morning breeze, Stone couldn't hear what was said.

Stone went back to his room to lie down. Maybe he could sleep for an hour after having been awake most of the night. He tugged his boots off before stripping out of the uniform he'd pressed yesterday, folding it carefully to maintain the military creases. Once under the blanket, he closed his eyes, forcing his breathing to slow to a steady rhythm as he pushed all thoughts from his mind. The more he tried to blank his mind, the more scenarios played out where she rejected him. But he forced himself to try.

Stone must have dozed at some point because he sat up just as the wall clock outside his room chimed ten—time for him to cross the street. Stone's heart raced, and his stomach churned. This wait had been worse than the anticipation of battle. With battle, guns needed oiling, ammunition pouches filled, bayonets sharpened, breastworks strengthened. The activity kept thoughts of death's immanence at bay.

This was different. After the first few days touring the city, he was left with little to do to keep his mind off the impending meeting. Imagination and fear took over. Rejection seemed far worse than death. What would he do if she had a beau already calling on her? Or if she thought him a fool? His throat dropped into his gut like a rock down a well. Charging an enemy line bristling with cannon and carbines induced far less fear than the thought of asking this angel if he could call on her.

Yet, ten minutes later he walked into the shop. He blinked at the change from the bright street to the dimness of the shop. The angel sat behind a large sewing machine, working the pedal as she pushed material through. Blood pounded in his ears, blocking the steady tapping of the needle rising and falling. Focused on her work, the angel didn't notice him, and the older, gray-haired lady he'd seen enter after her approached him.

"Can I help you, sir?" A slight French accent touched her voice.

"Oh, ah, I'm back to pick up a uniform jacket." Without looking at the woman Stone nodded toward the angel. "I dropped it off to her last week."

"I remember that jacket. That was a challenge." She turned to the angel. "Sally, you have a customer." When Sally looked up, a smile dimpled the older lady's cheek as she used her head to point to Stone. "Are you done with this young man's jacket?"

Sally. Even her name seemed angelic to Stone.

"Thank you, *L'Oréal.* I am." Turning to Stone she added, "It's in the office. I'll be back in a moment."

Stone watched as she retreated to the back of the small shop— her movements pure grace to Stone, her voice a melody. Sweat broke out on his brow. What interest would a woman like her have in a broken-down soldier like him? Maybe he could leave now before she came back. It wouldn't be stealing—the work was paid for. He swallowed hard. His feet shuffled as if to obey an order to retreat.

Sally returned to the front of the dress shop, jacket in hand, before the bugle officially sounded retreat. Stone swallowed hard. He could still back out—just take his jacket and run.

"Here we are, Major Stone." She held the coat by its epaulettes, front toward Stone. "Come try it on. We need to make sure it fits." Her voice held a light-hearted teasing tone. She signaled him to come to her.

"Let me help you with that." *L'Oréal* held his uniform coat as he shrugged out of it.

He allowed Sally to help him into the Zouave jacket, then turned to face her.

L'Oréal's eyes widened, and her hands covered her mouth. "Oh, just like my home's foreign legion. You look dashing, young major." With a twinkle in her eye, she shot Sally a knowing, sly smile, then put her hand over her mouth.

Sally nodded, an appraising smile on her face. She tugged at seams and smoothed wrinkles. Once again, her touch sent warm jolts up and down his torso.

"Major Stone, what do you think? Meet your approval?" Sally's tone was level and businesslike.

Stone blinked, his throat dry.

"Major Stone?"

Stone nodded while he tried to work some moisture into his mouth. He coughed. "It's perfect."

"Good. Now take it off, and I'll get it wrapped up for you."

Sally took the jacket to a counter in a back corner. Paper rustled and soon she had it ready. "Here you go, Major." She held the package but made no move to hand it to him.

"Th... thank you." Stone reached for it, but Sally shook her head.

"Just a moment. You overpaid me for this. I owe you some money."

Stone stared. "But I paid you what you asked."

"You did." An emerald sparkle flashed in her eyes. "Just how imprudent you are with money? Do you not know what services are worth?" She shook her head slowly. "Makes a girl wonder how such an irresponsible man became a major in the army."

"B... but you told me that was the price."

"And you just paid it without even questioning the amount? Why, a body could buy an entire suit of clothes for thirty-five dollars." She set the package on the counter again and laid thirty dollars on top. "No, I'm afraid that if I were to marry, it would have to be to a solid, sensible man." A stern look replaced her smile, but the twinkle never left her eyes.

"Well, I'm—" Stone stopped for a minute, looked at her, and screwed up all his courage. "You know, you never did tell me your name, and I would like to see you again."

"What do you take me for? A fancy lady, that I would consent to let you come by my home? I hardly know you." The indignation in her voice didn't touch the light in her eyes.

"N... no, of course not. I just wanted to, you know—"

"No, I don't know, but I'm sure you're going to explain, aren't you?"

"Yes, ma'am. I wanted you to know that I think you're about the prettiest woman I've ever laid eyes on. And, well, I thought... that we could step out one night." He blurted it out before his nerve drained. "If... if you wanted to, of course."

Sally eyed him, as if considering whether to throw him out on his ear or boot him in the ass. Damn. He'd gone too far. Stone's heart fell into the deepest pit in his gut. His chin touched his chest. Life was over.

"Well." She cleared her throat and scrunched up her face. "You can certainly be direct."

Silence. She said nothing.

Stone stared into those sparkling green eyes but said nothing more.

"Sally Quinlan. You can find me at the Hightower Boarding House for Women."

CHAPTER 12

STONE WOKE OF a sudden, primal instinct on full alert—the exhaustion of short sleep and long days in the saddle vanished the same instant. The hairs on the back of his neck stood on end. Heart slamming in his chest, he fought to maintain steady even breathing. Years of war had taught him how debilitating fear could be if allowed to take root, so he shoved back at the welling in his throat.

He opened his eyes—mere slits at first to preserve his night vision, a moment later, fully open. Under his blanket, his right hand fell naturally on the Colt Army he kept near to hand, and he palmed the butt, the worn walnut comforting in his grip despite the decade since the last time it had dealt death. Predawn gray shrouded much of the prairie. Fields of varying shades of deep blue hung roof-like over the earth. Some of the brightest stars remained visible overhead. Rolling his eyes right, yellow and orange scratched short, thin lines on the edge of the horizon, the glow indicating where the sun would rise.

Something hard thumped his head above his ear. He rolled his eyes left—and stared into a black hole exactly fifty-eight one hundredths of an inch wide—the muzzle width of an old Springfield. Stone forced down the bile that threatened to rise from his guts.

A brave, twenty winters old at most, held the weapon. Cords stood out on the man's neck and the gun wavered in his grip. The broad whites of his eyes flashed as they flicked side to side.

Stone recognized the symptoms. The young man was on a wire's edge and every beat of his heart wound him tighter, making it even more likely he would accidentally pull the trigger.

Watching the brave was like watching a cannon ball loft toward you, sensing the immediacy of death but knowing nothing you did could prevent it. Stone wasn't sure he could move his hands quick enough to knock the carbine away without tangling them in the folds of his blanket, leaving him unable to get out of his bedroll.

His palm rested on the Colt's handle, but so many things could go wrong. Maybe it was best to wait to make his move. Stone recounted the potential problems. The hammer of his Colt could catch on the blanket, either in its cocking or firing. What if a cap had fallen off in the night? For now, he should wait. See how this played out.

Stone glanced at the brave. Had that trigger finger twitched? Size and experience played in his favor. If he slipped inside the muzzle, he could wrestle the gun away from him. That would end the standoff.

Unless the kid fired while Stone made his move.

To hell with waiting.

Stone threw his blanket over the Springfield and rolled toward the man holding it, getting out from under the blanket in one sudden, quick movement. His upward lunge caught the brave still fighting to untangle from the blanket, and in an instant, the two wrestled for the Springfield. Stone had thirty pounds on the young warrior, not to mention years of experience. A well-placed knee and a vicious twist of the gun barrel and Stone had the weapon. Still wrapped in the blanket, it was useless, so he tossed it aside and lifted his fist to lash out. One blow, then a second. Nasal cartilage crumpled with the second. Blood gushed.

He drew his fist back for yet another punch, but something smashed into his skull from behind. The stars Stone saw weren't in the sky. He crashed forward.

WHEN HE CAME to, Stone found himself lying on the ground, his hands bound in front of him. Buffalo hide thongs bit into his wrists. Blood stained the skin around the bindings. Voices came from close by, but he didn't see the speakers. The language he recognized from his trading excursions—Sioux. By twisting back and forth, he worked himself to a sitting position. He took it as a positive sign that he was still alive and didn't seem to be in immediate peril.

He examined his surroundings. The sun was just peeking over the horizon. Birds and insects chirped and buzzed, oblivious to his plight. The ubiquitous prairie breeze brushed his face and neck, carrying the dry scent of a hot, rainless day. Two young braves stood near his hobbled horses. The one he wrestled with was average height while the other was taller, though not as tall as Stone. Ribs and spine protruded from both their backs. A scarred welt crossed the shoulder of the taller one as if a bullet or arrow had grazed him there.

Next to the horses, Stone had laid a ground cloth the night before and stowed the packs of supplies, mostly food stuffs, and saddlebags there and covered them with an oilcloth. The pair threw back the oilcloth. Scar, as Stone thought of him, squatted to dig through the saddlebags, the other slashed open a bundle of supplies. Stone's Henry lay at the feet of the one going through the saddlebags. A Springfield lay at the feet of the other, though Stone didn't know if it was the one he'd wrestled for earlier or a different one.

As if sensing him staring, the two turned, a mixture of unease and anger written on their faces. The one he'd started beating sported a nose swollen to the size of a green walnut and the beginnings of a shiner under his left eye. Shiner wore Stone's Colt buckled around his waist, the Bowie sheathed on the opposite hip. With a scowl toward Stone, he muttered something to his companion who nodded and stalked away. The cruel smile Shiner offered drew a matching smile from Stone who refused to acknowledge fear. Shiner bent to grab the Springfield. He used it to wave Stone toward the horses.

―――――――――――

STONE'S FEET ACHED. His captors had stolen what supplies and weapons they wanted, tying them to his horses in packs, leaving the rest, including his saddle, to rot or provide for prairie wildlife. Thankfully he'd been allowed to pull on his boots. While they weren't designed for walking, it beat walking the plains in his stocking feet.

His captors rode ponies, taking turns leading horses or him. By his estimation, they'd covered about ten miles, and this was the first break. Not since forced marches in Grant's army had he walked so far so fast. The bandana around his neck was soaked in sweat, as was his shirt. Stone fumbled with the canteen still tied to his packhorse—had to restrain himself to keep from draining it. Who knew when he'd be able to refill it.

The braves sat atop their ponies chatting in low voices and scanning the expanse of prairie to the south. Scar pointed southwest as he spoke, and Shiner seemed to agree.

The lump in Stone's gut grew. This was taking him farther and farther from Sally's murderers. He'd hoped to catch them before they reached Fort Pierre, but they'd likely make Fort Pierre by late tomorrow. From there a riverboat ride and a few days overland would have them in Deadwood. Hundreds of miners had flocked to the area around Deadwood Gulch since gold was discovered. To hear tell, mines had sprung up on every plot of ground for miles around. He'd play hell finding the killers once they blended into that environment.

If he could just free himself. The black mare was fast and while she'd been ridden hard the last few days, Stone was confident she'd outrun the Indian ponies.

He dropped to the ground. The boot knife was still sheathed in his right boot. As long as they continued to ignore him, he had a chance. His poor mare would have to take him bareback, but they'd

be okay. Worse, though, he'd have to leave the guns and supplies behind. Toughness was etched into his every fiber, but taking on two
full-grown men would be difficult under any circumstances. Add his
injuries and exhaustion, and he'd need Lady Luck and every four-leaf
clover in the territory to beat them.

No, he'd leave the pack horse and weapons and just race away.
Once he made it to Fort Pierre, he could always use some of the al-
ternative acquisition skills he'd learned in an often on-the-march,
short-supplied infantry regiment.

With a wary eye on the braves, he edged up his right pant leg. One
still-tied hand slid inside the boot cuff, when, as if sensing his intent,
Scar whipped his pony around, a suspicious scowl on his face. Heart
in his throat, Stone began scratching furiously at his leg. Scar laughed.

"What are you laughing at?"

Shiner turned.

Stone hadn't expected an answer, so it came as no surprise when
neither said anything to him. While still scratching the non-existent
itch, he tried again in French. Many of the older Sioux spoke at least
some since it was the language of the fur trappers and traders who
settled Fort Pierre, but the younger natives seldom if ever used it.
They looked at each other, laughed some more, and turned back to
the vast prairie to the south.

No longer scratching at a non-existent itch, his fingers brushed
the hilt. With his hands tied, it was difficult to get deep enough in the
boot for the job, but he kept tugging the weapon higher a half inch at
a time, all the while watching that his captors didn't catch him.

The top of the hilt peeked over the top.

The braves turned their ponies and started shouting at Stone.
He dropped the knife, and it slid back into the sheath. Stone's heart
stopped, and he held his breath. Had they seen the blade? A quick
swallow, a final scratch, and he pushed his pant leg down over the
boot. A minute later, he was once again double-timing behind Shiner.

"I NEED THAT deed." Charles Willis's voice held tension bordering on desperation—both unfamiliar to him. It made him uncomfortable.

The man across the desk from him leaned back in his leather chair and stared with unfocused eyes over Charles's right shoulder. Elias Davenport, Esquire, was long and lean. Light from a wall sconce reflected off his smooth head. He laced his fingers together and bounced his forefingers—which were steepled church-like—gently off his pursed lips.

"Elias." The big man jumped to his feet and slapped the hand-carved walnut desk in front of him. Rage set fire to his cheeks. The chair he vacated tipped over behind him and fell to the floor with a loud clatter. "Did you hear me? I need that deed."

"I heard you just fine." Elias focused his eyes and lifted his chin to stare at Charles. His voice a calm whisper, he continued to speak while his fingers maintained their rhythmic bounce. "If you have damaged my chair, I shall add the cost of a replacement to your already exorbitant bill. Now, sit down and be quiet. Let me think." He shifted his gaze, and his eyes once again became distant.

Charles blinked three times—surprised at the cool demeanor of his friend and advisor, and the ease with which his own anger had been salved. After a moment's hesitation, he bent down to right his chair and returned to it. He stared at Elias who, for fifteen years, had assisted in the negotiations and written the contracts for all Charles's land deals. The calm patience Elias exhibited both frustrated and amazed him. There was no question in his mind that the lawyer was the best attorney west of the Mississippi—even east of it few matched his prowess. Thus, Charles tolerated the arrogance and air of superiority as he had numerous times before.

After his unfortunate meeting with Emerson Lockhart, Charles wired Elias in St. Louis, one of several cities the jurisprudent maintained an office. The telegraph encouraged Elias to return to Yankton as quickly as possible to assist Charles with his crisis.

The lawyer continued to stare beyond his client. Charles tapped his foot—the rhythmic sound soothed his anxiety—until Elias returned his attention to Charles with a glare intense enough to back down an angry grizzly. Charles forced himself to still his foot and shifted in his chair.

"The challenge is that Judge Thompson is not going to just issue an order for an investigation." Elias's soft, controlled voice carried the authority of experience. "I shall have to present some evidence of possible malfeasance. Did you retain the telegram that ordered Mister Stone to stay in town? From the United States marshal, correct?"

"Correct." Charles reached into his vest pocket, producing a yellow slip of paper. "It's right here." From the satchel at his feet he withdrew a single sheet of paper. "And this is Marshal Burke's statement that confirms the order was conveyed to Stone at least twice."

"Mister Stone has abandoned his homestead?"

"No one is there. He left without leaving word of his departure or destination. Fields haven't been planted or even fully plowed for planting. He left his livestock. A young man from town has been riding out to care for the animals. Doctor Brady arranged that, not Stone. Sounds abandoned to me."

Elias nodded. "Before you leave, please write out your statement and give it to my secretary. He'll witness it, and I shall add it to the filing I will prepare for the judge."

"Is there anything else you require?"

"No. I can prepare any additional documents necessary. By this time tomorrow, I shall have the order from Judge Thompson. Under normal circumstances, the Land Office would take a week or more to even assign an investigator, but I know some people there and believe I can have that accomplished tomorrow as well."

Elias paused and seemed to consider something. He leaned forward and grinned. "I know both investigators for the Dakota Territory and feel comfortable saying that once one is assigned, you should have no problem... shall we say... directing him to the... ahhh... correct conclusion."

"I'm confident that should not be a problem." For the first time in the two days since his meeting with Lockhart, Charles smiled.

CHARLES STRODE DOWN the boardwalk, headed for his bank. He needed cash to cover the bribe he must pay the investigator tomorrow. He disliked such an obvious transaction, but he would not have time to return to Stockman to retrieve it from the stash he kept in his safe for such occasions.

A man working to hang a placard blocked the way ahead. *Palms Read, Séances Conducted. Madame La Vay—Medium.*

"Such rubbish." He muttered to himself as he moved to slide around the workman. He glanced back at the storefront and stopped. Silently, he stared through the window—eyebrows knitted. "Still, it would be nice to know if Judd Stone was dead." Then he stepped through the bank's open doorway.

STONE AND HIS captors topped a small rise as the sun reached its zenith. From the rolling ridgeline, the vast expanse of the undulating prairie once again opened to their view. The gentle, south-facing slope descended into a shallow basin. Excitement, or what passed for it among a typically stoic people, showed on the young warrior's faces.

A hard lump formed in Stone's gut.

Gathered in the depression at the bottom stood twenty Sioux warriors and a pair of chiefs. They were a hundred yards away, so details blurred enough that a positive tribal identification remained difficult but Yanktonai like his captors felt right.

Damn.

This development would make his escape significantly more challenging. Alone, Scar and Shiner would undoubtedly make a mistake Stone could exploit to escape—but that would be far more difficult with this many warriors.

Scar whooped, lifting Stone's Henry high in the air, shaking the weapon with the prideful ferocity of a young brave who'd counted his first coup. Looked like there'd be stories around the campfire tonight—with Stone as the butt.

A second later Scar tugged at the lead tied to Stone's hands, and he had no choice but to scurry after. Warriors formed a circle around them. Crow feathers adorned black-haired scalps swinging from a dozen lances.

Stone turned to one of the chiefs. He opened his mouth and started to speak, but before he could utter the first word a shadow flickered in the corner of his eye. A sledge-like fist slammed into his jaw, sending him crashing to the ground. The biggest, ugliest Indian Stone had ever seen loomed over him. A prominent brow hung like a cliff over his wide-set black eyes and flowed into a thick, blunt nose, the bridge broken and crooked. A puckered and jagged scar ran from his septum, followed the slope of his nose, crossing the cheek under his eye to end an inch below his earlobe—had to be the Devil's own brand.

Stone worked his jaw, tongue pressing against a tooth loosened by the blow. He snarled as he staggered to his feet. Exhaustion evaporated and adrenaline took over. Stone lunged for his attacker but pulled up short when Scar jammed the business end of the Henry into his chest.

Scar and many of the others laughed as if this was the funniest thing they'd ever seen. Nothing but contempt was written in the glare of Big Ugly, who seemed not to find the same humor as his companions.

Stone gathered the festering anger of the last week and put every bit of it into his return stare. "Coward. Let them untie me, and I'll take you." He spit a bloody wad into the big warrior's face.

Angry voices rose among the braves and an argument ensued. Big Ugly, face contorted and dark, arched his back, raised his fists, and roared to the sky. A sneer formed on his lips as he grabbed the knife at his waist and with a quick, violent movement slashed the air in front of Stone's face.

Stone refused to flinch, his stare holding his assailant's, and the knife passed harmlessly two inches in front of his face. Big Ugly took a step closer.

A low yet firm and authoritative voice spoke behind Stone. One of the old chiefs? Big Ugly stopped, turning his glare to someone behind Stone. He stalked past, screaming as he went. Stone turned to keep an eye on him as he marched past him. None of the words being spoken made sense, but Big Ugly's angry gestures and the old chief's steady tone gave him a clear picture. After a few minutes, Big Ugly grew more aggressive, swinging his arms in wide arc with an occasional fist jabbing in Stone's direction. At last, the old chief responded with angry sounding words. Everyone quieted.

A cruel grin spread across Big Ugly's face.

Shit. That look could only mean trouble. Stone steeled himself for whatever was to come.

Big Ugly wrenched the lead still tied to Stone from Scar's hand. Drawing his knife again, he sliced the leather strap binding Stone's wrists, then grabbed a long buffalo hair rope. He bound Stone's wrists, pulling the knots so tight the rope dug deep into flesh. Twenty-five feet remained dangling when he finished. In seconds Stone's hands throbbed.

Warriors yelled as they raced to jump on their ponies. Big Ugly grabbed the free line and mounted. Kicking his pony hard, he took off at a fast trot. Stone had no choice—follow or be dragged.

THEY TRAVELED INTO the afternoon. Stone's throat burned, and he struggled to swallow the few drops of water allowed him during their brief stops. Even the marches on the Peninsular Campaign back in '62 hadn't been this grueling. To make matters worse, he could no longer feel his hands, despite working them regularly.

Stone fought to keep pace. His breathing grew more ragged. His heart pounded against ribs already sore from the effort of sucking oxygen. He dared not fall, sure that would result in him being dragged across the hard prairie, left for dead, a feast for scavengers. Instead, he gritted his teeth and pressed on.

Mid-afternoon brought another water stop. Big Ugly approached, his brow furrowed and smile wide. For what seemed several minutes, he stalked around Stone, contempt and hatred written in the stare of his eyes and the slant of his mouth.

Stone forced himself to remain stoic and unconcerned, while he held the brute's stare, only breaking it to turn enough to catch it as Big Ugly rounded behind him.

Then, the water break ended.

The Indian spit in Stone's face and jumped back on his pony.

An hour passed. The image of Sally's lifeless body kept him upright when by rights he should have already fallen. His fury at the three men who murdered her burned like a drought-fed conflagration. He channeled the rage, the need for vengeance, to keep himself moving when every muscle screamed to stop. Another hour passed. He felt the oozing blisters covering his feet, his soles trapped in an endless cycle—form, burst, re-form, burst, repeat.

Then, with a sudden flicker, his anger searched for more fuel, but nothing remained.

Stone stumbled, caught his balance, staggered, and fell.

Big Ugly roared with derisive laughter as if anticipating this moment. He kicked his pony into a fast gallop. The rope grew taut and snapped Stone's arms against their sockets before he could re-act. His body hurtled forward over the hard, rocky ground, bounc-ing erratically on the uneven terrain. He twisted from one side to the other uncontrollably, like a weathervane in a storm. The prairie smashed against his back, his hips, his chest. Every bump pounded the breath from him.

He focused on protecting his head as best he could.

Seconds became minutes. Minutes seemed an eternity.

At last, Big Ugly stopped. Stone slid several feet through the grass before he came to a halt on his back. Like a drowning man, he gasped at the air. His diaphragm spasmed, unable to expand his lungs. He was suffocating, fighting to breathe in an airless vacuum. With his bound hands, he clawed at his chest.

Finally, his body relaxed and the dam burst. His lungs filled with fresh, life-giving oxygen. Breath after breath, he sucked it in and blew it out.

Thunder roared in his ears. The ground shook. Twenty horses, one in front of another, raced at him. By sheer instinct, Stone rolled to his stomach and ducked his head under his hands and arms just as the first hooves slashed viciously over him. Pain exploded through him as a hoof caught his leg. Another struck his ribs, followed by a second and a third. He thought he would pass out from the agony.

As quickly as it started, it was over.

He hurt. Every breath stabbed through his chest from ribs surely broken. Determined not to show weakness to the warriors, he kept quiet. The old chief called out, and two of the braves jumped off their ponies. Without a bit of gentleness, they hauled Stone to his feet and threw him hard across his horse. He stifled a gasp of pain.

Under no circumstances would he allow Big Ugly the satisfaction of surrender. Despite the pain and exhaustion, he would sit upright like a man. With the last reserves of strength, he twisted and sat tall on his saddleless mare. Now if only he could stay here. Cordelia stood still for him and gave him an apologetic look.

They traveled on. Every step sent jolts through his body. The bullet wound was bleeding again, but with his hands bound, there was nothing to be done for it. Hopefully he wouldn't bleed to death.

Willpower kept Stone on Cordelia's back. More than once he'd almost fallen off, either half asleep or nearly passed out, yet each time he'd clenched his legs and torso, determined to stay upright, if for no other reason than to avoid giving them an excuse to drag him again.

At last, the procession halted along a flat expanse of several acres. The top half of the angry orange sun hung over the tops of the grove of cottonwoods growing in a nearby stream's draw. Pinks, oranges, and lavenders brushed the sky around it like an artist's strokes. With the butt of Stone's own Henry, Shiner prodded him off his black mare. Too tired, too sore, and too stiff to catch himself, he fell hard. A lightning jolt raced up his injured arm, through his shoulder, to ignite a fire that engulfed his brain box. A quiet groan rumbled in the back of his dry throat.

Shiner motioned him off to the side, using the carbine and a scowl for emphasis. His hands were still tied. His arm and head throbbed in the wake of the lightning, while the ache in his legs made them difficult to control, so like a caterpillar, he dragged himself out of the way. When he stopped to rest, Shiner poked him with the barrel of the rifle until Stone began moving again. If his progress slowed, hard kicks increased his effort. Shiner spoke, his gestures telling Stone he could stop, then he spun on his heel and stalked away.

Braves busied themselves making camp—horses cared for and picketed, fires started, blankets laid out, meal preparations begun. More warriors joined them as more parties rode in. All the while, Stone seemed to be ignored. Even Big Ugly paid him no more attention than a cur.

As this fact penetrated Stone's consciousness, the fire in his head rapidly subsided to a dull throb. With the care of a man who knew he might get only one shot, he swiveled his head to take in the entire camp. He had been backed up to the edge of a cottonwood grove, his back to a trunk no more than three feet around. The stream bubbled behind him. Women and children had joined the encampment. The buzz of activity filled the camp. Shiner had joined the tumult.

No one watched Stone.

A second scan of the camp, this time long and slow—examining every individual warrior, casting a wary eye on each woman, assessing the children in case one or more had been tasked with watching him—assured him. He was invisible as a ghost.

The antler handle of the boot knife dug into his calf.

Cracked or broken ribs made every breath painful. His legs ached like a bad tooth from the day's travel. Scrapes and gashes crisscrossed his torso. Deep scarlet colored Stone's hands as if blood threatened to burst through the skin. Feeling had long since abandoned them. Stiffness in the finger joints rendered the digits almost useless despite near constant efforts to flex and work them. He'd seen amputations of digits and appendages when prisoners had been left tied too tight for too long.

Escape was his only hope. And it had to be tonight. Whatever his captors had planned for him would not be pleasant and would very likely kill him or near enough to not matter. And they'd do it soon. Maybe as soon as tomorrow.

The horses were picketed on the south side of the camp, his among them. The new moon was tomorrow night, so there'd be no moon tonight for all intents and purposes. The darkness could be both a curse and a blessing, but either way, one thing was sure—when his opportunity came, he better know his way around. With what little light remained he mapped the terrain in his mind. As he examined every rill, tree, and swale, a plan came together.

THE CAMP'S ACTIVITY hid under the darkness that settled over the prairie, but glowing embers, shifting silhouettes, and the aroma of roasting game gave witness to the cookfires in use. Stone's stomach rumbled, and he realized he hadn't eaten since yesterday. Maybe they'd feed him tonight—if anyone even remembered he was here.

Being forgotten would be better than a meal.

Escape right now might be possible, and the temptation continued to niggle at him, but waiting for everyone to bed down was still the safer bet. While he waited, Stone went over the plan he'd developed. Every probable contingency had to be examined, factored in, and planned for—just in case. Even a couple of unlikely scenarios wormed their way into his thinking. Preparing battle plans taught him to anticipate problems and have an idea how to deal with them. Planned complications rarely developed, but the sheer act of anticipation allowed for more rapid decision making when trouble interrupted.

So, he schemed and prepared. Escape was his sole priority. He had to get back to the trail of Sally's murderers. Already too much time separated him from them. He was farther behind now than he'd been when he left the homestead.

Conversations in the Sioux language drifted on the same currents as the cooking aromas. In the distance, crickets, various owls, and whip-poor-wills sang while coyotes yipped. No doubt accustomed to nature's sounds, the gathered natives seemed to ignore them. Until the screech of a barn owl spurred rapid but silent activity.

Weapons materialized seemingly from nowhere and warriors dispersed ghost-like into the shadows. Stone considered the possibility of a retaliatory Crow attack. The confusion would aid his flight, but also increase the likelihood of his being killed if he were discovered. He needed the knife and began working his pant leg up his calf.

Owl screeches answered from inside the camp, and activity calmed. Moments later, another party of Yanktonai trotted into camp.

Despair rose like bile from the pit of Stone's gut. So much had happened in the last week, and he couldn't remember the last time he'd felt this low. Not even when last summer's grasshopper swarm destroyed their entire crop.

But Sally had been there then, standing beside him. His throat clenched.

Who walked beside him now?

Only his new companions—pain and agony, with their offspring torment, torture, and death.

The new party carried their teepees and other supplies on travois dragged behind ponies. Shifting shadows from new campfires obscured the details as they made camp, but it was clear the group included women and children.

The Treaty of Fort Laramie, which ended Red Cloud's War, set aside a large hunting ground in north-western Kansas for the Sioux. The Western Dakota tribes—Yankton, Yanktonai, as well as Oglala, Brule, Miniconjou, Sans Arc and others of the Lakota gathered at various times for the hunt. No doubt this group intended the same, despite those just returning from making war on the Crow.

Could this be an opportunity? Reason to hope?

Resolve had defined his life. He'd never surrendered, not once. Not at twelve when his father was killed. Not at eighteen when forced to fight older, bigger men jealous he'd been made a supervisor on the docks. Not during the war when death sought out his friends as he led them in battle. Not during the early, hardscrabble life on the homestead. And not when grasshoppers destroyed his crops last summer.

And not now. He would not quit. Somehow, some way. Sally's murderers would suffer his vengeance, and nothing—not Marshal Zebulon Price, not this damned unending prairie, and certainly not these Sioux warriors, regardless of what they thought they had planned for him—would keep him from it.

Women set up teepees, assembling the poles and then attaching skins made of scrapped, stretched, and dried buffalo hides. By the light of the fires, many of the designs painted on the tough hides looked garish, though by daylight the intricate patterns would show their beauty. Children were either given tasks or knew what was expected as they pitched in to help. Several wandered into the night to collect dried buffalo dung. Soon fires were ready and even more aromas joined those already wafting along the breeze. Nearby, the men of the new arrivals mingled in small groups and their conversations and laughter filtered through the dark. Occasionally, one would turn and point to him.

So much for being forgotten.

A dozen men, mostly older chiefs, but a couple of braves, including Big Ugly, gathered around a fire not far from where Stone sat. The soft murmur of their voices was unintelligible. Tongues of flame licked at the pile of dried buffalo chips, casting queer, elongated shadows across the prairie, each bending and twisting with the rolls of the land. Frequent gestures and glances in his direction were all the clues he needed regarding the subject of their debate.

The discussion heated, and men shouted. Big Ugly sat on the far side of the circle where he could see Stone as he shouted louder and louder. Shadows distorted his nose and the scar, while blood and bronze-colored flames glinted from his obsidian eyes. If he hadn't appeared demonic before, he did now.

No more than a line of light, the thin crescent of moon crawled across the night sky. More braves gathered around the circle, most standing behind Big Ugly. A pair of old chiefs spoke, their tones at times gentle, other times sharp, but when they finished the assemblage quieted and the argument calmed. Most of the braves wore sullen expressions, but the grin on Big Ugly matched the scar for meanness. With a loud whoop, he stood, pumped his fist toward Stone, then walked around the fire to a spot about halfway to where Stone sat. Big Ugly turned his back to Stone, bent forward, and dropped his buckskin pants. The braves around the fire roared with laughter as he hitched his pants back up and returned to his place in the circle.

As the laughter died, a stoop-shouldered old chief turned toward a group of boys watching silently from the slope above the fire. He spoke, his words too low for Stone to hear. One of the boys rose and dashed off toward the women.

The old-timer produced a pipe from beneath his blanket. After lighting it, he took a long draw and passed it to another old chief. Low chatter resumed as the pipe made its way around the circle.

Stone watched the circle, wondering when they would disperse so he could make his break. He intended to be long gone by sunrise. With any luck they wouldn't follow. He sensed someone approaching but heard nothing. A moment later a tall woman stepped into a patch of moonlight. Her long, gently curved silhouette swayed with the lithe grace of an antelope as she walked, but her features were shrouded in shadow. She clutched something in her hands.

When she reached Stone, she laid a basket of fry bread and buffalo jerky at his feet. Silvery moonlight gleamed off long, silken black hair that only partially hid her high, prominent cheekbones and smooth skin. He gestured his thanks as best he could.

Baser, primal instincts took over, and he didn't wait to grab a piece of the bread. His fingers refused to work properly, so he held the flat disk between his palms and tore a bite off. His numb hands hadn't warned him that the bread was still hot, and he burned his tongue, but Stone didn't care. He was ravenous and before long he'd devoured the entire basketful of bread disks. He glanced up briefly, but the woman had walked away.

As he gnawed on the third or fourth piece of jerky, she returned. She stood in front of him, patient while he ate what he held in his hand. Stone paid more attention to her as he chewed. She wore a soft, beaded buckskin dress that fell midway between her knees and ankles.

Fringe adorned the sleeves, waist, and hem. She stopped him when he reached for the last sliver. Blood-red firelight shone in the metal of the knife in her hands. Where had that come from? Stone's eyes grew wide as she grabbed his hands. With a single deft movement, she sliced the buffalo hair rope from his wrists. Blood rushed back into his hands. Red hot pokers stabbed his palms and fingers as surely as if a torturer had applied them, and he gritted his teeth against the pain.

The Sioux woman watched as he worked his hands, trying to restore circulation. At some point, an exasperated expression crossed her face, and she knelt beside him. She grabbed one of his hands, massaging the flesh, working into them an obnoxious smelling ointment she'd pulled from a basket he hadn't noticed. Her thumbs worked their own form of magic. Pain in that hand lessened and soon dissipated to nothing. Moments later she'd repeated her magic with his other hand.

"Thank you."

She looked at him, eyed him with concern and wariness etched into her expression, but she said nothing.

He tried again in French, but she said nothing.

Dark eyes searched him from head to toe. Her strong hand grabbed his chin and turned his face to one side, then the other. Her visual exam paused at the dried blood on his arm. He winced when she began prodding the wound through the bandage. With the other hand, he used his thumb and index finger to mimic the firing of a gun while he imitated the sound.

She nodded and continued her work. She tugged at rips and tears in his clothing, shifting to see behind them. A scowl crossed her face, and she made signs that he should remove his shirt. Hesitation invited her frustration to take action—she tugged at the hem to pull it off.

Stone's face warmed, and he shooed her hands away—he'd do it himself. The woman then bent farther and gripped a boot.

Shit. The one with the knife.

What would she do if she discovered it?

His other task forgotten, Stone gestured that he would remove the boots himself. Her brows furrowed in puzzlement, but she relented. As he removed the right one, he held it in such a way as to hide its contents. If she saw the knife, she made no indication.

Stone took short, rapid breaths to control the sudden pain of exertion. She knelt beside him and cut away the tattered shirt he hadn't slipped over his head. Newly formed scabs ripped away as she pulled the fabric from his wounds. More tore open when she removed his socks. She helped him lay flat and tugged at his pants. Even in the dim light her wince was obvious. Stone followed her eyes to the large abrasion on his thigh where he had been kicked by one of the ponies— it was already dark and swollen.

With a firm hand, she scrubbed the dried blood and dirt from his face and body. Her first touch to his ribs brought a sharp inhalation of breath and a wince. She ground roots and other plants she'd brought into a foul-smelling paste which she applied to his cuts and bruises. Flesh touched by the ointment tingled and the muscles warmed. Using long strips of cloth, she bound his ribcage tight and gave him another long drink of water. Stone made signs of appreciation as she withdrew.

The concoction worked its magic, and the pain eased. He clenched his jaw to stifle a yawn, but soon wave after wave crashed over him. Heavy weights dragged at his eyelids. His chin thumped against his chest—he shook his head twice to clear it. Minutes later, the weights returned, and he shook his head again.

As the woman worked, Stone glanced over at the council fire. Pipes were passing among members. The old chief who had earlier sent the young buck on an errand rose to his feet. As if on cue, Big Ugly also stood, but the old man waved him back down.

The woman grabbed her supplies and hurried away as the old man approached. Stone sensed trouble and struggled to sit up—if something was about to happen, he needed to be ready.

AS HE MOVED closer, moonlight illuminated the old chief's face. A big grin cracked Stone's face like an egg—Chief Runs With Deer, his trading partner from the reservation. The wizened man squatted next to him.

"You are in bad shape, Judd Stone," he said in French. Many of the older Sioux had learned the language from the French-Canadian fur traders along the Missouri and Mississippi Rivers. Stone was thankful his own mother had forced him to learn it.

"Beat up. My daughter, she cared for your wounds?"

Stone nodded. "I didn't know she was your daughter." His throat raw from ragged breathing and not speaking for several hours, his voice was raspy.

"She is quite skilled. Much medicine lives in her." He was silent, and his serious expression held Stone's tongue.

"It is dangerous for a white man where you go. Do you chase the gold, also?" The niceties were over.

"Chief, I'm not here for the reason you think. I don't care about gold. Miners, on their way to the Black Hills, killed my wife. I'm hunting them—hunting vengeance."

The old Sioux nodded and crossed his arms. "I told the council you were an honorable man and would not invade our sacred lands without cause. But, the young warriors insist all white men are the same. They come to our sacred ground like locusts that come in a mighty cloud and eat everything—destroy everything." He waved an arm in a long arc. "Then they move on, leaving only dust behind them."

"I'm truly sorry for what they're doing. White men chase gold like young braves chase glory in the buffalo hunt."

The old chief nodded.

Stone touched his chest. "What is to happen to me?"

"They planned to leave you staked-out on the prairie, naked, for

the coyotes to feast on. It would be a sign to other white men of what
happens to those that come to our lands."

A shiver slithered down Stone's spine.

"I argued that you should be questioned. Released if your inten-
tions were honorable. The young ones refused. Black Buffalo, the one
with the scar across his face." He made a slash along his cheek with his
thumb. "You know who I mean?"

Big Ugly. Stone nodded.

"He insisted that you had insulted him. Demanded the privi-
lege of killing you himself. I could not deny him, and many of the
others fear him."

Stone stared at the old chief.

What could be worse than being eaten alive by coyotes?

"You will fight—knives—to the death. If you win, you go free. If
not...." Runs With Deer let the thought hang. They sat silent for a time.

Stone wanted to protest—he was in no shape to fight the brute.
But the argument would be futile. The old Indian could not change
the decision. Stone nodded. "When?"

"When the sun is highest in the sky tomorrow." He stood and
took two steps. Turning back to Stone, he shook his head and stared
at his feet. "I wish you well. You are a good man, Judd Stone. That
is a bad man you fight. He has only hatred in his heart." The old
chief walked off.

———————

FIGHT BLACK BUFFALO or be staked-out for the coyotes to feast
on. A wealth of options.

Escape? An hour before, it had been his only chance, but now?
What about now? Something about Runs With Deer's tone made
Stone wary of considering such an action. Had it been concern in his
friend's voice? Warning?

Of course the old chief had brought him hope. All Stone needed to do was defeat a physically healthy man half-a-head taller and sixty pounds heavier than himself, while hindered by broken ribs, a gun-shot wound, bruises over his entire body, and a hostile environment.

Fight to the death.

Win and go free.

Easy as rolling off a log.

Stone closed his eyes and took three deliberate short breaths to steel himself and filled his lungs to a slow ten count. At four, he winced, and a shiver ran the length of his spine. At seven, his breath caught—he held it and pushed the pain from his mind. Then he completed the inhalation. Release—slow.

Again.

His heart quieted.

Again.

His shoulders drooped and his hands dropped to his sides.

In one sense, the news of the fight was a relief. This path placed his fate directly in his own hands. Regardless of the long odds, they were better than if the braves staked him out on the plains. He was no stranger to fighting, white or red men. Black Buffalo was huge, powerful, and fast, but he had weaknesses. At their first encounter, Black Buffalo displayed the temper of a jealous suitor. The corners of Stone's mouth turned up, but a yawn overpowered the smile.

Anger will fuel his strength, but will drive him to make mistakes, also. They can be exploited. Would that be enough? Shanghai Pete had been a known commodity the day Stone gave him a beat down. He had known Pete relied on his wicked right hook—had seen him use it. Knowledge led to the big man's defeat. He would have no such advantage tomorrow.

Stone yawned again and shook his head. Thinking was like slogging through mud pits. Gravity pulled at his eyelids. He slumped to the ground.

Sleep, however, failed to come—too fatigued to sleep and too weary to think. In this half-conscious state he visualized the fight with Black Buffalo again and again.

CHAPTER 13

STONE JERKED AWAKE, startled by the light touch on his shoulder. Runs With Deer's daughter squatted next to him. The early morning sun highlighted details the moon's rays could not—the faint hint of crow's feet, scattered strands of grey hair, a frown line.

As he sat up, she placed jerky and fry bread before him. Deep onyx eyes stared at him as he devoured the meal, but she remained silent. Stone plopped the final bite of fry bread into his mouth. Before he finished, she again tended to his wounds.

"What is your name?" The coarse rasp of his voice contrasted with the elegance of the French language—his cheeks warmed.

She spoke without lifting her head to look him in the eye or pausing her work. "I am Dancing Waters."

"Why are you helping me?"

Her eyes seemed to probe deep into his being, as if she read his entire life, his soul, and took his measure—he was powerless to look away. She did not speak.

Finally, she lowered her head and went back to her labor. "What did my father tell you?"

"Only that I am to fight Big Ugly over there at noon."

"My father likes you. You are one of the few white men who treats us with respect. Most act as if we are children or animals. They get angry when we won't trade for cheap knives or useless guns. Some trade us blankets filled with sickness. Others rape our young women." She paused to scoop more ointment from the hide bag at her side.

Kneeling next to him, fingers holding the thick paste, she again held his gaze. "Not you. You traded your best wheat and corn and treated our people with kindness."

Stone shrugged.

"Father says you are a mighty warrior. He can see it in your eyes. One of the soldiers at the fort told us he fought with you in the white man's war—said you were brave and fierce."

"Sergeant William Blose. Saw him at Fort Stanley when we first moved here." Stone shook his head. "He talks too much."

She averted her eyes and bent back to her work. "Did my father tell you that Black Buffalo wants me to come to his teepee to be his woman? He wants to be a chief and thinks if he marries a chief's daughter, he will gain the respect of all the warriors. Twice he placed the bride price outside Father's teepee, twice Father refused."

Tapping his arms, she said, "Lift." He pulled his elbows up even with his shoulders. "Hold this." She stuffed one end of a long heavy bandage into his hand and wrapped the rest around his ribcage several times. Then she took the end tucked in his hand and tugged the cloth tight. Stone grunted as she tied them off.

"Today when you fight, you will also be fighting for me. Many of the others wanted to leave you for the coyotes and wolves to feast on. The only way Father could save you was to offer me to Black Buffalo if he killed you in a fight. Father is confident that despite your injuries, you will defeat him. I pray to the Great Spirit that is so. I do not want to go to his teepee." She turned away and spat on the ground.

"Wish I was that sure. He's a lot of man." Stone frowned. "I'm surprised you're not already married."

Dancing Waters straightened her back and lifted her chin. "I was.

To a great warrior. Many years ago. He was killed during the buffalo hunt." Her shoulders drooped. "I returned to my father's teepee. Many have asked Father for me, but Father will not force me, and I do not wish to marry a young brave. So, here I am."

"What happens if I win?"

"You will go free."

"And will I be expected to marry you?"

Once again, she paused in her work to stare at him. "Would it offend you? Am I ugly like Black Buffalo that you do not wish to take me into your teepee, Judd Stone?"

He sighed. "That's not what I meant. You're a beautiful woman. Any man would be proud to call you his wife. But, my Sally...." Stone left the thought dangling, a thickness in his throat, unable to finish.

"I know about your wife." Sympathy filled her voice. "My father told me you hunt those who killed her. I am sorry, Judd Stone. Your spirit aches, and I should not have teased you. No, I only have to marry if Black Buffalo wins."

They remained silent while Dancing Waters tended to the remainder of Stone's wounds. She gathered her supplies and rose. After three steps, the Sioux woman stopped and turned to him.

"Remember this, Judd Stone. Black Buffalo is big and dangerous. All fear him. But he is not smart. He bragged all night at the fires how he would kill you and take me for his wife." She shuddered and clenched a fist to her chest. "I have seen him fight. He is strong like a buffalo bull, but he has never fought Coyote, someone clever he could not defeat on strength alone. His might has always been enough. I think with you"—she stared at Stone—"it will not be enough."

SHORTLY BEFORE THE sun reached its zenith, Dancing Waters came for Stone. After she left him that morning, he had pulled on his dungarees and boots and wandered the camp. The Sioux had posted no guard, and he had not been re-tied after she cut him free the previous evening. So, he took advantage of the freedom and stretched his legs to work the stiffness from his muscles and joints.

No one objected when he moved among the horses. He was surprised to find Cordelia and Ulysses. He pulled clumps of dried grass and rubbed down each of them, first his black, then the pack horse. Work helped him think. Black Buffalo would give him one hell of a fight. His jaw was still swollen and ached from the stunning punch the big man had delivered yesterday. He'd have to avoid the fists while landing his own blows. Not easy against an opponent with both a height and reach advantage. Maybe he could goad Big Ugly into being over aggressive, draw him inside to take away the length advantage. His body would be battered in the process, but inside Stone's own blows would pack far more power. By the time Dancing Waters appeared to escort him, his plan was set.

"I wanted to thank you for everything you've done for me."

"Are you well? You limped around camp."

"I'm as fine as I can be." He winked. Other than the pain that every breath caused, he was better than he had any right to expect. The muscle tightness was gone. The minor aches were gone. Even the knots where the horses had kicked him were loosening. Whatever that ointment was, it worked.

"I have one more thing for you."

Stone stopped. "But you've done so much for me already."

"It is a small thing, but maybe helpful." She produced a pair of thin, tan, leather riding gloves. "These belonged to a white soldier. My husband took them off his dead body many years ago."

"They're wonderful." He tugged them on—the fit was perfect.

They continued the short distance to where the entire camp had gathered in a circle. Just outside the group, she stopped and took his hand. Eyebrows knit together, she gazed up at him. "Remember what I told you, today you must be clever like Coyote." She glanced down at his feet and back to his eyes. "Use every advantage. For your Sally. For me."

Realization struck him.

Dancing Waters knew about his boot knife. How?

Stone nodded once.

She dropped his hand, stood tall, chin high, and led him into the assemblage. A murmur worked through the crowd as it parted for them. He limped into the makeshift arena.

Ahead, the men formed an inner ring twenty feet in diameter. Each brave held a long lance decorated with feathers and trophies. Many had scalps that dangled from beneath the feathers, but one bore the faded and tattered battle flag of the 2nd Cavalry, its emblem visible among the folds. Fetterman. An involuntary shudder crawled up his spine, thinking about what the Sioux had done to his men.

At the very center of the arena burned a small fire. Heat radiated from the orange and red coals and singed Stone's legs as he approached it. Runs With Deer stood at the edge of the fire to Stone's right, erect and proud in his brightly beaded buffalo hair shirt and breeches. Between his feet was a knife, its blade buried in the soil, its hilt pointed straight up. The other chief from yesterday, adorned in ornamented buckskins, stood to Stone's left—a knife also buried hilt-up in the ground between his feet.

Between them, facing Stone from the far side of the fire-circle, waited Black Buffalo, clad only in a breech cloth. His wide, massive shoulders, barrel chest, and thick arms looked like he could snap a man in half if he got him into a bear hug. Only his skinny legs looked out of proportion.

The Indian glared at him. The scar on his cheek glowed scarlet. Stone limped to the fire, his shoulders hunched and head low—his eyes glanced furtively at his opponent. He took his place. The fire's heat shimmered in the air between them.

The older chief began speaking and gesturing while Runs With

Deer translated. "Runs With Deer claims that you are an honorable white man. We will see. You have been challenged by Black Buffalo who says you have insulted him. The fight is to the death. No mercy should be expected. None given.

"You will stay within the circle of warriors." The old chief pointed to the braves around them. "If either of you are thrown outside of it, you must return immediately."

Black Buffalo shouted something and spit across the flames at Stone. Runs With Deer didn't translate, but no translation was necessary.

The old chief scowled before he continued.

"You will begin when Running Bear's arrow plunges into the fire." With that the two proud chiefs exited to seats next to each other among the warriors. Dancing Waters slipped in behind her father.

The Indian continued to glare and a thin smirk creased his face—his intention to crush Stone like an insect under foot was clear.

Stone muttered under his breath. "Keep thinking that way, big feller—just keep thinking that way." Stone shifted his weight to the balls of his feet, ready. All the while he kept his head low and shoulders hunched.

Black Buffalo flicked his eyes from one knife to the other.

Which way would he go?

Running Bear's arrow plunged deep into the bed of hot coals. Sparks flew like fireflies on a summer night.

The crowd howled.

Stone lunged straight across the fire. His boots provided protection from the hot coals as he churned his legs through the flames. The quick attack caught Black Buffalo as he half-turned to his right. Stone's shoulder drove through the larger man's left knee—there was a loud pop as tendons and ligaments ripped and tore. The Indian grunted but kept his feet.

With arms locked around the bigger man's legs, Stone hurtled ahead and slammed Black Buffalo to the ground with a thud that rattled teeth. The attack carried the combatants several feet from the knives.

Stone pressed his advantage, sliding forward quickly to straddle the surprised Indian. Even as his knees locked onto Black Buffalo's hips, he dropped a left overhand hammer fist.

Followed by a right.

And another left.

Violent, powerful blows rained down, all intended for Black Buffalo's heart.

The big man wheezed, unable to breathe. His eyes bulged—darted side to side. The Indian grabbed at Stone and wrapped his thick arms around him.

He tried to hug Stone to him, but a hard head butt into the bigger man's chin snapped his head against the ground. Black eyes rolled up in their sockets and then tumbled back like Sisyphus's boulder.

A cacophony of whoops and hollers exploded from the gathered warriors—lances rattled.

Stone renewed his assault, crashing hammer fist after hammer fist onto Black Buffalo's chest, not daring to stop.

Black Buffalo roared. Powerful arms grabbed hold of Stone's torso and lifted him straight up.

The Indian's raw strength startled Stone. He fought to stay mounted—tried to drive his knee into his opponent's groin, but the angle was wrong and the blow glanced off.

Still laying on his back, the brute flung the smaller man to the side like a sack of feed.

Flying through the air, Stone's stomach flipped. Packed earth met him. Cracked ribs screamed. He blinked against the pain. As Stone scrambled to his feet, Black Buffalo ripped one of the knives from the ground. Stone dove for the other blade, rolled forward on his shoulder, and into a crouch as he tore the weapon free.

Knife held low, its edge up ready to disembowel, the Indian charged.

The heavy limp that was the result of Stone's earlier work slowed him, and Stone tumbled hard to the right, easily avoiding the big man's thrust. A quick forward roll, and he bounced to his feet, turning to face the Indian.

The two men circled each other, arms wide, crouched, and wary. Stone eased to his left to force the big man to move into his injured leg.

Feint and dodge.

Attack and parry.

Around and around—they probed each other's defenses.

Black Buffalo thrust, Stone danced back. He hesitated to close with the Sioux, cautious of the big man's strength. Twice, Stone thought about the knife his father had given him still hidden in his boot— twice his challenger pushed forward and forced Stone to shove the thought away as he shuffled aside.

The watchers cried out encouragement, though Stone had no idea for whom.

Anger burned in the Indian's eyes. Using his empty hand to beckon Stone forward, he yelled something unintelligible. Then he lunged. Stabbing high, then slashing low, he opened a shallow cut across Stone's leg.

Blood oozed down his wounded thigh—he stumbled on the uneven ground and fell to one knee.

Stone pushed back to his feet as Black Buffalo, teeth bared, howled his excitement, and charged in.

Unable to avoid the rush, Stone used his free hand to grab ahold the attacking knife hand. He struggled to keep the bloody blade away. The bigger man's weight carried Stone backward, and he landed on his side with a loud *Oomph*. While he fell, he pulled Black Buffalo with him and planted his foot in the big man's mid-section—a lever to throw him with.

But the Indian twisted away and landed beside Stone.

Black Buffalo leapt.

Stone scissored his legs and caught the larger man mid-leap. Wrapping them around the big man's waist, his roll to the right caught the Indian's left knee under their combined weight.

Black Buffalo screamed with the primal fury of an injured grizzly.

Atop the Indian, Stone snapped his head into Big Ugly's already broken and misshapen nose.

Screaming, the big man again flung Stone to the side.

Stone's breath caught as he staggered to his feet—sure another rib had cracked. His sides heaved. Every gasp brought searing pain. Crimson stains soaked through the bandages on his arm. His vision swam. He shook his head to clear it.

Black Buffalo was already on his feet. Blood dripped from his chin. Multiple cuts stood open over one eye and the big man's nose skewed to one side. Yet his breathing seemed normal, as if he'd just walked around the circle.

Stone's heart dropped into the pit of his stomach. He had known this man was powerful and his own condition poor, but he'd allowed himself to believe that he could beat Black Buffalo if he out-witted him. Early surprise allowed him to deliver a fearsome beating—a beating that would have crushed most men—yet seemed to hardly faze the Indian.

Stone's knees wobbled. How much longer could he keep going? If he stopped, he'd die.

Triumph lit Black Buffalo's eyes. Lunging forward, his knife slashed upward.

Stone twisted. The blade bit deep but glanced off a rib. Blood flowed from the wound and ran down his side to soak into his dungarees.

Black Buffalo feinted, and Stone gave ground.

Sweat stung his eyes. He shook his head and swiped at the sweat with his hand. The warrior rushed forward, grabbed Stone's knife hand, and drove him to the hard packed soil. He landed hard, Black Buffalo's full weight atop him. Stone grimaced and gritted his teeth.

Heat singed his scalp—his head was mere inches from one of the rocks that comprised the fire circle.

The combatants locked hands around each other's wrists to hold back certain death—Stone's muscles shook from fatigue. How much longer would he be able to fend off that knife?

The monstrous man mounted his hips and this time there was nothing Stone could do to prevent it. Bile rose in his throat.

Black Buffalo lifted Stone's knife hand and bashed it hard against one of the rocks of the fire circle. Once, twice, a third time the brute slammed the wrist down. Finally, Stone's grip loosened. His blade fell into the flames.

Every breath was a fight—his chest heaved against the weight lodged on it—the agony of his cracked ribs threatened to overcome his consciousness. His arm shook as he fought to hold the big man's knife away. With his other hand he groped for a weapon—anything.

A flurry of blows smashed like sledgehammers into Stone's face. His nose broke for the second time in a week. Blood gushed and splattered over Black Buffalo.

Stone's vision blurred. Even the Indian on his chest seemed no more than an indistinct blob. The whoops and hollers of the nearby Sioux warriors sounded faint and garbled through the roar in his ears. Nausea gripped him. Strength ebbed by the second and soon what remained would be gone. When that happened, he'd be as dead as Sally, without having extracted his vengeance.

No. That could not be the end. Stone refused to surrender to the inevitable.

Groping with his hand, he found the rock that his wrist had been beaten on only moments before. He clamped onto it, its heat stung his hand even through the leather glove. Gathering his strength, he swung it toward Black Buffalo's head.

With a loud laugh that held contempt rather than mirth, the big man blocked the blow—then easily pried the rock from Stone's fingers.

Black Buffalo jerked his other arm from his opponent's grip and slammed his thick forearm into Stone's chest. The breath was driven from his lungs. The blade grazed Stone's cheek. The Indian twisted his wrist to draw the edge against the stubble there. As the tip touched the corner of Stone's eye, he stopped. With a snarl he then leaned over the smaller man and allowed his spittle to drizzle onto his face.

A weak hook landed on the big man's muscled shoulder. It drew a smirk.

Black Buffalo raised the rock high over his head. Stone's vision cleared and his eyes grew round.

Motion seemed to slow to a crawl. The rock descended. Stone turned his head and thrust his arms up to protect his face.

Too late. It struck the ground an inch from Stone's head with a loud thump.

Surprise. Shock. Disbelief. A quick blink.

Black Buffalo laughed as his stare sought a single face in the crowd. A lustful, leering expression soon painted his face.

Stone knew—Dancing Waters. He would fail her just like he'd already failed Sally.

"Noooooo!" The primal scream ripped from Stone's throat. Energy coursed through him. With both arms, he raked at the ground above his head near the fire circle. A weapon. Something. Anything. He tipped his head back for a better view.

Rocks, coals, his knife—everything lay inches beyond his reach. Desperation fueled his effort. Boot heels dug into the ground for leverage, Stone heaved. His hips lifted the big man atop them and his legs churned.

He gained an inch.

Again.

Another inch.

Black Buffalo lifted his rock high, the leer of lust replaced by a murderous growl.

A gloved hand closed around burning coals and embers. They seared Stone's flesh through the leather even as he flung them.

Hot cinders caught the warrior full in the face. Black Buffalo bellowed and leapt backward. He released the rock, which landed on the far side of the circle. His blade tumbled harmlessly to the ground as his hands clawed at his eyes and nose.

Free of the big man, Stone grabbed for the weapon in the fire. He missed it, but his eye caught Running Bear's arrow. Sap boiled out from the top of the shaft cut from a green shoot of a chokecherry tree.

Face covered in wicked blisters, mouth twisted into a snarl, teeth bared, Black Buffalo rushed Stone. The force of the impact carried them both up and over the fire.

Stone clutched desperately at the shaft and his fingers curled around it—boiling sap immediately raised blisters through his gloves. He ripped it from the earth as he flew over the flames. On the far side of the circle, the combatants landed hard.

Black Buffalo rose, a savage scream on his lips.

Stone rolled to his knees, while he gripped the arrow's shaft with both hands. With one hard thrust, he slammed it upward to meet the charge, plunging it under Big Ugly's rib cage.

Weight fueled his momentum—carried him into Stone, his impetus drove the arrow deeper and higher into the brute's thick chest.

Stone collapsed beneath Black Buffalo's lifeless body.

The next few minutes passed in a vacuum for Stone. He lay still, unable to move. His heart raced. His vision blurred. The shakes rolled over him, and he couldn't stop them. Dancing Waters came to him. She ran, yet her movements seemed spasmodic, as though he watched through the slots of a zoetrope.

The assembled warriors leapt and shook their lances, their mouths moved, but the staccato throb that roared in his ears drowned out any noise they made. Blackness enveloped him.

MARSHAL PRICE SAT on the ground, back against a rock, and
knees folded to his chest. He peered over the cup of coffee he held at
his lips and surveyed the men sleeping by the glow of the small fire.
Their soft snores mingled with the crickets' chirps. The peaceful setting did little to help his foul mood. He had intended to ride out with
no more than eight or nine experienced men, but here he was saddled
with an extra dozen, all shave tails between hay and grass—and all
because Charles Willis had insisted.

Gathering the supplies and animals to outfit the larger crew took
an extra day, so they hadn't left until this morning. Price hated delays.

Yet, it wasn't the delay that had him on edge. Inexperience had cost
him good men in the past, and he feared one of the green horns would
start trouble. Telling the wives or mothers was the hardest part. Made
no sense that Willis would insist on so many kids, yet he had.

He'd pondered this since leaving town but had no answers. Riding
the trail gets monotonous, and men chat—about familiar things. Price
listened, gathering information, but kept his own council.

The marshal checked his cup and frowned. He poured a refill and
then rummaged in a nearby pack to secure a second cup, which he also
filled with the dark liquid. Only the marshal and one other were awake.

Angus Hoeckerman—owner of the Stockman livery—had volunteered to take second watch every night. It wasn't likely any roving
band of Sioux would attack the posse, especially with such a large
group, but if they could steal the horses, they would. A moonless
night like this was perfect for horse thieving.

Price found him on the hillock that overlooked the camp.
"Thought maybe you could use some Arbuckles."

"Could at that." Angus accepted the cup and sipped the steaming
liquid. "Needed that. Been a quiet night, so far. Even the horses been
still. Tough to stay alert."

The two men chatted about nothing—horses mainly. Marshal Price stood to leave, then hesitated, uncertain. Turning back to Angus, he asked, "So, what's this I hear about Willis buying out Flater?"

"It's true. Last week. You know Flater?"

"Rode with me on a posse once. Good man. Not much of a farmer, though, I guess."

"Oh, no," Angus shook his head. "He's a helluva farmer. Had him a nice place till last summer. Locusts destroyed his crop. Lot'a the others too. But Charles wouldn't extend the loan on Flater's place this spring. He did for some, but not Flater. Foreclosed on him. Did the same thing to Ahlgren and Niequist."

"Any idea why?"

"Rumor has it the railroad's coming through. Paying big money for land's what I heard. All three of those places are on the planned route. Stone's too."

Marshal Price grunted. It was true—the railroad was expanding, and he had seen the proposed plans in the Yankton courthouse a couple of months back.

"Willis rode out to Stone's place a month ago. Made him an offer."

The marshal nodded but remained quiet.

"Yup, Stone turned him down flat."

"How do you know this?"

"Willis returned a horse to the livery one evening. Rode in real reckless like. All red-faced. Asked him if everything was all right." Angus shrugged. "All he did was mutter 'stubborn Stone woman'. Wouldn't say no more.

"Asked Stone about it next time I saw him. Told me Willis tried to buy him out. Most of the farmers rely on bank loans for seed and such and pay it off every year at harvest. Not Stone. They don't borrow from anyone, so Willis had no hold over him. Got angry when Sally told him no. Guess he got adamant with Stone. Well, Stone's been married long enough... he told Willis that Sally already gave him their answer. Made Willis madder'n a sheep in a haggis factory. Then she called him something that questioned his momma's purity." Angus guffawed. "Wish I could a seen that."

Price chuckled with him. "Thanks." He rubbed at his stubbly jaw as he returned to camp.

CHAPTER 14

STONE BLINKED OPEN his eyes. A thick mist swirled, and an ominous aura pressed around him like a weight. The sense of impending danger drove him to his feet. Phantoms floated in the translucent haze. Ghosts of the men he'd led in battle—their chanted accusations maddening.

"You, Major Stone. You're responsible. You killed us."

Heart beating like a charging buffalo, hammering to escape his chest. "But I didn't mean to." A sob escaped him. "I loved you all, Brothers. It was war. The cause was just." His voice cracked as he cried out his denial.

Still the chants continued. "You killed us. You are responsible. You killed us. You. You. You."

Stone howled his apology. "I'm sorry. I had to. War."

More spirits joined the chanting parade that swirled about him. Parents. Grandparents. Siblings. Spouses. Children. Deceased loved ones of the murdered soldiers. "Why? Why? Why? They trusted you. And you lead them to their deaths. Why? We needed them. We trusted you with their lives." The chants grew louder. The throng thickened as more joined.

The chanting grew more frenetic.

"I didn't mean to." Stone clamped hands to ears, as if he could shut out the cacophony.

Faster they whirled about.

"It was war."

"Why? Why? Why?"

"No. Please no. Loved them."

"Dead. Because of you!"

Till Stone reeled. Almost collapsed.

Then, through the mists, beyond the tormenters—faint, indistinct. Movement.

Through the thick, white brume someone ran toward him. A woman. As she drew closer the specters dispersed. A few at first. Families. Slowly. The closer she came the faster they fled.

The haze of apparitions drifted away, but not gone—straining to return but held at bay by the woman. Strawberry-blonde locks cascaded over her shoulders in an avalanche of curls. Dressed in an ivory-colored wedding dress, she raced to him. Something familiar—

"Sally!" His voice broke and his heart skipped a beat.

"Judd." Only Sally called him that. Her voice was a melody as beautiful as ever he'd heard. His heart leaped into his throat. Oh, such joy.

Out of the phantasmic mist a darker figure broke. A monstrous black wolf, nearly shoulder height to Sally, gave chase. Golden eyes hungry with need, its jaws slavered and snarled. Stone's stomach clenched and twisted, yet Sally had eyes only for him. Skipping and rushing to him, seemingly oblivious to the danger, she laughed and waved, calling his name.

Panic swept over Stone. Only yards separated the wolf from her. She wouldn't reach him in time.

Stone opened his mouth—tried to yell a warning—but no sound came out. He cleared his throat and tried again. Nothing. She wasn't far. There was still time to reach her if he ran hard. He tried but unseen bonds locked his legs in place. The wolf was closer. He had to get to her. With all his strength he wrenched against the force that held him fast. Stone couldn't move.

His chest ached from the sledgehammer pummeling his ribs.

Forced to watch, he clenched and unclenched his fists as if he could beat the gag that held him silent or the bonds that held him in place. They soon ached from the exertion.

And he continued to struggle against unseen bonds—tried to scream a warning.

At the last second, fangs nipping at her heels, Sally realized her danger. Before she could turn, the wolf's head-long rush bowled her over. Her heart-rending scream died with the snap of powerful jaws. Bright red blossomed from her throat and sprayed her dress in spurts.

Stone's gag shattered. "Noooooo."

Invisible shackles dropped from his legs, and he stumbled, falling headfirst to the ground. The wolf turned to him with a glint from golden eyes. The predator ignored Sally's bloody, torn, and lifeless body to sneer at Stone. When he scrambled to his feet, the wolf raced off.

Stone knelt, cradled her in his arms. Tears stained his face. "I'm so sorry, Sally. So sorry." The world went dark.

BRIGHT SUN PIERCED his eyelids, and the heat pricked his cheeks. A lump stuck in his throat and every breath came in ragged gulps. His hands ached, though he couldn't remember why.

Stone climbed to his feet. A mountain meadow carpeted with yellow mustard and daisies spread around him. Tall grasses bent in the gentle breeze. A woman skipped up from where the lea met the purple mountains, her red dress bounced around her ankles with each step and the bloused bodice billowed in the gentle breeze. Strawberry-blonde hair tumbled over her shoulders, curls springing with her leaps. She carried a basket, a gingham cloth draped over the side. Somehow, he knew she carried a picnic lunch to share with him.

As she neared, she waved while full, ruby lips formed a smile capable of beguiling a eunuch. She seemed familiar, as if he should know her, though he was sure he'd remember meeting a woman as angelically beautiful as this one. Yet, he was sure he knew her from somewhere. He paused.

"Sally!" Joy filled his heart. That dress was the same one she wore the day he proposed marriage.

She looked up and noticed him. Her smile widened. "Judd."

A loud roar from behind her snapped his quiet reverie. A massive grizzly rose on its hind legs—easily three times Sally's height. Razor-sharp claws slashed the air as hungry eyes found her and dropped to all fours before the beast broke into a lumbering run, intent on its prey. Sally had eyes only for Stone and seemed unaware of her danger. She continued to skip toward Stone.

Stone started to yell a warning, but his voice froze—he couldn't speak. He tried again. Nothing.

He tried to race to her, but again unseen bonds held him immobile. Every muscle strained as he tried to break loose, but to no avail. He stood frozen in place.

A noose of despair tightened about his neck. He couldn't breathe.

The grizzly closed the distance with Sally, every stride chewing up distance at an alarming rate. Stone tried to scream his warning yet again.

Nothing but silence.

Just as the monstrous beast reached her, Sally turned. The terror in her scream ripped at Stone's heart, even as he remained helpless to aid her. A mammoth paw, claws long and razor sharp slashed at her throat. Bright red blood spurted from the gashes.

"Noooooo." Stone's voice broke loose from its prison of silence as his feet slipped free. He dashed toward Sally.

The bear, busy sniffing its kill, lifted its head, roared in defiance, and loped away.

Sally lay still. Blood and gore covered the bodice of her pretty dress. Tears flowed down his cheeks as he dropped to his knees. He pulled her to him and hugged her against his chest.

"I'm so sorry, Sally. So sorry." Blackness enveloped him.

There were more visions. Many more. Always Sally ran or skipped to him, happy and joyful, unaware of the dangerous creature that chased her. In every vision, Stone witnessed her death, helpless to warn her. His scream broke the spell in each, too late to rescue her but in time to drive the beast away before it feasted on her bloody body. Over and over, he re-lived the gruesome tableau. Each time, he cradled her to his breast, tears in his eyes, as he murmured, "I'm so sorry, Sally. So sorry."

CHAPTER 15

MARSHAL ZEBULON PRICE sighted down the length of his Winchester '73. An antelope stood two hundred yards up wind. It grazed on a clump of prairie grass, unaware of its impending doom.

Price took the slack out of the trigger, breathing out as he did so.

The boom of a single shot thundered from across the silent prairie.

The antelope dashed away—its tail flashed warning white with each leap.

Startled, Price released the pressure on the trigger and snapped his head around toward the camp he'd left that morning. Damn. That was Jackson's Sharps—no mistaking the sound of that cannon.

His pulse quickened, and he scanned the grassland for danger. A salvo of rifle fire erupted in the distance.

The lawman raced to his picketed steed.

Price worked the reins. Zeus's long mane streamed behind as he galloped across the plain. He seemed as anxious to get to the action as his rider.

The camp had been quiet when he left. What happened? Indians?

As he closed to within a half mile of the camp, Price heaved back on the reins to stop his big mount's headlong rush. Rifle in hand, he dismounted and dropped to all fours. Sporadic shots barked as he scrambled through a buffalo wallow, but the Sharps remained quiet. A lump formed in his throat as he belly-crawled up the far side.

Price doffed his hat and lifted his head over the lip of the wallow. Fifty feet to his left, a Sioux pony nuzzled at the prone figure of an Indian. Crimson stained the surrounding grass, and a soft moan reached his ears.

Were there others? How many?

His heart thumped. A survey of the grassland revealed nothing, but a hundred Sioux could be hidden in the casual undulations of the prairie.

The camp was visible five hundred yards ahead. No one had seen him leave. Would the posse think he had been killed or captured? He feared one of the inexperienced young men might mistake him for an Indian.

Movement caught his eye, and he glanced back toward the injured Indian. Another Sioux had slipped up and now tugged at his injured companion.

Price slapped his rifle to his shoulder. As he took the slack out of the trigger, the brave stood. And the marshal froze. They were only half-pints. Maybe twelve, certainly no older. Damn. Sweat poured into the lawman's eyes and blurred his vision. Was it all sweat? He blinked several times to clear his sight.

The bead of his rifle centered on the boy's back—he once again gently squeezed the trigger. What was he doing? Price hesitated. He might not live long enough to regret it, but he'd be damned if he'd shoot a squirt just because he's an Indian. Besides, Sioux don't bring children with war parties. He snapped the rifle to his side. It clacked against his leg, loud in the stillness.

The buck whipped around, clearly startled. For a brief second, the marshal thought he saw fear on the youngster's face.

Angry shouts rose from the direction of the posse, but he couldn't understand what was being said. Ignoring them, he held his hands up in what he hoped was a peaceful gesture and hurried to the injured brave. The boy stepped back and reached for his bow. Price swallowed hard, but still dropped to one knee beside the prone figure.

Blood pooled around the boy, soaking into the dry ground, taking on the appearance of oxidized metal. Wide black eyes stared at nothing from a hairless, cherubic face. Just a boy. A lump formed in Marshal Price's throat. He slammed a fist into his thigh. With a gentle touch he pulled the eyelids closed and stood to face the other youth.

An arrow protruded from the boy's drawn bow—pointed at Price's gut. Forcing his eyes to glide past the projectile and lock with the boy's wide orbs, Price offered what he hoped was an expression of sorrow. He shook his head. Anxious to be gone, he spun on his heel and strode away. An itch formed between his shoulder blades where he imagined the arrow would strike him. He kept walking. Zeus grazed where he'd been left as if nothing had happened.

Astride his stallion, he returned to the spot where the body had been, but both boys were gone.

"WHAT THE HELL just happened?" Marshal Price roared his question through clenched teeth. The men milled about in two groups. Howard Willis and his young friends formed one. The second group consisted of the remaining posse members, most of whom were veterans of the Civil War. They had been shouting back and forth when Price entered the camp.

Emmitt Jackson, dark eyes squinted in anger, pointed into the crowd of young men. "He took my r—"

"Shut your baz—" Ernest Crawford, one of Howard's friends, shouted over the blacksmith.

"Enough." Price stared at the men, his gaze swept over both clusters.

The older men met his scowl with their own steady scrutiny, but the young men stared defiance until he locked eyes with each one. Then chins dropped like the recalcitrant children they were.

He purposely left Ernest for last. Fixing him with his best "don't mess with me" look, he growled, "Ernest, not another word out of you until I ask for it."

Not waiting for an acknowledgement, he said, "Emmitt, please tell me what happened."

The story came out in pieces.

Someone had spotted a pair of Indians riding past the camp to the west. Men seized guns only to realize a minute later that the travelers were children and not a threat. The veterans stowed their rifles and returned to their half-drunk coffee. Howard and his friends, however, kept their firearms out and continued to watch. At some point, Ernest stole the Sharps from Emmitt's saddle boot. Light-hearted banter between the young men grew loud and one of the Sioux boys spotted them.

Ernest decided they could not be allowed to leave. He fired and the Sioux boy dropped from his pony. Scared, the young posse opened fire despite the distance.

Emmitt, angrier than a she-bear with cubs, jerked his rifle out of Ernest's hands and punched the tenderfoot.

Price huffed through his thick mustache—the course hair rippled. With a scowl that alternated between Ernest and Howard, he spoke, "You boys have dropped a hot potato in my lap. In less than an hour I expect a party of Sioux to ride up, looking for bear. If they don't start a fight right off, they'll demand I turn you over to them to be punished. I can't do that, even if I was so inclined. What I can do is arrest you."

"Fer killin' injuns?" Ernest's voice somehow managed to sound both incredulous and sullen.

His friends took up the chorus.

Dumb kids—they were unaware of what they had started. Price clenched his fists, his breaths came in short, rapid pants. Before he realized it himself, he drove his fist through Howard's jaw and knocked the much larger man to the ground.

Howard glared at the marshal.

Price stalked up and stood over him. Glowering down at him he growled, "I told you to be quiet. Now shut your trap and listen."

Howard tried to crab-crawl backward.

"Stop." The marshal leaned down until his nose was inches from Howard's. Price stabbed his index finger into Howard's chest. "I'll tell you when you can move. Until I say so, you sit right there like the little schoolboy you are."

"Why you—" Howard started. His hand reached for the revolver strapped to his hip. The distinct chink of a rifle round being chambered stopped him mid-reach.

Sven Larson held his old Henry repeater aimed right at Howard.

The normally quiet man wore an air of determination—the rifle never wavered. The lawman nodded to the shopkeeper and turned back to Howard, whose hands were still frozen mid-reach. Price guessed he had never stared down the barrel of a rifle.

"Ja, go ahead, Marshal."

"Now, Howard, you sit right there and don't even think about interfering."

The big man scowled but kept quiet.

"Good." Price sought out Ernest, but the young man was gone. "Where d—"

The sound of a galloping horse answered the unfinished question. The whole posse gawked as Ernest rode hard to the southeast toward Stockman.

"Well, I'll be damned, slipped off while I was fussin' with Howard."

"What'll we do, Marshal?" Emmitt Jackson's face held an odd expression—part fear and part determination. "Should we mount up and chase the boy down?"

"Ja, vhat ve do?" Sven echoed.

The lawman reached his hand to his chin and stroked his thumb over it. His mind raced. The rider rapidly receded against the horizon.

"No, let him go. I can arrest him when we get back to Stockman, if he manages to make it back." He stared at each member of the posse one at a time beginning with Howard and his friends. One of the youngsters started to open his mouth but Price's glare snapped the mouth shut. "When the Sioux get here, and they will come, I do all the talkin'." Price eyed Howard as he spoke.

Howard's eyes were mere slits as he returned the glare.

"Understand?" Price bent in closer to Willis.

The big man remained silent.

"If anyone tries to interfere while I'm chattin' with the Indians, I'll arrest that person." He continued to stare at the son of one of the most important men in the Dakota Territory. After several minutes of complete silence, Howard dropped his eyes.

Only then did Price return his attention to the rest of the men. All around him youngsters gaped. The older townsmen's shoulders slumped in unison as the tension drained from them.

The men packed up the camp.

Price gathered Jackson, Larson, and Hoeckerman together, and they huddled alone for several minutes. When they finished, all but Price mounted and slipped out of camp. Some of the younger men noted the departure. Price ignored the silent questions in their eyes.

———————

TRUE TO THE lawman's prediction, a party of four dozen Sioux warriors rode up at a fast lope. Half of the warriors held Winchester repeaters. The remaining force was armed with bows and lances. Marshal Price, who expected twenty Indians at most, worked his mouth to clear the cotton that filled it. A posse of seasoned cavalry might have stood a chance against even odds, but he was outnumbered more than two-to-one, and half of them were green kids. This was a massacre waiting to happen.

He turned to the men stretched out in a line behind him and said,

"No one reach for a gun unless I say so. Otherwise just stay as relaxed as you can. And stay here."

Nudging Zeus forward, he considered the angry natives before him. Many of the faces held scowls, and most radiated a sense of barely restrained rage. Not that he blamed them. An old chief broke away to meet him. The marshal realized he recognized the man as someone he had dealt with in previous years.

He swallowed hard. While the old Sioux chief had been reasonable in the past, he would have the pressure of a grieving mother and warrior, as well as the increased tension because of the situation in the Black Hills. At the touch of his rider's knees, Zeus stopped midway between the groups.

"Elk in the Trees, I'm sorry for the boy's death," Price said in the Sioux tongue. As the territorial marshal, he had learned the Sioux language over the course of many years and numerous dealings with the various tribes that called the reservation home. He scrutinized the old man's face for any sign of his intent.

"Marshal," the chief said. "My heart is broken." He brought a fist to his heart as he continued. "The boy was my grandson. The heart of my daughter is broken. What happened?"

"One of my young men. Fool said he was just trying to scare the boys as they rode. I wasn't in camp, or it might not have happened." The marshal hoped his tone conveyed the sadness he felt.

"We take that man with us to face our people. Be punished by our people." The Indian stared at the lawman, steel in his eye.

"We have known each other a long time. You know I can't do that. I don't like it, but that is our law. I—"

"I believed you would say this. We have had many dealings." There was bitterness in the old man's tone. "Today, though, we are many, and you are few." The chief waved a hand at the line of men behind the marshal. "You will give us the man, or we will take him. Many men, yours and mine, will die if it comes to that, but we will have the man that killed my grandson."

"I couldn't give him to you if I wanted to—he rode away right after he killed the boy." Price pointed east.

The Sioux's eyes widened, and he turned his head back to his own people, rattling off something too fast for the marshal to follow. At once, a dozen men broke from the group and raced east. The remaining warriors rode out of rifle range and formed a loose circle around the white men.

The chief locked eyes with the lawman and said, "We wait."

Price rode back to his posse with the reluctance of one with disturbing news.

"Marshal?" One of the older posse members—Price couldn't remember his name—swallowed hard. "What's going to happen?"

"Rest easy. There's no sense planning a fight. We'll wait to see what happens."

"Where'd you send Angus, Sven, and Jackson?" Howard's tone demanded an answer.

The lawman stared at the younger man.

Howard fidgeted, like he wanted to ask again. He rubbed his bruised chin but remained silent.

The posse remade the camp they had so recently broken down. Wary eyes cast furtive glances at Sioux who continued to sit and wait but made no move to attack.

Dusk's grey was shifting to the indigo of twilight when a dozen Indian braves galloped into sight from the east. A figure, indistinct in the gloom, was being dragged behind one of the ponies. Sure it had to be Ernest, a weight settled on Price's chest.

Howard approached him. "Marshal, that's Ernest they brought back. You have to do something."

"Sixteen men—more than half untrained—against fifty of the finest light cavalry in the world. *What* would you have me do that would not get every damned one of us *killed*?"

"We can't just let savages kill Ernest."

"If that fool shot a white boy back in Stockman he'd be hung."

"That's different. No jury would convict him of murder for killing an *Indian*."

"An Indian jury would." It was a weak retort and the marshal knew it. Regardless of Price's personal feelings, Howard was right. Ernest murdered that Indian boy today, yet in the eyes of the law, the Sioux had no authority in the matter and a trial in Yankton would result in a verdict of not guilty.

Part of the marshal was glad the Sioux had caught the man. They would execute their own justice and Price, in spite of his sworn duty, was trapped with no way to protect the fool.

The big man glared at the marshal for several seconds before walking away. None of his friends came to support him, though the lawman knew they felt similarly.

As Price reached for the coffee pot, a blood curdling scream broke the quiet.

"What was that, Marshal?"

"Was that Ernest?"

"Are the savages attacking us?"

Questions peppered the lawman, but he ignored them all. Several men grabbed for weapons, but he silently waved them off. He stared into the darkness in the direction of the yell. He knew what it was and that more would follow. Depending on how strong Ernest was, the cries might last all night. Bravery was a virtue valued by the Sioux. If Ernest showed courage, they might be merciful and kill him early on. If not, Ernest would be kept alive and tortured all night.

———————

DAKOTA TERRITORY, MONDAY, MAY 10TH, 1875

THE MEN KEPT watch through the night. Those not on patrol lay in their bed rolls, but no one slept. Ernest, it seemed, was not brave, and his screams didn't cease until the Eastern sky began to lighten with the first coral rays of dawn. Fifteen minutes after the last muffled scream reached the camp, the Sioux rode away.

They found Ernest staked out, spread-eagle and naked. Blood congealed across his head where his scalp had been taken. Burns blackened much of his skin. The nauseatingly sweet smell of burnt flesh soured the air. As a final insult, his manhood had been slashed off and stuffed in his mouth. Price hoped Ernest had not lived to feel it.

The sounds of stomachs emptying reached him. How long had it taken him before he no longer lost his last meal after witnessing the after-effects of Lakota torture?

They had buried the body and were replacing the sod when Angus, Sven, and Emmitt rode up. A troupe of U.S. Cavalry from Fort Sully trailed behind—too late to save Ernest.

CHAPTER 16

THICK FINGERS PLUCKED the fine cigar from the humidor and snapped the mahogany lid shut. The delicately carved box canted on the desktop from the force of the closure.

"Serves that pompous little man right for always keeping me waiting," Charles Willis growled under his breath. He struck a match and lit the tip as he puffed to ignite the tobacco.

The rhythmic tapping of his foot was the only sound as he waited for his host. Since there was no ashtray in sight, he knocked the grey cinders onto the carpet. Charles leaned back in his chair, the cigar's stub nestled in the crook of two fingers while blue smoke billowed from between his lips. The office door opened, and the diminutive vice president of the Dakota and Montana Western Railway stepped into the room.

"I see you managed to raid my fine Burmese supply." Annoyance accentuated his already nasal tone. "One of my British clients secured those for me. If only you were as proficient in securing deeds." A thin smirk punctuated his comment.

Charles's face heated and both hands curled into tight balls as he exploded to his feet. "Why, you...." The remains of the expensive cigar tumbled to the floor—Charles ground it into the carpet with the heel of his boot.

Emerson's eyes grew large, and his body stiffened. Though he worked his mouth, nothing came out.

Charles stopped before he took his second step. He closed his eyes, sucked in a deep breath through his nose, and blew it out between pursed lips. Business was more important—nothing good could come of any type of outburst, let alone a physical one. He needed to calm himself. The pressure had him behaving so far out of character that he almost didn't recognize himself anymore. By the time he reached ten in his silent count, his fists were relaxed.

Composed, Charles stepped back and looked the elfin man in the eye. "I'm sorry. I should not...." His tone terse, he paused and inhaled—a long, slow, breath before continuing in a more conciliatory manner. "I should not have responded that way. Please forgive me."

Owl-like, Emerson blinked twice. The tiny man's jaw clacked shut, and he shook his head. "F—fine. Sure. It's fine." He shook his head again and knitted his brows together. He waggled his finger at Charles. "But the next time you pull a stunt like that, I'll have you tossed in jail like some common miscreant."

It took an effort of will for Charles to fight down the cringe that threatened to rear its head. He knew he deserved the dressing down, although it galled him that it came from Lockhart. The little man's day would come, but for now Charles needed him.

"Now, where were we?" Emerson strode to his chair. As he sat, he seemed to notice his humidor for the first time. Scowling, he stepped to the side of the desk and adjusted the box to re-align it evenly with the edges of the desktop.

Upon his return to his seat, Emerson stared at Charles and smiled. "Ah, yes. You were just about to tell me all about this deed you have been unable to secure for me. Please. Sit." He waved a hand in the direction of Charles's empty chair.

He waited, eyebrows raised, for his guest to be seated. The visitor opened his mouth to speak, but Emerson shook his finger at him and Charles closed it again.

"Please tell me that you are here with the deed you promised to deliver by last week."

"These things take time." Charles waved his hand. "I've taken steps to secure it. Should take possession in two weeks."

"Doesn't leave me much time. What if it takes longer?"

Charles shook his head. "Let's just say that I've, ah... ah, purchased... certain assurances. We'll have plenty of time."

Emerson smiled. "I also took steps. Contacted Cyrus Clinton three weeks ago."

Clinton! Charles fought to maintain an even expression. Enemies of the railroad died suddenly when that man was around. If rumors could be believed, the gun-hand had killed a dozen men in fair fights. In quiet corners, it was whispered that he may also have dry-gulched almost twice that number.

"I was quite confident you would not be able to talk Stone into selling or bully him into leaving, as you did the others." He stood and paced behind his desk, arms clasped at the small of his back. "Of course, who could have predicted those miners would show up and murder poor Sally." He laughed. "How fortuitous."

Charles forced himself to chuckle. "Indeed. So you sent Clinton back?"

"Absolutely not." The tiny man stopped. "I know you made sure your son was on the posse. You told him to find a way to dispatch Stone, if possible."

"I did no—"

"Please." Emerson waved his hand in dismissal. "It's the only conclusion. Why else would you let the boy go on such a dangerous mission? No, you wouldn't have been foolish enough to murder the woman, but you aren't above taking advantage of it. Well, neither am I. When I heard about the killing, I knew Stone would take off after them. Surely they're headed to Deadwood, so I sent Clinton there too. He'll take Stone, fair fight or in the back, and I don't care which."

Charles slapped the arm of his chair. "That'll be it for Stone. I hear Clinton's faster and deadlier than Hickok."

Emerson walked around the desk and picked up the humidor. He opened it and extended the box toward Charles. After the big man took one, the smaller man plucked his and replaced the box on the corner of his desk, perfectly aligned with the edges. "That he is."

———————

CONSCIOUSNESS RETURNED LIKE the slow march of the condemned. His face felt tight. Someone nearby chanted in a language he didn't understand. Melodic. Rhythmic. Hypnotic. An acrid, sweet smoke tickled his nose.

Stone forced his eyes open against the crust that held them shut. Ebony darkness surrounded him. With slow deliberateness, he reached into the emptiness. His hand appeared, deep black against the ebony backdrop. At least he wasn't blind.

Cotton filled his mouth. "Water." It came out as a croak so faint he wasn't sure he had even spoken aloud. Except his throat ached after.

The chanting stopped, then continued, as if the person had paused to listen.

"*Calme.*" Hush. The soft whisper floated to him. He recognized her French—Dancing Waters.

As his eyes adjusted, he was able to distinguish between the walls around him and the night sky filtering through the hole at the top of the teepee.

How had he gotten here?

The fight. He fought Black Buffalo.

Memories jumbled together.

Hot coals. He touched his palm. A thick cream coated his unbandaged hand. It didn't hurt.

Bindings around his ribs restricted his breathing. Discomfort accompanied each breath. But no pain.

Someone or something nearby stirred. The murmur of cloth on cloth marked their presence. The flap of the teepee was pushed back, and Dancing Waters stood silhouetted by the fire beyond. Stone tried to rise. She glided to him, ghost-like, and pressed her hand to his shoulder. He groaned, and she held a finger to his lips.

She knelt next to him and pulled a bowl to her—the contents sloshed. "You have slept a long time, White Warrior. I began to fear you would not return from the land of visions." Touching a rag to his lips, she squeezed, and water drizzled onto them. Rough, chapped skin caught on his tongue as it retrieved the precious drops.

"What time is it?" He worked his mouth to find more moisture to ease his raw, hoarse throat. "How long have I been asleep?" Less rasp this time.

"Just past moonrise. But the sun has risen and set seven times since you battled Black Buffalo."

"Seven days! I need to be after Sally's killers." Stone raised his shoulders off his pallet, but Dancing Waters laid a hand on his chest and gently guided him back down.

"Shhhhh. Not yet. You're still healing. Give your body time."

Silken strands brushed across his bare chest as she leaned over him. He roughly pushed down the feelings it stirred.

"You saw many visions while you lay resting." Her tone changed from the tender voice of a healer to the more authoritative voice of a medicine woman. "Many times you called out, then whispered something. I could not understand what you were saying. Many times I wiped tears from your eyes."

Stone laid still, looking at nothing, remembering his dreams. Were they visions?

"The spirits spoke to you."

"I'm not sure what they said."

Dancing Waters touched the center of Stone's chest. "Listen to your heart. The spirits will make themselves known if you listen."

They sat silent after that. She sponged more water for him.

Dancing Waters placed a reassuring hand on his shoulder as she rose. "Rest now. We'll speak in the morning."

"GIT ON WITH you, now, Frankie. I got other fellas to attend to." Ida's roots were obvious in her drawl.

"But I ain't done, yet."

The girl giggled and tossed her sheets aside. "Seems to me you finished." She stood, naked but for her stockings. "'Sides, you used up the time you paid fer. Ya gonna have to talk to Cora if'n you're want'n more."

Frankie stared at her—his gaze followed as she walked casually to the washstand on the far side of the room. Blindness—or desperation—often helped when it came to visiting the brothels of Deadwood, but Cora recruited and imported only the prettiest girls from all over the country, and Ida stood out among them. Long blonde curls tumbled over creamy white shoulders and cascaded down her supple back, to stop just above the soft curve of her hips. The smoky, mirrored glass of the chiffonier reflected other assets. An elegant chin turned back to him, and he imagined a twinkle in her azure eyes. Full, plum-colored lips parted.

"I'm serious, Frankie. Git dressed and be gone with ya before Miss Cora has an apoplexy."

"Oh, all right. I'm goin'." He swung his body to the edge of the iron-frame bed. As she sponged off and slipped into her petticoats, he contemplated her beauty. "I shore am gonna miss you, Ida." A smile tugged at the corners of Frankie's lips. "Come with us into the hills. We'd have a grand time. You could cook our meals and wash our clothes, and we'd all git rich t'gether. Wha'd ya' say?"

The young beauty giggled and waved her hand. "Wherever do you git such ideas? Why, what would all the fellers here 'bouts do without me? Now hurry and git dressed, or Miss Cora'll tan my hide and set the boys on you."

Five minutes later, Frankie stepped out of Cora's Palace of Delights. He pushed through the line of men that snaked around the corner and slogged up the dark street toward the saloon. Streets in Deadwood remained a churned-up mess of mud and horse pies—no rain required—and clumps of the semi-soft muck formed thick pads that stuck to the soles and sides of his boots. Soon he found himself stumping and tottering as he struggled to drag his bad leg.

Frankie hefted the coin purse in his coat pocket and cringed. Excursions with Ida were almost extortionate. Cavorting with her represented a departure from his normal frugality that he couldn't explain. Perhaps the near-death experience with the Indians had changed him—he had never been more scared than at that moment. No matter, wealth beyond his wildest dreams awaited.

Gold flowed like water in Deadwood. Men gambled thousands of dollars' worth of dust on single hands of poker or a turn at the faro tables with no more thought than if they wagered pebbles. Claim-stakes and sluices littered Deadwood Gulch and seemingly every turn of the spade produced sparkling flecks that waited to be plucked.

Prosperity also created problems. For every claim in proximity to Deadwood, three or four men hoped to find a stake others had missed. Easy, though not honest, gains drew professional cardsharps and thieves, alike. Two men were buried at the Mount Moriah Cemetery the day that Frankie and his friends rode in. One of the men had been murdered, the other lynched for the killing.

The day following their arrival, Curly sent Shorty and Erik to reconnoiter possible sites far removed from prying and dangerous eyes. They were expected back tonight.

Flickering lantern light spilled out of the open flap of the tent that comprised the Pageant, the largest and most popular of the four drinking establishments that called Deadwood home. The saloon was two connected structures—the larger was devoid of furniture except for the bar and a piano, while empty crates and barrels made do as tables and chairs for gambling in the second.

From inside the tent someone banged out "The Glendy Burk" on an out-of-tune piano, while a choir of drunken voices bellowed the words.

> The Glendy Burk is a mighty fast boat,
> With a mighty fast captain too;
> He sits up there on the hurricane roof
> And he keeps his eye on the crew.
> I can't stay here, for they work too hard;
> I'm bound to leave this town;
> I'll take my duds and tote 'em on my back
> When the Glendy Burk comes down.

Frankie stepped through the flap into a swirling, stinging smog of blue and black smoke from the array of cigarettes, cigars, and lanterns. A single tear formed in the corner of his eye, and he blinked to clear it. Curly waited for him somewhere in this tumult. Men shouldered their way to the makeshift bar, a thirty-foot rough-hewn plank stretched over whiskey barrels. Others clustered about the piano against the back wall. The song ended, and the music quieted, which created a lull in the din. The clink of mugs and buzz of conversation filled the void.

Curly waved from among the singers. The friends locked eyes, and the bald man lifted an empty mug high. Frankie nodded once and elbowed his way to the bar. By the time he reached his companion with their beers, the pianist was half-way through "Camptown Races." Curly bawled out the words as lustily as the rest of the throng—Frankie joined in on the final verse.

ABOUT MIDNIGHT, A gentle nudge stirred Frankie from where he had fallen asleep in a corner. He lifted his head. Curly nodded toward the open doorway where Shorty stood with a grin so wide it almost couldn't fit through the tent flap. The pair worked their way across the room to join their friend.

"What's got in to you, Shorty. Ya ain't frownin'," Curly yelled to be heard over the ruckus.

"We gots to talk. Ya won't believe what Erik and me lit on."

"Well, out with it."

"Where is Erik?" Frankie's heart beat a little faster as he contemplated the cause of his friend's absence.

"He's guarding our claim. Let's get outta' here. Somewhere private."

Now Frankie's heart thumped from excitement rather than fear, even as his temples throbbed in time to the current tune. They found the mother lode. His hands shook and his knees weakened. It took restraint to fight down the smile that attacked his lips.

"How big is it?" The song ended as he started, so the shouted question sounded through the whole tent. Men stared at him from all over the room, and his cheeks warmed.

"Hush, ya idjit." Shorty spit. He shook his head. "Outside."

I'm gonna be rich!

CHAPTER 17

"I'M PULLING OUT tomorrow." Stone stood outside the encampment next to Runs With Deer.

"Mmm." The old chief nodded and cocked his head to peer at his friend. "I think you have not mentioned this to my daughter."

"I will. Tonight." Stone tried to jam his hands into the front pockets of his pants. When he missed, he remembered that he wore buckskins, a gift from Dancing Waters. "She's been busy with whatever she took from the buffalo carcasses yesterday." He paused before continuing. "I think she's angry. Tried to talk me out of going after them."

The chief only nodded.

"I told her I had to do this." Stone flicked his wrist in a backhanded wave. "That's when she stormed off muttering something about the buffalo hunt and having work to do."

"My daughter is wise. Revenge is for young men with tempers like the bull buffalo. Killing these men will not return your wife to you. Besides, they are four, and you are one. She does not wish for you to die after she saved your life."

"I owe her more than I can pay. For fixing me up, for caring for me." He glanced down and pointed to his new buckskins. "For all this. For not leaving me. Don't know what would've happened to me if you had left me there after the fight."

"She insisted on tending your wounds." Runs With Deer chuckled. "Ordered a couple of braves to drag Black Buffalo's body off you and more to take you to my teepee. When the buffalo were found, she rigged a travois for you, to bring you along."

"Whatever it was she did, the pain is mostly gone, and I feel better than I have any right to." To emphasize his point, Stone swung his arms and twisted his body.

"She is a gifted healer among our people. She would be a fine wife to some brave. Maybe one whose own died too soon. Or was murdered." The old chief's stare held miles of unspoken meaning.

Stone shook his head. There could never be another after Sally. At least not yet. Maybe later. Right now he was focused on his mission, but he didn't want to offend his friend or his daughter. "I have to do this. I've already lost too much time as it is. I owe it to Sally to see this through." He looked at the sky, then all around. "Where, exactly, are we?"

Runs With Deer smiled and paused for what seemed an eternity to Stone. "The trail my people use to cross Mako Sica, the bad land, is a day's ride that way." The old man pointed northwest. "Five suns to the sacred hills from here."

"Will you tell me how to find the trail?"

His expression blank, Runs With Deer gazed into the distance. He didn't speak for a long time, but at last he turned back to Stone and shook his head. "No. I—"

"Chief, pl—"

A gnarled old hand rose, palm out, to quiet his friend.

"I will send my daughter to guide you through."

"You shouldn't—"

"It is decided."

CHAPTER 18

THE NIGHT AFTER picking up his package, Stone came calling. One hand, pressed into the small of his back, clutched a bouquet of daisies, while with his other hand he turned the crank of the doorbell. The loud whir of the gears and the clink of a bell announced his presence. He stepped back to wait.

A stooped and gnarled old woman opened the door. She eyed Stone, her head moving from his face to his boots—he still wore his Uncle Sam issued pair—then drifted back to his face, her disapproval as obvious as the long tuft of hair that grew from the mole on her chin. "Well, state your business."

"I'm Maj—ah, Judiah Stone, and I'm here to call on Miss Sally Quinlan, please, ma'am."

The hidebound old woman sniffed and muttered under her breath. He caught a few words, "gentlemen," "officers," and "in her day," as she closed the door without even inviting the young man into the parlor.

The wait seemed an eternity. Stone's palms grew clammy, and his breathing sped up. What if she wouldn't see him? What if she sent the old woman out to shoo him away like a lost puppy? Mrs. Fedick had warned him about Mrs. Hightower. Supposedly the widow of a naval captain who served with Captain Perry during the Battle of Lake Erie, it was said that her husband's old flintlock pistol was primed and ready to shoot unsatisfactory gentleman callers.

Stone dismissed the story as rumor. Still, when the knob rattled and the door opened a few moments later, he caught himself wondering if he would be shot.

Sally stepped through the open door. Oleander and honeysuckle perfumed the breeze that played with the ruffles around the bodice of her dress. Her eyes locked onto his.

Stone's tongue felt swollen. He worked his mouth to find some moisture. "Good evening, Miss Quinlan."

"Good evening, Major Stone." Her tone was flat, noncommittal, as if she had greeted many suitors and was as unimpressed by this one as the last.

He swallowed and hoped that the bob of his Adam's apple wasn't obvious. Pulling his hand from behind his back, he thrust the daisies at Sally.

"These are for you." Her stoic face broke into a grin too wide for her cheeks to contain, forcing it to spread to her eyes.

The couple soon moved to the swing that hung at the end of the porch. Periodically, Mrs. Hightower pushed aside the curtains in the window to check them. Once, when the suitor appeared too close to the naive and vulnerable young woman, she tapped on the glass. When they looked up, she pointed a gnarled finger at Stone and gestured at him to move away from Sally.

Stone complied and the widow retreated. No sooner had the curtains closed and Sally laughed. She then proceeded to slide closer to him.

"Are you trying to get me in trouble with the woman? I'd rather face an army of angry Rebs alone than have her mad at me."

Sally giggled. "She is not the one you ought to be concerning yourself with."

CHAPTER 19

LEATHER BIT INTO the back of Stone's neck as he allowed his field glasses to settle against his chest, their weight supported by the thong draped around his neck. The Bad Lands, Mako Sica to the native Lakota, seemed to rise out of the vast prairie to form a desolate maze of spires, hoodoos, mesas, and low peaks. Pastel yellows and reds formed distinct cake-like layers along the geological features. Even from here, nearly half a mile away, the foreboding presence of the place loomed over them.

The setting sun cast deep shadows, so when he could learn no more, he returned to the small fire that crackled nearby. Skewered on spits over the flames, a brace of hares roasted. The aroma of grease and boiling coffee, carried on the ubiquitous breeze, wafted about him as he stared at the sunset. A deep, soft rumble interrupted the stillness.

Dancing Waters chuckled. "Hungry?"

"More than I realized, I guess."

"We rode hard today."

Stone glanced at their mounts who munched on green clumps of grass. "I still can't believe your father was able to get my horses back. Cordelia's been with me since Sally and I married. Even my saddle. I thought sure that was lost when the braves that captured me left it behind." He touched the revolver on his hip. "And my guns. I'll never...."

"My father and I owed you a great debt. It was worth the six ponies we gave to Little Elk." She pulled a rabbit off the fire and handed it to her companion. "Although I begged father not to trade for your weapons. I hoped that if you didn't...." She let the thought trail off.

"I'd have gone after Sally's murderers anyway." As he tore a bite from the carcass with his teeth, juice dribbled down his chin. He wiped it away. "Either picked up a gun along the way or found another means to exact my revenge."

"My father said the same thing. Better that you have your own weapons."

The pair ate in silence.

From someplace east of camp a whippoorwill called. Another answered. Stone touched the butt of his Colt, the tips of his fingers still slick with grease. "Visitors?" His whisper was no louder than the rustle of the grass in a gentle breeze.

She shook her head. "We're alone. That was only the song of the night birds."

He let his hand fall away, but his eyes scanned the grassland around them. There was nothing to see in the darkness, and he soon gave up the search.

"You have not answered my question, Judd Stone."

"What question? Did I miss something?" He glanced up, and her obsidian orbs stared at him.

"In my father's teepee. Why do you insist on finding these men? On killing them?"

Seeking a distraction, he bent down to rip up a tuft of grass from between his feet. One at a time, he tossed individual blades to the ground. The last piece he threw hard.

"Men that would attack a woman need killing."

"Then why not let the posse do it?" The Sioux woman cocked her head. "Surely they will capture the men and hang them."

"I need to do it if I can. For Sally. So she can be at peace." His voice was unconvincing, even to himself.

"Vengeance is for the living. The dead are past caring. Is this what she would want?"

Without lifting his head to look, he sensed her eyes boring holes, drilling deep into him to force a response. He shifted his weight from one foot to the other, then wiped an imaginary speck of dirt from the front of his shirt.

Finally, he spoke. "No." Stone shook his head and was quiet for a few seconds.

Dancing Waters waited without speaking.

"Used to argue about this. Oh, not argue like fight, but debate. Something to pass time during the winters. We'd sit by the fireplace. I'd be mending a harness, or something. She'd do her needlework. Whatever topic came up is what we discussed.

"One week the Kansas City Star reported on a lynching farther out west. Cattle rustlers. The news was two, three months old when we saw it, but it gave us something to talk about. She hated it. Figured if they could be caught alive, they should be tried. Rule of law. Trial by jury of your peers. That's what she believed in."

"You don't?"

"No, not always. Seen murderers released on technicalities. Not right. Law's often days or weeks away out here. Hundreds of miles away even. No, in those cases frontier justice is better. Protect you and yours."

"It won't bring your woman back."

Stone's hands curled into tight fists at his side. The hare he'd eaten felt like a roiling cannon ball in his gut, threatening to come back. His lip curled, and he snarled his retort. "But I'll feel better knowing they've paid for their murdering."

"By murdering them? And at what price to you?"

He met her gaze and stared at her for a minute. The even demeanor of Dancing Waters's argument reminded him of Sally. No anger, no yelling—just calm self-assurance and logic. "Wouldn't be murder. It'd be justice." Silence hung over them again for a minute. "May not matter. I've been delayed so long the posse may get to them first." He spit as if disgusted by the thought. "If so, I'll have to figure a way to kill them without hurting my friends, if possible."

"Would you do that? Hurt your friends to avenge your wife."

Stone stared into her dark eyes, his own mind a jumble of thoughts. Would he? Without answering, he turned and walked into the darkness.

CHAPTER 20

HIS HANDS WERE mostly healed from the fight with Black Buffalo, but a few crusty scabs remained on his knuckles. They scratched his face as Stone tried to rub the soreness from his eyes. His tongue twisted in revolt at the first quick swallow of coffee—cold bitter dregs left from the previous evening. A measure of alertness had seeped into his mind by the time he tossed the last of it into the grass.

Curled near the remains of their fire, Dancing Waters slept while he pulled his boots on. In the pre-dawn darkness, the slight rise and fall of her chest was almost imperceptible. Long dark hair fanned out around her and shimmered in the faint light. The peaceful glow of sleep enveloped her and reminded Stone of how much he missed watching Sally sleep. His heart ached at the memory.

He stood. One touch on Dancing Waters's shoulder woke her. "I'm going to get the horses ready. Be light by the time I'm finished."

A yawn and a stretch accompanied her nod.

WIND AND RAIN had eroded away the regolith over many millennia leaving only bare rock. Their horses placed each hoof with care on the slick surface of the hardened sandstone. House-sized rocks with muted yellow and faded burgundy striations and oatmeal caps surrounded the travelers. The trail led between shale cliffs that rose on either side. Their height blocked all but a thin sliver of the azure sky, leaving Stone and Dancing Waters in deep shadows that would not dispel until the sun reached its zenith. Soon after the gloom would return as the orb began its descent toward the western horizon.

An ominous air laid heavy across Stone's shoulders, as if evil spirits kept watch over Mako Sika.

"You feel them, don't you?"

Dancing Waters's whisper startled Stone. He nodded without looking at her. His responding whisper was so quiet he almost couldn't hear it himself. "There's something here. Something that hates us. We're disturbing it. Almost like we've awoken something evil."

"Yes. We must be careful in this place. The spirits here are very old. Very angry. If there were any other way, I would not have led us through here."

"I know. Reminds me of some of the battlefields during the war. So much violent death. Sometimes the morning after the battle, while mist lay heavy still, it was almost like you could feel them, the dead. Could almost hear them on the breeze asking 'Why?' Feel them clawing at you." Stone paused, unsure if he should continue. He shrugged. "I never was sure if they were clawing to try to come back or trying to claw me to hell with them."

This time gooseflesh raced along his spine from the small of his back to his neck and lingered under his ears before touching his cheeks. He glanced over his shoulder, half expecting to see a hooded specter reaching a boney finger for him—but there was nothing but shale cliffs and sandstone rocks. As he turned back to watch ahead, he allowed his gaze to linger along the tops of the cliffs.

A hundred yards into the cut the trail split.

"Our way goes there." Dancing Waters waved to the left, toward an artery that ran beside a dry creek bed.

She led them on a dizzying trek of twists and turns through canyons and gorges, over grass covered flats, along draws and animal trails.

"You must've been through here many times to remember all these turns."

"Only twice."

"Then how?"

"Ask the hawk how it flies or the trout how it swims." She shrugged. "I do not know how, only that I do."

Stone lifted his hat and wiped his brow with his bandana. He wrung it out and swabbed the back of his neck. Using the hat to shade his eyes, he examined the cliffs above them. "Midday and hot already."

"When these rocks heat up, it'll be worse." She pointed to the path ahead with a casual wave of her hand. "This canyon opens up soon. For many miles there will be little shade."

"Aren't you full of cheery news today."

———————

HEAT SHIMMERS DISTORTED the trail. The afternoon sun bore down on them, an unrelenting and oppressive fever. Stone's head swam, and he wobbled in the saddle.

A hoodoo along the trail had broken twice to form a rough arch. Dancing Waters stopped her pony and turned. "We'll rest in the shade."

He nodded as he dismounted.

Cordelia lapped at the hatful of water he offered. Each in turn, he allowed the others to drink, careful to keep them from consuming too much.

Stone slumped next to the horses and closed his eyes.

"Rest for a few more minutes. I'm going to ride ahead and check the trail."

"I'm fine to go on." Stone started to sit up.

She touched his thigh. "No, your body is still healing. I won't be long."

Ten minutes later she returned, her eyes pinched, and brows knitted. "We have a problem." Her voice was tight. "The ravine is blocked." She indicated back the way she had come. "A shelf collapsed, and the debris blocks the trail."

"Can we get around it?"

She shook her head. "We must take a different route." She eyed the water sacks tied to Stone's packhorse. "We'll have to conserve water."

"Why? How far around is it?"

"Two days. We—"

"What?" Stone jumped to his feet. "Two days? Impossible. I've already lost a week. I won't lose more."

"But we can't get the horses past the dam."

"Then let's go have a look. I'll find us a way."

They walked the horses. As the trail bent, the canyon floor widened, but the cliff faces seemed menacing, narrowing as they rose, leaning far out over them. The trail curved more. A wall of rubble blocked the way. The left side of the makeshift dam stood almost twenty feet above the floor of the creek bed. Its slope, a jumble of shale and rock fragments, was too steep to climb. The right side was much lower with a long gentle slope. The horse could be led over this section, except the trunk of a tree grew out of the opposite cliff face at an odd angle, its branches dense and tangled like each fought the others for light.

Stone squatted under some of the low-hanging limbs and craned his neck upward. A pair of thin grey squirrels played there. One of them stopped to watch him from atop a tangled web of branches entwined within the wall of debris. It chittered at him from its perch, then disappeared behind the impenetrable tangle.

"You and I could pick our way through this tree and move on, but not with the horses." Stone used his thumb to scratch at the stubble on his jaw. "We'll have to walk them over the rubble."

"The shale underneath is slick. Likely to slide if one of us puts our weight wrong. A broken leg, ours or one of the horses, would be very bad."

After a long pause, Stone glanced back at his packs. "Think I'll get a better grip if I change into moccasins."

When he returned, he pointed toward the far side of the ravine where the rubble was highest. "Stand over there. I'm gonna try climbing. To test it." The raised eyebrows and tilt of her head prompted him to follow up. "No sense in you being buried, too, if I cause a slide."

"Humph." Still, she glided to the opposite side of the gorge.

Stone placed a foot on the pile and tentatively eased his weight onto the loose rock. Shards of shale bit into his sole through the soft leather. It held. Hot breath whistled through his teeth as he sighed his relief. Each footfall placed with the same care one used to approach an enemy encampment in the dark, Stone worked his way up the wall of debris.

At the crest, he allowed a satisfied smile to touch the corners of his mouth. It would hold the horses, though the job would have to be done one animal at a time. While he squatted atop the rocky apex, a soft but distinctive rattle pierced the stillness like a rifle shot on a quiet night. Stone's breath caught, and he froze.

He scanned the prominence.

Perched on a flat rock ten feet away to his right was the coiled rattler, head and tail held high. A forked tongue whipped back and forth before a blunt nose. Black vertical slits stared at him.

Stone kept his eyes locked on the rattler as he eased to a standing position. No sudden movements. He slipped his hand to his hip and palmed the holstered Colt.

"Don't shoot." Dancing Waters's horse whisper held a note of urgency. "You could start another slide."

Stone's hand released the weapon. The shale cliffs towered a hundred feet above him and leaned far over the valley. His mouth went dry. Glances flitted from the snake to the horses to the top of the cliff, then back to the snake. "Gotta do something. Can't bring the horses over with him there." Stone tilted his head toward the rattler. "And the other end is too tall and too steep."

But Stone couldn't see any way to rid them of the snake. Tossing rocks at it would just anger it. He'd never been much good throwing knives, or he'd give that a shot. There weren't any fallen branches around the tree. The thought spilled out of his mind. Grabbing the Bowie from his left hip, Stone poked around the branches until he found what he was looking for. Grabbing hold of a branch, he hacked at the inch-thick base.

"What're you doing?"

Stone ignored Dancing Waters.

"I could—"

The quick glare Stone shot her had the effect he wanted—she stopped talking. It was hard enough to focus on maintaining his balance on the loose scree while cutting the branch and watching that damned snake without trying to listen to her as well.

The sound of the blade hacking at the branch sent the rattler's tail shaking, and it hissed a warning. Stone assessed his distance and adjusted his stance to be able to watch the snake as he worked. A minute later he held the branch. He stripped off the suckers and smaller branches until he held a five-foot-long stick with two tines of a fork at the far end. "This should do it."

"What do you have planned?"

Stone began working his way across the loose shale slope with careful steps. "Catch him and then kill him."

"And how exactly do you plan to do that?" Skepticism dripped from Dancing Water's voice.

Stone ignored her.

"I could help."

The rattler eyed him. "I'm fine. Now be quiet so I can concentrate." Stone could not take his attention from the snake. As he drew nearer, the buzz of its tail grew louder, filling the air with threats of dire consequences.

Dancing Waters muttered something he couldn't understand, and he didn't have time to worry about what she said right now. At least she didn't start talking again. He inched closer.

At ten feet, the upper torso reared back as if preparing to strike. Stone shifted his grip to hold the stick out in front of him like a pitchfork, while the snake's forked tongue flicked its own warning.

By the time Stone had closed to within five feet, one fork of the stick hovered over the snake's head, but its steady stare never wavered from Stone's eyes. With a quick flick he dropped the fork and pushed hard, pinning the rattler.

The snake thrashed like some great Homeric sea serpent. Stone pressed harder on the forked stave. Rolling the Bowie in his hand, he eased closer while reaching the blade closer to the hissing head. A rock squeezed from under his foot like a bar of soap.

His arms flailed as he fell backward.

The reptile, caught between the forks, was lifted from its perch and thrown upward, spinning through the air with the staff Stone had also thrown.

He landed hard and the sharp shale bit into his back. Sliding headfirst down the slope toward the tree, Stone's heart threatened to pound its way out of his chest.

"Watch out."

As the rattler's momentum caused it to flip mid-air, it also separated from the branch and landed high in the web of tree limbs.

Loose scree carried Stone under the same tangle of branches—limbs whipped at his face, and he closed his eyes against the assault. With a violent thud he slammed against the floor of the canyon. His hat tumbled down next to him.

A cloud of dust swirled around him. It clogged his throat and stung his eyes—a violent coughing fit doubled him over. He clutched at the pain that knifed through his ribs.

Finally, clearing his lungs and temporarily forgetting about the snake, he snatched at his hat. Onyx slits only a foot from the brim glared at him. At that moment, one of the squirrels that had been playing fell through the branches above and startled the angry reptile.

It lunged at Stone.

The rattler struck—too fast to follow.

A blur flashed in front of Stone as a soft hum whispered off the canyon walls.

The snake's body lashed violently, impaled on a Sioux arrow anchored in the debris.

A dozen yards away, Dancing Waters clutched a bow as she stood poised for a second shot.

He gawked at her for a moment. Then his wide eyes and open mouth morphed into a scowl. "If you had a—" Another coughing fit interrupted his thought.

"If you close your mouth when you breathe, the dust will not get in your throat." Dancing Waters's voice was quiet and matter of fact, but a twinkle in her dark eyes betrayed her underlying mirth.

When the spasm finally subsided, he clutched aching ribs and glared at her. "Funny." He spit the word out like a sour apple and stabbed a finger toward the top of the rubble. "I almost got myself killed." He paused long enough to point at the rattler whose death throes had subsided to mere twitches, "Why'd you let me go back up there after that thing when you had a bow?"

"I tried to stop you. Twice. But you had an idea." A mischievous smile tugged at the corners of her mouth. "You did not ask for mine. Sioux or white, men are the same—act now, think later." She cocked her eyebrows. "Be thankful I saved you. I should've let it bite you." The grin returned. "I'm sure you'd have sucked the venom out yourself." Then she turned and strode back to her pony.

Stone stared after her while he beat his hat against his dusty clothes. With a shake of his head, he moved to join her. "We still need to get the horses over. I think the wall will hold if we take them one at a time. You agree?" A smile punctuated his question.

She nodded.

———————————

THAT NIGHT THEY camped on an open patch of prairie dotted with rock mounds and bordered on all sides by mesas, low peaks and spires. Coyotes yipped in the distance and the scream of a catamount sounded faintly from somewhere. The horses were picketed for the night where they had good graze.

Stone stared into the darkness, one hand perched on his hip, the buckskin pants soft against the scabs. In his other he held a half-full cup of coffee. A quiet rustling behind him made him aware of Dancing Waters's approach.

"What troubles you tonight?" Her gentle touch on his shoulder sent familiar, pleasant shivers all through his body.

"Just thinking."

"About the men you follow?"

A shrug and a nod were his only response.

"Talking about it may help. Tell me about that day, please. What happened?"

Stone didn't look at her, but he felt her eyes on him. "I think about it every day. While I ride, before bed. Can't get it out of my mind." He thought back to that day. "Still piecing things together. Big chunks of my memory are missing. Later is clearer. I remember the boy, Howard, and I being fired on by three men fleeing on horseback. Someone else covered their retreat from over the ridge."

"Howard is your son?"

"What? Oh. No." Stone shook his head. "Local kid. Not really a boy, seventeen or eighteen. Huge. Almost as big as Black Buffalo." A hand held a few inches above his head added emphasis.

"Said he was riding past my place when he saw the three men

run out of my house. Shot at him when they spotted him, so he took cover inside. I was unconscious on the floor. Came to just as he made it through the door."

"What happened to you?"

"I came in from the barn. The door was ajar. When I went in, Sally was on the floor, all bloody, her best dress torn." His voice wavered and a tear formed. Thankful Dancing Waters couldn't see it in the darkness. "Guess someone hit me on the head with a shovel and then shot me. Don't remember it."

A memory from that day played in bits and pieces in his mind. He was watching the homestead from the barn. He knitted his eyebrows and tensed.

"What is it?" She grabbed him by the shoulders and stared at him. "Tell me."

He shook his head. "I'm not sure. I thought I remembered seeing their horses tied up in front of the house. All I've been able to think about was those three mounts. One of the riders was quite short. The fourth had long narrow feet and walks with a limp. He was the one over the ridge. Saw his sign later.

"But just now, the memory—there *weren't* any horses at the rail when I came out of the barn. I only imagined that part."

"Maybe they tethered them on the side."

"No post there. Or anything else to tie them to." Stone chewed his lower lip. "Howard specifically said their horses were in front when he came up. Why would he lie about that?"

"Could they have come later? After someone beat you?"

He didn't want to dismiss her question, but the idea didn't make sense. Who else could it have been? His stomach clenched. Had he been chasing the wrong men?

"No, that doesn't make sense. Howard was the only other person there, and he wouldn't have killed her. It had to be the miners. I'm just missing something."

DAKOTA TERRITORY, SUNDAY, MAY 16TH, 1875

IT WAS EARLY afternoon when Stone and Dancing Waters climbed the sandstone slope and exited the Bad Lands. Ominous clouds hung on the western horizon, but here the sun shone bright and hot.

"You could still go back with me. Abandon your quest for vengeance. You can't bring her back." Dancing Waters touched the stubble on his cheek and gazed into his eyes.

"We've been over this. I'm going to see those men dead."

Tears leaked down her cheeks. She turned her mount and rode away.

CHAPTER 21

STONE HELD THE field glasses to his eyes, scanning the gulch below. Dust hung heavy in the air after the brief rain shower that ended only five minutes prior. Dark clouds promised the short misting would not be the end of the rain today. Ponderosa pines, tall, straight, and sparse, dotted the hillsides around the town. Near their tops, branches poked out from the trunk like ascending, ever-shortening spokes from a wheel hub. In the center of the quarter mile stretch that was the town's only street stood a pair of conifers, one to a side—like sentinels standing guard over the hidden gold.

Deadwood Gulch began as a mining camp—it was fast transitioning into a mining town. A mixture of wooden construction and tents lined the lane. Signs were either painted on the false-fronts or protruded from the buildings like grotesque beaks. Some named the establishment—Palace Gambling House, Two Sisters Café and Hotel, Oriental, and many others. Others announced the service provided— barber, blacksmith, laundry, assay office.

Directly under one of the ponderosa protectors, a group of men mingled on the boardwalk that ran the length of the largest tent. A man separated from the crowd and tossed an angry gesture back at them as he stepped down into the street. Mud pulled at him and his boots sank to the ankles into the mire. One exaggerated step at a time he slogged across the way. On the other side he climbed to the walkway and strode toward the two-story edifice there. A petit woman, broom in hand, met him at the entry and shooed him back out. After knocking each foot against the boardwalk and dragging his soles over the boot scrape beside the door, she nodded, and he disappeared into the building.

A quick smirk broke his grim expression as Stone lowered the field glasses. Cordelia required only a gentle nudge to begin weaving through the ponderosa forest and over the ubiquitous deadfalls that littered the hillside giving Deadwood Gulch its name.

———————————

CLUMPS OF GOOEY muck splattered behind the horses. An unkempt man ducked to enter the pharmacy—a small once-white tent now spotted appaloosa-like with mud and soot. Cordelia swung wide around the wagons gathered at the double doors of the next structure. The rhythmic ring of a hammer on iron drifted from within.

A group of men loitered outside a large double tent. The garishly painted sign read "The Pageant Saloon." These were the same men he had seen from above. Long scruffy beards covered faces lined from weather and worry. Their tattered, dirt-smudged overalls and shirts covered bodies hardened by lifetimes of physical labor. They chatted and smoked amongst themselves. An occasional guffaw or expletive punctuated their conversation.

Stone halted his black mare in front of them.

Like the sudden silence that precedes a storm, all conversation stopped. Almost as one man, their eyes shifted from Stone's face to his holstered Colt. No weapons were visible among the men. Even in a place like Deadwood, few carried sidearms. Those who did usually stuffed the gun into a waistband or coat pocket—holsters were rare, and often meant trouble. Wary eyes slid back to his face.

"Afternoon, Gentlemen. Anyone know where I might find a livery and a good meal?"

Silence hung like a black storm cloud for twenty seconds as the men stared at him.

"Keep ridin' the way you're headin', Yank." The deep voice came from the shadows beyond the tent's entrance. Texas had surely raised the man behind the voice. Spurs jingled as the man stepped onto the boardwalk.

Silver hair and beard framed cold, steel-grey eyes. His anvil-like chest and shoulders caught Stone's attention. His eyes fell on the tied down holster on the man's narrow hips. The wooden grip of the revolver was worn smooth.

The miners scrambled back against the canvas wall. Their eyes darted back and forth between the two men.

"Clinton." One of the men hissed it, but Stone caught the name.

"End of the street on the right. Only liv'ry in town." The thick man used his chin to point across the way. "Singer sisters o'er there serve up some mighty fine grub."

"Much obliged." Stone nodded to the man and nudged the black. He worked his way down the muddy street.

So, Cyrus Clinton was in Deadwood. As he rode the short distance, Stone pondered Clinton's presence. Possible he was looking to strike it rich, but didn't seem likely. Men like Clinton only knew one thing. Folks claimed he was as dangerous a gunman as his fellow Texan, John Wesley Hardin. Word around was that he worked for the railroad as their fixer—and when he fixed a problem it stayed fixed—and dead. What would the railroad need fixed here?

A young grulla mare, along with a couple dozen other horses ran loose in a split-log corral next to the livery. Stone thought a few looked familiar but wasn't sure.

"Put yer horses up fer ya, mister?" The short, wiry boy appeared sixteen at most. His threadbare canvas shirt and denim pants were stained with days-old stable grime.

"Sure. You the owner?"

"Naw. Just the stable hand. I gots a knack with hosses." The boy's smile widened.

"I'll bet you do."

"Micah. My name's Micah, but my friends call me Turkey." The boy must have caught the puzzled expression on Stone's face. He added, "It's 'cause I kin call a turkey better'n anyone I knowd."

"Orvis. Orvis McLean." Stone decided it was best not to use his real name.

"Glad to meet you, Mister McLean." Micah shook Stone's proffered hand.

"Please, just call me Orvis. Mister McLean makes me nervous."

"Okay, Mister Orvis." The boy led Stone and his mounts toward the back. He paused to stare at a huge, speckled stallion. It wasn't the kind of horse that could easily be mistaken, and he'd seen it before. No doubt about it—the posse was already here. At least they hadn't found Sally's killers yet or they'd be gone.

Turkey led him to a pair of empty stalls in the back. Stone unsaddled his horses while Micah forked some hay for them.

"I'm looking for some fellows, Micah. You seen four miners together? They'd have come in sometime during the last couple of weeks."

"Several groups like that, Mister Orvis, what with all the gold an' such."

"One of these men would have been short." Stone held his hand level across his chest to indicate an approximate height. "And one walks with a serious limp, dragging one foot."

"I seen 'em. Last of 'em left outta here 'bout a week ago. Rumor is they gots a big strike, but no one knows where."

He began prattling on, asking questions, and commenting before Stone could answer. Local gossip—the Martin mine found a big nugget, Indians got old Finn, and Winter's mule was pregnant which is why it wasn't in the livery now. Stone paid enough attention to be polite while he brushed out his stock, but his mind was on a hot meal, soft bed, and whether the marshal planned to arrest him.

"...lookin' fer some sod buster."

Stone stopped brushing mid-stroke. His head jerked around to stare at the stable hand. "What did you just say?"

"That Cyrus Clinton's in town?" Micah acted perplexed, like everyone knew about the gunman.

"Yeah. What about him?"

"Been here a'most a week. Sez he's huntin' some dirt farmer. Gonna kill 'im when he finds 'im."

"What's he wa—"

"Folks say he's kilt a dozen men in fair fights an' dry-gulched twenty or more, or least ways, that's what they sez."

Stone had heard the rumors too. Supposedly a railroad benefited by the demise of each man. But rumors weren't getting him any information about Clinton's presence here—he needed to get the conversation back to that.

"Who's he after?"

"Some fella name a Stone."

A sledgehammer pounded in his chest. Clinton was after *him*? Why? It didn't make any sense.

"Stone? Hmmmm." Stone cocked his head. "Don't think I know anyone by that name. Sure wouldn't want to be him, though." He chuckled and hoped it didn't sound forced.

A BRUSH WAS mounted on the side of the boot scrape and remembering the lesson learned from atop the gulch, Stone stomped, scraped, and brushed the muck off his boots before stepping through the double doors into the Two Sisters Café and Hotel. He paused to allow his eyes to adjust to the dim light. A staircase climbed along the far-right wall—a simple standing-desk next to it. Mounted to the wall behind the desk was a grid-work of numbered boxes. Keys dangled from a few of the boxes, and letters poked out from others.

A woman stood at the desk with her face buried in a ledger. She muttered something Stone didn't catch while she scratched her pen over the page. Ink-smudged fingers rubbed her nose. A smear of black appeared across its tip.

Stone coughed.

Without lifting her head, she peered over the top of her spectacles. Chocolate eyes locked onto his gaze, and she pulled herself erect. A wisp of pecan-colored hair fell across the bridge of a long slender nose, and she attempted to push it back into place with the back of her delicate-looking hand. "Oh, I'm so sorry. I didn't hear you come in." Her smile creased otherwise smooth cheeks. "How may I help you?"

Stone guessed her age somewhere between late twenties and early thirties. "A room and a hot meal." He looked down at her and hoped his tired grin appeared friendly.

"We have both, though the only room we have available is at the top of the stairs. It's small but clean. I hope that'll be acceptable?"

"It'll be fine."

She spun the register around and showed him where to sign in. When he finished, she turned the book back to examine his name.

"Mister McLean, we don't start serving supper for another hour." She pulled the glasses from her face and looked him over. Her eyes lingered on the scar along his jaw, then shifted shyly to a spot on the desk. "But you look as though you've been traveling hard. I'll bet my sister can roust something up sooner." She batted again at the recalcitrant wisp. "Oh, I must look a fright."

He offered her the most charming smile he had the energy to muster. "You look beautiful."

"Oh, you shouldn't tease me." But her bashful smile widened, and a bit of pink touched her cheeks.

Stone sniffed as he palmed the key she laid on the desk. His smile broadened. "Something that smells suspiciously like fresh-baked biscuits is calling my name. Be down in a few minutes for that meal."

THE WORST OF the trail grime had scrubbed off well enough, and he managed a quick change into cleaner clothes, though actual clean would be a stretch. His clothes hadn't seen a real scrubbing since Dancing Waters had them while he was unconscious. Now he was ready for a hot meal.

Heavy flowered draperies separated the empty reception area from the dining room. After checking the street with a quick glance through the front window, he slipped behind the reception desk and grabbed the register. He didn't recognize any of the names on the page he'd signed. He flipped back a page and ran his finger down that list. Nothing. On the next page, he stopped half-way down the page. He recognized several names. Price and the posse signed in to this very hotel three days back.

The thought of moving out crossed his mind, and he pondered on it for a few seconds. He could set up camp away from town out in the hills, but even by just being around asking questions he was bound to run into them sooner or later. And if he was going to find out where the bastards were, he would have to ask lots of questions to piece together their location.

How much had the posse discovered? Could they have already found Sally's killers? Would Price arrest him for disobeying the order to wait? He'd only met the marshal once—rode on a posse with him a few years back—but believed the no nonsense lawman would have behaved the same as himself in a similar circumstance. That should count for something. In the end, the real bed won out. And home cooking that wasn't his or some Sioux concoction.

Stone stood behind the wall on the reception area side and inched the drape aside enough to scan the room beyond. Then he pushed it a little farther aside to the entire room. Six long plank tables filled the room, each surrounded by chairs. There was sufficient seating for almost a hundred people.

At the moment, only one other person shared the room with Stone—Cyrus Clinton. The gunman sat alone in the front right corner with his back to the wall. Stone pushed the curtain aside. As he stepped into the room, Clinton's steel grey eyes locked on Stone's and never wavered. So much for stealth.

Stone returned the stare long enough to let the other man know that he wasn't afraid of him but not so long as to challenge him. Then he turned his back to Clinton and took a seat in the other front corner where he wouldn't have to stare to keep an eye on the fixer.

He could feel Clinton's eyes study him. The petit woman from earlier stepped into the dining room, a coffee pot in one hand and a cup in another.

"Why, Mister McLean, I was just getting ready to set you a place." She hurried to Stone and quickly set the cup in front of him.

Clinton's eyes widened for the briefest of moments at the mention of the name.

"Let me pour your coffee. I'm so sorry I was rude earlier." Dark, steaming liquid filled his cup. "I'm Ophelia. Ophelia Singer. My sister, Lizzie, and I own this establishment." Her demure smile returned, and she batted her eyes once as she glanced at the table.

Stone sipped at his coffee. Seated, he could look her straight in the eye. As she prattled on about the place, he allowed his gaze to slide past her to Clinton. The gunman shoved his chair back and stood. As he slipped through the curtained exit, he cast a final glance at Stone, which was acknowledged with a nod.

Ophelia seemed oblivious to Stone's inattention. "Why, Mister McLean, where are my manners today? I haven't brought you anything to eat. You must be starved." Her hand squeezed his arm and a quick smile touched her lips. "I'll be right back." A low rumble from his stomach emphasized her point, and she giggled as she retreated.

Cyrus Clinton had been a distraction. With him gone, hunger pangs gnawed at Stone. Kitchen aromas filled the room, and he tried to remember the last time he'd eaten beef. Meat in the Stone house consisted of whatever wild game he killed—sometimes rabbit, other times antelope or pheasant. On occasion he traded for buffalo.

Moments later, a plate piled high with sliced beef, boiled potatoes, and carrots landed in front of him. From the looks of the place, the sisters did a booming business. He should take advantage of her interest in him, feigned or otherwise. "Are you planning to join me, Miss Singer?" He nodded toward the plate and winked. "Enough food here for two."

"Ophelia. Call me Ophelia. And don't be silly. I... I have work to do. Place'll be packed in twenty minutes. Besides, you look ravenous."

"Packed? Really?"

"Wall to wall." She squared her shoulders and straightened her spine. "We serve two dinner shifts in here, and three breakfast shifts. Over five hundred meals a day, total."

"So many? Amazing."

"Even more here on bear sign day."

Stone's eyebrows lifted to his hairline, and he couldn't control the smile that broke across his face. "Bear sign?"

"Tomorrow morning." Her fingers caressed his shoulder. "Get here early."

Ophelia returned as Stone savored the final bite. "Pie, Mister McLean? Get yourself a slice now 'fore the crowd picks us clean." She pointed toward the curtained entry where the shuffle and banter of men could be heard.

"I'm sure it's as delicious as this meal, but I couldn't eat another bite." He glanced toward the curtained entryway and lowered his voice. "I do have a question, though."

Ophelia leaned in close. "Of course, darlin'."

Her warm breath in his ear sent a tingle over his scalp. "Ah...." He paused to regain some composure and tried to remember what he was about to ask. "Ah... um... since you see so many here, I'm wondering if you've seen some men. Four of them. One's got a bad limp and one's only about as tall as you, and—"

"They friends of yours?" Her tone grew cold, and she tensed.

Stone fought to contain his surprise. He shook his head. "No, ma'am. Met them back in Yankton before I started this way. Said they were coming here. Wondered if they'd made it."

Ophelia harrumphed. "They were here. That short one called me a name suggesting I worked for Miss Cora. Why, I never."

"I'm sorry he insulted you." He allowed himself a mischievous smirk and winked at her. "I'll kill him for impugning your honor if you wish."

She slapped lightly at his shoulder and grinned. "I guess that won't be necessary. He was all mad 'cause we ran out of bear sign. Might've still been drunk from the night before, I suppose. Besides, the bald one broke his nose. Got blood all over. Worth the effort of cleaning it to see him get his."

"I'm glad he got what he deserved, but my offer still stands." They shared a laugh before he continued. "You wouldn't happen to know where their claim is, would you?"

She nodded. "They were trying to hide it. Didn't want anyone to know, but I overheard them talking about Strawberry Creek. Only remember it because Lizzie made jam the day before."

Butterflies set to flight in Stone's stomach.

STONE STEPPED FROM the tent to the boardwalk. Dim light filtered through the canvas and spilled from the open flap, but most of the street remained in darkness. As he strolled down the boardwalk, he hummed along with the piano tune that emanated from the establishment he just left.

Humming helped him think sometimes, and there was much to think about. The last two hours had been spent in one saloon after another. Seemingly no one knew the four men or anything about them. Ophelia's information helped, but he needed more. A reference to Strawberry Creek didn't tell him where they were. It could have meant anything. Was their claim along the creek? Past there? In the general area? At least it was a starting point.

A yawn came from nowhere. He was tired. The ordeal to get this far had taken its toll, even with the week-long rest under Dancing Waters's care. It would be nice to sleep in a real bed for a change.

As he neared the dentist's office, a scratch followed by the flare of a match in the alley caught his attention. Dark shadows filled the narrow passage and only the reddish glow from the end of a cigarette gave away the man's presence.

"Thet you, Yank?"

Stone stopped where he was. "Clinton. Nice night to be out."

"Yep. Step down here. Wanna chat."

The butt of his Colt rested inches from his hand, but Stone fought the urge to reach for the weapon. The light from the saloon on the east side of the street backlit him—a perfect target for the gunman. If he planned to backshoot Stone, he could have done it. He licked his lips and stepped into the darkness.

"Heard you're lookin' for some men."

"You see them?"

"Commentin's all. Killed your wife, or so I've been told."

Stone's throat tightened. He hadn't told anyone why he was looking for them.

"What're you talking about? They're acquaintances."

"Sell that story and your phony name to the sisters, Stone. I know who you are and why you're here." Clinton waited a second, then added, "And you know why I'm here."

Silence hung like a hangman's noose. It's one thing for the stable hand to say it, and quite another to hear it from the man who planned to do the killing. Stone tried to swallow the lump in his throat, but it refused to be dealt with so easily. "I heard." Stone paused—forced himself to relax before speaking again. "What's next?"

"You got twenty-four hours to take care of your business. Then I'm comin' for you."

"Why not get it over with now?"

"That anxious to join yer bride?"

"No. Just wondering?"

The gunman drew on the cigarette between his lips. The sudden glow of the tip illuminated his shrug. "Let's say I respect what you're doin'. Do the same thing thet were my wife."

"What if it takes me longer?"

"It won't. They're close by. And I know the kind of man you are."

"What happens after?"

"I kill ya. Maybe a shoot-out in the street, maybe dry-gulched in the hills. Regardless, you'll be dead."

"Good luck. Won't be the first Johnny Reb to try." Stone turned and strode from the alley.

Behind him, Clinton chuckled.

TWENTY-FOUR HOURS WASN'T long and the only information available was that Sally's murderers might be prospecting somewhere near Strawberry Creek. Not much to go on. Laying on his bed and staring at the ceiling, he searched for answers. The creek could take days of riding over rugged terrain to explore. Yet, Clinton seemed confident Stone would find them tomorrow. Unless he planned to lure Stone deep into the hills and dry-gulch him there—a possibility to be considered.

Then there were the murderers. How would he kill all four? Once found, he would have little time to devise a plan. The risk of discovery would increase with every minute. He scrubbed at his fresh-shaved chin.

At last, he decided the punched tin ceiling held no more answers and the iron frame bed sure beat the ground. He stifled a yawn. For now he needed a night's sleep.

CHAPTER 22

SILVER AND PEWTER haze diffused the first rays of the morning sun. Already heavy slate clouds pushed in from the west. A strong breeze swirled bits of straw and hay dust from the barn floor. He strode into the stables, past Price's stallion who was still in its stall. He'd taken his breakfast in a napkin to avoid any of the posse members. He ate leaning against the wall in the very alley he'd encountered Clinton the previous evening.

Both his mounts nickered their greeting. A pair of carrots purloined from the Singer's the previous evening earned him a nudge from each.

"Morning, Mister McLean," Turkey called from the hay mow.

"Call me Orvis. And good morning to you, Micah. I didn't mean to disturb you. You sleep up there?"

"Most nights. Keep an eye on things, and they's fewer fleas here than m' own bed." He laughed and slapped his knee. "You pullin' out?"

"I'm getting ready to find my friends. You don't happen to know where Strawberry Creek is, do you?"

Micah's eyes widened and an awkward smile turned up the corners of his mouth. "I shore do. Let me jump down from here an' I'll give ya directions whilst I git your hoss saddled fer ya."

The young man climbed down and had Stone's black mare saddled soon after. While he worked, he provided a verbal map of the area surrounding Deadwood Gulch so vivid he might have painted it for Stone.

When he finished, Stone tossed him two bits. "Thank you. Shouldn't have any trouble finding it." He double-checked the Henry and eased the rifle into the saddle boot. As he led the black from the stable, he turned back to Micah. "Say, didn't see the grulla this morning."

"That's Cyrus Clinton's hoss. Rode outta' here two hours ago. Ya reckon he found that Stone feller?"

"Could be." The bear sign Judd ate at breakfast suddenly turned into an iron ball in his stomach.

STONE TUGGED THE brim of his hat lower over his eyes and turned up the collar of his duster—it rubbed at the backs of his ears but kept his neck dry. The misty rain brought out the fresh earthy scent of the pine—a reminder of the western New York forests of his youth. The slight gurgle of the creek below, the occasional scolding from a nearby jay, and the creak of saddle leather were the only disturbances in the otherwise silent wilderness.

His black followed one of the game trails that crisscrossed the gulch. This one mirrored the ridgeline above Deadwood Creek from a few yards below the crest. She stopped at the fork where the West Strawberry broke off.

He pressed the field glasses to his eyes. Holding a hand over the end to keep the lenses clear, he scanned the creek.

A man plied the waters with a pan. The gulch had been littered with men working pans and sluices for the first mile out of town, but this was the first he had seen since. As Stone observed him, the man pinched something from the muck in the tin plate and held it to his eyes, before depositing it in a canvas bag at his waist.

When the course's meander prevented him from seeing farther,

Stone turned his attention back to the branch and again traced the creek until a bend took it from sight.

Disappointment clenched at his gut, but he hadn't expected it to be that easy. Cordelia moved along at his nudge. Stone turned to check the back trail. Clinton was out here somewhere. Was he ahead? Behind? Maybe he had a different reason for an early morning ride, but if the war had taught him anything, it taught him coincidence didn't exist. It'd been a hard lesson—one that cost him too many friends—but once learned he'd never forgotten it.

The morning wore on, and the West Strawberry turned into the Strawberry. A whitetail fawn startled him once, though from its eyes he suspected that the baby was even more surprised. Mom snorted from the field of ferns below, and the fawn disappeared as quickly as it appeared.

As he rode, Stone pondered his choices once he found the men. They deserved to die, yet the thought of ambushing them sickened him. If he discovered them bunched together, he could ride into them—probably kill them all if he did it right. Sally's voice floated across his thoughts then. *Bring them in for trial. Rule of law.* He shook his head.

A flash of grey on the other side of the gorge jarred him out of his reverie. Slapping his field glasses to his eyes, he searched the far crest. A grey squirrel leapt from one tree to another. Was that what he saw? Didn't seem right. The flash had seemed larger, like a horse. Whatever it was, it was gone now—maybe it had been the squirrel. He shrugged and nudged Cordelia on.

A rider topped the rise twenty yards ahead on the opposite side. A gray campaign hat, then a grizzled face. The grulla appeared next, confirming the identity of the rider.

Cyrus Clinton.

The gunfighter smirked as he stared across the gorge at Stone. His hand rested on his thigh within easy reach of either his revolver or the rifle visible above the grulla's withers. The fingers of his left hand dipped into a pocket inside his duster and pulled out a small disk the size of a pocket watch.

Stone scrutinized the man but didn't react.

With a casual flick of his thumb, Clinton flipped open the cover. He tapped the glass with his index finger and slipped the instrument back into his pocket. Then he turned his horse and disappeared over the ridgeline.

He'd been right. Now what? Nothing changed—his purpose remained the same. If Clinton wanted him dead, good luck.

————————

BY MIDDAY, STONE had worked his way along the entire length of Strawberry Creek, which turned out to be significantly shorter than he feared the previous evening. More times than he could count he'd gotten close enough to a camp to hear voices. He'd dismounted, crawled through the understory, and observed the camp, only to discover the miners weren't who he sought.

Maybe what Ophelia overheard was intended to misdirect anyone listening in on their conversation. Maybe it meant that they were close to this creek, but not on it. Could they be working on the hillside? Everyone in Deadwood placer mined. This opened up the possibility of days spent searching several square miles of rugged wilderness.

Why had Cyrus been confident Judd would find them quickly? The more he pondered the thought, the more sure he grew that the murderers were somewhere along Deadwood Creek. He turned to Cordelia.

The continuous drizzle made the path slick, but the black mare was sure-footed and managed the two-hour trip back to the mouth of the West Strawberry Creek without incident. Another game trail led to the bottom of the gorge.

Halfway down, the slope gave way and Cordelia slid. She extended her forelegs and lowered her haunches, riding the wave of mud.

As he fought to keep his weight balanced in the saddle without sliding forward or leaning, Stone risked a glance behind him. A wall of mud followed. His heart raced. The floor of the gulch rose faster with each second until it was only feet away. If he didn't time this right, he and his black would find themselves buried under tons of mud.

As her front hooves touched the bottom, Cordelia leapt high across the creek. The avalanche of muck that trailed them slammed into the floor behind them.

Stone gave Cordelia her head, and she picked her way up the opposite slope to the top and another game trail along the ridgeline. Here the forest grew thicker. Boughs slapped at him as they rode. The echoes of men's shouts drifted through the heavy vegetation.

Flashes of movement showed through the undergrowth and the voices grew louder. He dismounted and tied the black to a nearby limb. How many times today had he already dismounted to check on a camp only to discover it wasn't the men he sought. Rifle in hand, he ducked low as he slipped along the trail to a better vantage point.

The camp materialized through a gap in the ferns and timber—Stone counted four men. Two hauled buckets of material from the creek bottom. The other two worked a pair of long sluice boxes set into the water. Tin pans and rocker boards littered the water's edge. Four tents stood against the gorge's wall, and a low fire burned nearby.

Even from the distance, it was obvious that one of the men was much shorter than the others.

Their voices carried clear and distinct in the narrow chasm.

"Frankie, would you slow down. My legs can't keep up with you," the short one said.

"Not my fault, Shorty. If you'd et your veggies like your mama told you to, you might'a growed up to be a real man." The taller man laughed at his own joke.

"Why you ol' pole cat. I ought'a knock you on your keister and show you how much a man I am."

Stone ignored the banter as he worked himself to a better position from which to observe them. A spot behind some ferns allowed him a clear view of the camp. He separated the fauna and focused the field glasses on the four. The tall thin man walked with a limp and dragged his left foot.

Stone hadn't seen them since the day Sally was murdered, and that had been from a distance. But he was certain—these were her killers. His heart threatened to explode from his chest.

The glasses hit the ground and his body tensed. His breathing accelerated with his pulse. Before he thought about it, the Henry was in his hands and aimed at the short one. His finger pressed to the trigger, but his hands shook, and he couldn't sight in. He took a deep breath, held it for a ten count, and released it through a long, slow, even exhalation. Repeating the process twice more, he finally calmed.

The short one appeared beyond Henry's sights. He eased the slack out of the trigger.

And then he realized what he was about to do.

Not like this.

Jerking the rifle back, he rolled to a sitting position—his back to the miners below. Tears streamed down his cheeks. He scrubbed at them with the back of his hand. The pain of Sally's loss flooded him, and silent sobs shook him.

He couldn't bring himself to dry gulch the men below.

But they deserved to die.

What if he rode into their camp? Could he take them four on one? If he—

An argument from below broke his reverie.

"Never have told me what happened back at that homestead. I'm damn tired of not knowin'. People don't shoot at you for no reason," the tall man with the limp screamed.

"Ya wanna know? Fine."

"Damn straight I do. Ain't been straight with me since."

The short one told his story.

Stone listened from above—stunned.

THE PIECES SNAPPED together like a familiar puzzle. Everything changed—Stone knew the truth.

He raced to Cordelia. His instinct was to charge into the camp below and drag more information from them, but that would serve no real purpose. He had the answers he needed. Instead, he hurried back to Deadwood.

AS HE RODE up to the stables, the grulla chomped hay in the corral alongside Price's speckled stallion as well as several other horses he recognized. The bay Thoroughbred that Howard Willis favored was there as well. Stone thought about the horses he'd seen yesterday and didn't recall seeing the bay, but he'd been focused on Marshal Price's mount. He knew for fact he hadn't seen Howard's name in the hotel register, but Deadwood supported several such establishments. No doubt some offered entertainment of more interest to a young man with more money than sense.

"Mister Orvis, can I take 'er fer ya?" Turkey called from the shadows in the back of the building.

"Please. That would be perfect, Micah." Stone pointed to the corral. "Lots of new horses, today."

"Yep. Big posse rid in couple days ago. Asked after the same fellas you were lookin' fer. Been ridin' the hills ever' day since. Come back in lil' bit ago." The stable hand took Cordelia's reins. "Pointed to yer chestnut paint back there an' ask'd if a Ju-diah Stone were here. I told 'em I didn't know th' name, but I don' think tha' big feller on the bay believed me. He looked twixt th' paint an' me 'n stormed off."

Stone stared at Micah. "I'm sorry I lied to you. That is my name, but I thought it prudent not to advertise with Cyrus Clinton hunting me." He stuck his hand out and Micah took it and the two shook.

"No hurd feelin's Mister Or... I mean Judiah."

"Good. And call me Stone. You don't happen to know where the owner of that big, speckled stallion is, do you?"

"Went to the barber fer a shave an' a bath."

"Would you deliver a message to him?" When the young man nodded, Judd tossed him two bits and told him what to say.

THIRTY MINUTES LATER, a whip thin man of average height stepped into the stable. He had mutton-chop style sideburns, only narrower, and a moustache that crossed his upper lip and turned to follow his smile lines down to his chin.

"Marshal."

"Stone."

Stone wiped his hand on his dungarees and extended it. The two shook.

"You disobeyed my orders." The marshal stared at Stone, his eyes hard.

"You planning on arresting me?"

"Done anything I should arrest you for? Murder Sally's killers?" Price arched his eyebrows.

"We need to talk."

"THAT'S AN INTERESTING story, Stone." The marshal nodded. It was the nod of contemplation, not agreement.

Judd pointed to the corral. "I see Howard's horse out there."

"Him and almost a dozen of his friends. Couldn't keep 'em away.

Fools. Got one of them killed. Buried the boy out on the prairie." Price eyed him. "What're you thinking?"

The two men put their heads together and whispered for the next hour.

MARSHAL PRICE LIFTED the flap for Stone, then followed once Stone stepped into the saloon. Seated around three tables along the back was a group of men, Stone recognized them all, though he didn't recall everyone's name. Emmitt, Angus, Howard and several of his friends, other men from Stockman and the surrounding farms. "Look who I found." Price's shout turned heads all over the tent, but recognition drew a cheer from the back.

Emmitt Jackson and Angus Hoeckerman pressed through the crowd toward Stone and the marshal. The blacksmith raised two fingers above his head as he shouted to the bartender, "Two more mugs." The four men met in the middle of the room and shook hands.

"You must be a ghost." Hoeckerman laughed. "Expected you'd be here already when we arrived. When no one'd seen ya thought sure the Injuns got you."

"They did." Stone's tone was hard as he continued. "Spent about ten days in a Sioux camp. Thought I was dead at one point."

"What!" Emmitt's eyes almost bugged out of his head. "How'd you get away?"

Stone said nothing but tipped his head toward the others. Emmitt nodded.

As the four men rejoined the posse, men rose, some clapping him on the shoulders and back, others lifting their mugs to him. Emmitt dragged him to an empty chair next to him at the middle table. "Stone here was just about to tell us about being captured by Indians and how he escaped."

Eyes widened and all three tables quieted—a congregation anticipating the Bible waving preacher's next words.

"Ain't much to tell." He shrugged.

"You ain't getting off that easy."

"Spill it."

More calls for the story came.

"Fine." He held his hands up in surrender. "I'll tell it." He paused to collect his thoughts, but also deciding how much he wanted to say, especially about Dancing Waters. Not that anything happened, or would have. He was still mourning Sally in his own way while also hunting her killers. Thoughts of Dancing Waters as anything more than a friend who offered her assistance were unwarranted. But some of these men might not see it that way.

"I'd just woken up one morning when these two Yanktonai kids caught me unawares. Never saw the second one until after coming to from him clocking me a good one. They had rifles and—"

A woman in a long, ruffled dress delivered ale to the new arrivals. Emmitt shooed Stone's offered money and handed her four bits. Stone drained the tall glass—it had been weeks since he'd had a beer. Never had it at the homestead, so it was only when he made it to town that he indulged. Same with whiskey.

"Well? Come on." Marshal Price feigned impatience. "Get on with the story."

Cheers rose again.

Even some of the local patrons gathered around to listen to the tale. As he talked about being dragged, a chorus of "ouch" echoed from the throng. Later, during the fight, they *ooohed* and *aaahed*. His only reference to Dancing Waters was simply as the tribal medicine woman who cared for him.

As he finished the story, the crowd parted, and he spotted Clinton staring at him. The gunman flashed his watch and quickly turned away. Stone glanced around. None of his listeners seemed to have noticed the gunman. For a brief moment, he contemplated introducing Clinton to the marshal but dismissed the thought.

When Clinton came for him, he would find a time and place to do it privately or legally.

Price gathered the posse. The marshal shared the location and layout of the miner's camp. He laid out his plan for the next morning, while Howard stood alone and drank.

CHAPTER 23

DARKNESS STILL BLANKETED Deadwood Gulch when the men of the posse gathered at the stable. Ghoulish shadows of the men danced on the walls as they saddled their horses.

"Where are the young 'uns?" Angus waved toward the corral.

"Don't know. Their horses are gone." Stone wasn't sure of the name of the man who spoke, but decided it didn't matter.

Judd eyed Marshal Price and nodded as the others discussed the absence of Howard Willis and his friends.

Micah leaned over the edge of the hay mow. "Ya'll talkin' 'bout thet there big feller was with ya? Rides the bay Thoroughbred?" He didn't wait for an answer. "Him and seven others done rode outta' here o're an hour ago."

"Damn fools," Emmitt cussed. "Gonna try to be he-roes. Bring those miners in themselves."

"What do we do now, Marshal?" Angus tossed his saddle over his dun gelding.

"Let's ride. See if we can save them from their own stupidity." Price mounted Zeus.

Stone checked the corral one last time as he left the livery. The grulla was gone too. He urged Cordelia to a fast lope to catch up to the marshal at the front of the posse.

Price glanced at him as he pulled up. "Everything all right?"

"Just gave the stable one last look before leaving."

"Looking for anything in particular?"

"Tell you about it later. Let's worry about preventing more killing."

The men that remained rode as quickly as the still slick trail above the gorge allowed. As they approached the mouth of the West Strawberry, Stone warned them about his experience the day before. This time the descent went smoothly, and all nine riders made it safely.

At the gorge floor, the marshal divided the group. As the assignments were completed, a volley of rifle fire from upstream broke the early morning quiet.

"Stay behind me." Price motioned for everyone to form up. "Let's ride." He gigged his stallion and took off without waiting to see if anyone followed.

Stone nudged Cordelia, and she zigzagged her way to the top of the hill—Metterman followed. The marshal's stallion struggled up the steep slope, almost slipping off twice. It was a slow climb for the big horse and Stone didn't wait—the marshal would just have to catch up. He pushed the black mare to a high lope along the ridgeline.

The gunfire slowed and then stopped.

Seven horses blocked the path ahead. One of the young men Stone recognized but didn't know stood with them. An old single shot carbine shook in the boy's hands as he stared up the trail toward the gunfire.

Stone dismounted and ran ahead to the boy.

"Where are they?" Stone took the tone of an army major once more as he barked the question.

The kid pointed in the direction he faced.

"That thing loaded?"

The only response was a wide-eyed nod.

"Give it to me." He snatched the weapon before the boy could decide whether to obey or not.

Stone raced up the track on foot with Metterman at his heels. Price had made it and wasn't far behind. Howard, mounted on his big bay, Peacemaker on his hip, sat on the ridge above the mining camp. He cradled his rifle while he watched the action below. Stone slid to a halt in the thick mud and climbed to the crest next to the young man. When Metterman made to follow, Stone waved him to stay by the trail.

Twenty yards downslope, six of Howard's friends crouched behind trees for cover. Each pointed a rifle at the floor of the gulch where a body lay near the campfire. The body wasn't moving.

"Call them off, Howard." Stone spoke with a calm voice. He held his weapons at his side.

"Don't you want Sally's murderers dead? We're just taking care of business. Dad's poster reads 'dead or alive.'"

Price called from the trail. "Except your father doesn't have the authority to issue a dead-or-alive reward. Only a judge can do that." The marshal joined Stone. "If that man down there is dead, whoever shot him will go to prison for murder. Is that what you want, Howard?"

The young men below had turned to watch the drama at the top of the gulch. Several mouths were agape. Price glanced at them. "You men hear that? At least one of you is going to jail. Put your guns down and come on up. It's over."

Two of the young men lifted rifles to their shoulders, pointed in the general direction of Stone and the marshal. The other four cast questioning glances at each other and then Howard, clearly unsure what to do.

Marshal Price took a confident step forward. "Don't do it. Emmitt Jackson's on the west ridge with that Sharps of his. You've all seen him shoot. You want to die today?"

Eyes glanced furtively toward the opposite slope, but no one dropped their weapon.

One shot boomed from across the gulch and a pine bough splintered only inches above one man's head. "Next one won't be a warn-ing." Emmitt's voice carried across the void.

Six rifles hit the ground together.

Price turned to Howard. "Your turn—"

Howard spun his stallion back toward the trail and spurred him hard. The Thoroughbred shouldered Metterman out of the way as they charged past and galloped down the trail.

Stone brought his Henry up, but the rider had disappeared.

Price knelt beside Metterman, but the downed man waved them on. "I'm fine. Mostly missed me. Go after that fool. I'll round these boys up and meet you at the horses."

Stone and Price ran back along the slippery trail.

Emmitt's Sharps thundered once more.

From near where the mounts were tied, the piercing, high pitched scream of a horse filled the ravine. Stone's throat tightened. Memories of the war flashed through his mind. So many. The screams of horses and men flooded his mind. Men's pain he had learned to shut out, at least on a temporary basis. They'd volunteered to fight. It was the animals he never got used to. And it wasn't just the horses. Donkeys, mules, oxen, cattle, wild creatures caught between lines or struck by errant cannon fire—none of them had any choice about being there. With the chaos of the battle, soldiers were often too busy staying alive themselves to spare the time to put beasts out of their misery—at least until after the battles were over. Many suffered for hours before ei-ther succumbing to injuries, pain, or were finally released with a bul-let to the head. Stone shuddered.

The horse's wail turned into a loud whimper. Around the bend in the trail, the young man they left stared down the gulch. Sobs rocked his body like a rag doll.

The marshal got to him first. Grabbing him by the arms, he gently shook the boy. "What's wrong, son?"

The boy said nothing—just gaped down the slope.

Stone glanced in the direction of the boy's eyes. The lump in his throat dropped like a cannon ball into his stomach. A jagged trail of mud and crushed understory led toward the bottom. Manfred lay on his side. A white bone protruded from his forelimb. The beast whimpered.

Howard laid beside his horse, one leg trapped under the creature. The man had landed below his horse and wasn't moving.

"Damn fool, kid." Marshal Price spoke without taking his eyes off the scene below. "Tried to go around the horses that blocked the trail. Slick as it is out here and that big ride of his. Never had a chance."

Stone didn't respond—he had already started to climb down.

As he picked his way down, moving as quickly as prudence allowed given the muddy soil and slick foliage, he considered the problem of extracting Howard from beneath the bay. There were no other trees within ten feet of the one they came to rest against. The horse was between Stone and Howard. At his best, Manfred had never been friendly. Emmitt, who had a way with even the most temperamental horses, mentioned how difficult Manfred was to shoe. Now the poor beast was scared and hurt—likely to lash out at anyone that came too close. Yet, if Stone just shot the horse from this angle the bullet could ricochet off bone and catch Howard. He needed to get the rider from below.

"Should've brought a rope."

"Grab my hand. I'll help you." Price had rigged his belt around the base of a nearby pine. There weren't any low-hanging branches, so it gave him something to extend his reach without a root structure pulling loose from the damp soil.

Stone clasped the offered wrist and eased lower until his feet came to rest against a protruding rock ledge just below the tree. The horse continued whimpering, but now a faint human groan joined the wailing.

"Howard's still alive. I can hear him."

"That's great news." Angus Hoeckerman had somehow gotten to the floor of the gulch. "How bad is it?"

Stone risked a glance at his friend. "Manfred has a broken leg and bloody froth coming from his mouth. Don't know about the boy. At least one leg is pinned beneath the horse and the rest of him appears to be wedged between it and the tree." He scrubbed the back of his hand over his chin. "We'll play hell getting him out of there."

"Got a hundred feet of rope on my saddle."

"Can you climb up here with it?"

Angus eyed the wall of the gulch. For most of its height, the side was steep but climbable in the right conditions, but the final twenty feet to the base was a vertical drop. "I'd have to go the long way. Take a while."

"Time we don't have."

Quince Martin rode up. "I can get it up to you."

Moments later a rock arced over the underbrush, the rope followed like a kite's tail. Stone pulled the rope off. He worked himself back to the tree that supported the horse and rider. A loop tied around the trunk and his waist supported him as he knelt by Howard.

The big man's eyes were blank, and his body was twisted. Every thrash and kick by Manfred elicited another groan. Stone guessed that a normal sized man would already be dead. The marshal stepped onto the rock Stone had been balanced on. Stone arched his brows. "Not good." He more mouthed the words than spoke them, but Price nodded his understanding. The lawman used the other end of the remaining rope to haul himself up to join Stone.

Stone glanced at the Colts on Price's hips and then the horse. The marshal sighed before drawing the weapon. Stone placed a hand gently on Howard's shoulder.

"Son, can you hear me?"

"St...Stone? That you? Ohhh, God it hurts." His weak voice cracked.

"It's me. Rest easy. We're going to get you out of here."

"H—how's Manfred? Don't put him—"

"Got to, son. He's in a bad way." Stone glanced at the marshal and then at the horse.

The echo of the shot reverberated for several seconds. The stallion stilled.

"Stone? You still here?"

"I am."

"I'm sorry. Sorry 'bout Sally."

"I know."

"Don't kn… whole story."

"Okay, son. Be still." He exchanged a knowing look with Price. Stone continued to keep Howard still and talking.

Hoeckerman and Quince Martin must have made record time through the gulch and up to the top of the hill. They climbed down as Price began rigging a sling to lift Manfred enough to pull Howard out from beneath him.

Howard gasped for air as he told his story. Crimson froth bubbled from his mouth. He paused between some of the details of the events to gag or cough. More blood dribbled down his chin.

Stone struggled to make sense of what Howard was saying. Was this why Sally died? He glanced at the marshal, a silent question passing between them. Quince and Angus stood next to Price and Stone eyed them as well. "You hearing this?"

They nodded in unison.

"We're ready."

"That was fast. You sure?"

Price nodded toward the men with him. "Yankee ingenuity—and an assist from Quince and Angus."

"Will the three of you be enough?"

"We didn't have any pulleys lying around, but we used the trees as a sort of makeshift pulley. It'll have to be enough to do the trick. All we got." Price glanced at the other two men. "You ready?"

Nods were the only answer.

"Lift slowly. Let me check underneath to make sure that leg is clear of the stirrup."

The three men heaved in unison, the marshal calling a cadence. The rope squeaked and groaned in protest. They moved the horse an inch. Then two.

"Stop. Let me check." Stone leaned low. He shifted Howard's leg enough to pull the last couple of inches clear of the stirrups. "Okay, one more tug, and I should be able to get him."

Once again, the marshal called a cadence and the three worked. Their faces reddened.

"Almost there. Keep lifting."

The rope slipped a fraction of an inch. The dead horse lurched. Smoke rose from one of the trees the rope was strung around.

"No. No. Not yet. I need just a little more." Stone shifted his grip on Howard and took a quick glance at his footing. If he slipped while pulling Howard, they'd both end up at the bottom.

"Haul." With a last heave Manfred's body rose an inch and Stone stepped back, dragging Howard with him. When his boot cleared from under the horse, Stone shouted.

The other three men gasped and dropped the massive bay who slid, coming to a stop against the trunk of the nearest tree.

"Think we can use the rope to lower the boy down?" Angus pointed to the floor of the gulch.

Stone shook his head. A tear leaked from the corner of his eye. "No need." He brushed his hand over the boy's lifeless eyes to close them forever.

———

QUINCE MARTIN SCRATCHED his head. He and the remaining members of the posse gathered at the Singer Sisters. As a group, they milled around Stone and Price at one table, some sitting, others standing behind. "I still don't think I understand what happened. So, the miners we came after didn't kill Sally?"

Stone drained the last of the coffee and set his cup on the table. He started to speak but paused when Ophelia Singer brought a fresh pot of coffee. She refilled his cup, touching his shoulder with her free hand as she leaned in to pour. She flashed Stone a shy smile as she backed out, her bosom brushing his arm in the process. "Can I get you boys anything else? Ya'll must be starvin'."

Stone glanced at her and offered an appreciative but brief smile. He didn't want to be rude, but he also didn't want to encourage her attention either. "I think we're good for now. Maybe we'll indulge in whatever leftover pie you have in a little while."

Disappointment showed in her eyes for a brief second before she gave Stone a broad smile. "Very well. Ya'll just holler when you're ready for that pie." She paused and gave Stone a knowing look. "Or need anything else." She turned to go. Once only Stone could see her face, she winked.

"Thank—why, thank you, ma'am. We'll do just that." Stone waited for her to step away before speaking again. When she had retreated to the far side of the room, he made eye contact with Quince, then scanned the faces of the posse members. "The miners were just convenient scapegoats."

"How do you know that?" It was one of Howard's friends. His tone was quiet, and the question was a real inquiry, not a challenge. With first Ernest and now Howard dead, the attitude of the remaining youngsters changed dramatically.

"I had an inkling yesterday. I spoke to the marshal about that at length before we met you at the saloon."

Price nodded his agreement. Several heads turned his way as if they expected him to jump in, but he allowed Stone to tell the story.

"I overheard them talking about it. He confirmed the details with them later." Stone nodded toward the marshal. "Matched up with what Howard confessed to just before he died."

Quince Martin scratched at the days-old stubble on his chin. "So, Howard killed Sally?"

"No. He helped cover it up, but he didn't do the killing."

"So who did?"

"Charles Willis."

Excited murmurs raced around the table.

"How. Wasn't he with Burke when Sally was murdered?"

"He didn't arrive at the jail until later. I should have figured it out when I interviewed Burke, but I didn't." Marshal Price shook his head. "Sometimes we assign greater measures of truth to what powerful men say without subjecting it to more thorough scrutiny. Guess I was guilty. Willis is a big man in this territory."

"What happened?"

"Charles needed the deed to my place for the railroad. He had tried to buy it earlier and Sally refused him."

Marshal Price chuckled. "Heard about that. Wish I could've seen it."

Angus Hoeckerman nodded. "Me too." His chuckle soon had the other men joining him while the young ones looked from one to another quizzically.

"Oh, she laid into Charles that night. It was fun to watch." The memory drew a brief wry smile from Stone, but he turned somber again before picking up the story where he'd left off. "The morning she was killed, Charles took Howard with him to check on the Flater place. He wanted Howard in case the family hadn't left, and he needed someone with a gun to drive them off. As they rode past our house, Charles decided to ask Sally again." Stone shook his head.

"He left Howard and the horses on the road behind the house and walked down. I must have been in the barn at the time, but Charles didn't know that. When Sally refused him again, he slapped her. She fell and hit her head, and then he strangled her." Stone swiped at some moisture in his eye. "When he heard me coming, he panicked. Hit me with the fireplace shovel and knocked me out. Tried to kill me with a

Derringer he keeps, but he was shaking so bad he hit me in the arm."
His hand rubbed absentmindedly at the scar on his arm.

"That's about when those miners happened along. They were only
looking for water and directions. He bowled one of them over and
raced to Howard who had started for the house when he heard the shot.

"Charles raced into town to establish an alibi with Burke while
Howard started a gunfight with the miners to chase them off and
blame the whole thing on them."

The marshal picked up the story.

Stone's mind wandered from the conversation. He had other con-
cerns—like Sally's voice in his mind. The need for vengeance almost
turned him into a murderer, and that thought had kept him awake
half the night. Innocent men.

He picked up his coffee and the contents splashed over the
rim onto his hand. Quickly setting it back down, he glanced at his
still shaking hand.

He would let the law deal with Charles Willis.

There was still the matter of Cyrus Clinton. The grulla had been
back in the stable when the posse rode in. He was somewhere in
town. Clinton would have a hard time dry-gulching Stone with the
posse around and Stone wasn't fool enough to be goaded into a fight.
He doubted Clinton was interested in an old-fashioned brawl. Too
bad—be easier than Black Buffalo.

"The short one, they call him Shorty, got bowled over by Charles."
Price chuckled. "He looked through the door. Got sick when he saw
bodies and blood. Then they hightailed it out of there.

"Charles sent Howard along on the posse with the intent that
he make sure they never had a chance to tell their side of the story.
Figured if he went, some of his friends would too, and one of them
would get an itchy trigger finger. Got one killed by Indians and his
own son dead. Fool."

Quince Martin looked from Stone to Price a couple times as

if waiting for one of them to continue. He spoke up when neither did. "What now?"

Stone wondered the same thing. Wondering turned to pondering. What would he do? Go back to farming? Homestead wouldn't be the same without Sally and the constant reminder of her would drive him insane or at least to drink. The crop should have been in a few weeks ago. If Flater was still around maybe he could hire him to help out.

"Hey, Stone." Angus tapped him on the shoulder. "You gonna sit here all-night drinkin' coffee? Others went to their rooms twenty minutes ago."

Stone blinked and looked around. He and Angus were the only two still here besides Ophelia Singer, who flashed him a wide grin when his gaze swung to her.

"Maybe you need to get you a piece of that pie you were talkin' about." Angus nodded toward Ophelia and winked at Stone, his eyes dancing, and a mischievous smile wide as the Missouri River on his face.

"Funny. Why don't you?"

"Ain't me she's took a shine to."

Stone glanced at Ophelia. She was pretty and any shyness she'd displayed at first had since disappeared. He sighed. As he stood, he clapped Angus on the back. "Nope. More inclined toward Dancing." He smiled at his own joke, aware Angus had no idea what he was talking about.

"Dancing? What're you talkin' 'bout. I'm going to bed." He stomped off.

"Yah. Me too."

CHAPTER 24

THE RETURN TRIP to Yankton was without incident, but somber. Two young men dead—no one relished the thought of notifying their loved ones. Greed and hatred led to senseless tragedy once again. Both deceased young men were known to each member of the party, Howard better than Ernest. Yet, Ernest's parents belonged to the community, and the loss would impact the entire town.

The sun was high in the sky approaching its zenith as the remaining posse members de-boarded the riverboat that carried the men from Fort Pierre to Yankton. Much more river traffic headed toward Deadwood than away, so they'd found a boat able to accommodate everyone and the horses. The riverboat, working with the current, made the back half of the trip in a third the time and Marshal Price had been anxious to get back.

Price's speckled stallion was the first mount off the boat. Before any of the others were off-loaded, he had Zeus saddled and ready. Once mounted he gathered his posse. "No one leave here until I get back. I'm going straight to the courthouse to get an arrest warrant for Willis." He paused and stared at Stone. "Stone. We discussed this on the ride back. I'll handle this. You stay with the group and leave justice to the law. Have I made myself clear?"

Stone returned the marshal's stare but said nothing. After a minute had passed, he nodded.

"I want to hear you say it."

"I'll wait. Just don't take too long. Can't promise I'll wait all day." Despite Stone's realization in Deadwood, and his silent vow to leave justice to the law, his anger had grown over the course of the last five days. Standing on the dock, so close to the man who murdered Sally, he was no longer sure he could keep that vow. But he would try.

Price nodded. "That'll do. I'd hate to have to throw you in jail instead of Willis. Waste of a good man." He gigged the reins and rode away.

The posse men had long since run out of things to discuss, so they milled about watching the activity on the docks. Dock hands tied up a boat just arriving from St. Louis. Stevedores transferred cases to wheeled carts. The first down the gangplank were a stately old couple. They were followed by a well-dressed, middle-aged man with a young woman draped on his arm.

Men crowded the rails but were not disembarking, no doubt headed to the Black Hills to make their fortune. Why hadn't Frankie and his friends stayed aboard when they came through? The trip to Fort Pierre was faster by boat than overland. Stone hadn't thought to ask when he'd talked to them. What would have happened if they hadn't come along? He might never have known who killed Sally.

Emmitt tapped his shoulder. "Look there." He pointed to the street leading to town where a man on a smart little palomino charged toward them.

The man was young but carried himself like someone much older. Sunlight glinted off the silver star that adorned his chest. He and the pony both panted as if they'd sprinted from wherever they'd come from. "Which one of you's Stone?"

Stone stepped forward. "I am."

"Price told me to fetch ya. Gotta get ya to the courthouse fast. You others too." He whipped the horse around and galloped off. Passers-by scurried out of his way to keep from being trampled.

"You heard the deputy, let's ride." The posse hurried to mount up, and they raced to catch the lawman. Men and women, just recovering from the first rider, had to scamper to avoid the over-sized party.

———————

STONE DASHED UP the few stairs to the Territorial Courthouse and burst through the doors into the courtroom. The gallery benches held a smattering of men who scribbled furiously in their notepads. Stone recognized one as a newspaper reporter he had met a few years back. On the other side, a lean man in a fine business suit waved his arms in controlled arcs. He stood behind a table facing the judge.

"Your honor, he clearly abandoned his homestead, and thus, as the land bureau investigator has reported," the lawyer pointed to a document in the judge's hand, "you must revoke his deed and return it to my client for re-sale."

Seated next to the speaker was a large, dignified-looking man— Charles Willis.

Stone turned to Marshal Price. "Who're they talking about?" As if sensing the answer, his low voice held an unusual level of urgency.

"Before I tell you, you can't react. I got this handled so stay quiet." Price's whisper was so soft Stone had to strain to hear it.

"So, they're discussing my homestead." His whisper was louder but still quiet.

"Yes." He put his palm flat against Stone's chest when he took a step forward. "I told you. I'll handle this. Stay out of it until I tell you. Take a seat on the back bench." He glanced up as the posse men entered the courtroom, then waved them back out.

Stone scowled but sat as instructed.

"Marshal Price. What is the meaning of this? Can't you see I'm conducting a hearing?" The irritation in the judge's voice was also reflected in his face.

"Judge Thompson, I apologize for the intrusion, but I have information that pertains directly to the matter before the court. May I approach?"

The judge waved him forward. Stunned silence hung over the room so that the jingle of Price's spurs as he walked seemed an alarm of impending revelation.

The two put their heads together over the bench and whispered for a second.

"Judge," Charles's lawyer stood as he spoke, "am I to be allowed to be privy to this information?"

"In a moment, Mister Davenport." Judge Thompson waved him back to his seat. "Let me hear it first and determine if it does indeed pertain." He once again lowered his head to listen. Price handed the judge several sheets of paper. As the lawman continued to speak, the judge read the documents he'd been handed. His eyes grew wide, and his face reddened.

Stone's heart pounded in his chest. He couldn't take his eyes off Charles. The man poked his lawyer and pointed to the bench area. Davenport steepled his index fingers and tapped them against his lips. He shook his head at Willis.

At last, the judge motioned the lawyer forward. The three men whispered together. As Judge Thompson spoke, Davenport glanced back at Charles with his eyebrows knitted.

After several minutes, the judge waved the two men to step back. Davenport returned to his seat and whispered something to his client.

"Marshal Price." The judge eyed the lawman. "Please perform your duty."

"Yes, Your Honor."

A lump formed in Stone's throat. He couldn't swallow it.

The lawman turned to face Charles. "Charles Willis. You are under arrest for the murder of Sally Stone. Please come with me."

Willis's nostrils flared and the glare he shot his attorney might have killed the man. "What?" He turned his attention to Judge

Thompson. "How dare you? Do you know who I am? The governor shall hear about this." He spun on his heel to Price. "And you, lawman, had better start looking for a job because you'll be out of one before the end of the day."

"I don't think so. I have witnesses who will confirm everything. Including your son."

"My son would never."

"But he did. Strange what people will admit to when they're dying."

"What? Dying? My son is dead?"

"He is. Died trying to escape after shooting one of the miners you sent him after."

Life seemed to drain from Charles's face. Howard had been his only family, at least here. Howard's mother died of smallpox in 1869, and he was their only son. Charles had always doted on the boy.

Turning his attention to the judge, he sputtered, but nothing came out. Suddenly the big man exploded from his chair while he dragged a small pistol from his jacket pocket. He pointed it at the judge. "How dare you!"

Everything slowed down for Stone. He glanced at Price—thongs still held the hammers of his twin Peacemakers.

A woman screamed—he didn't remember any women in the courtroom.

The small caliber hide gun in Charles's hand wavered, but he had it cocked. His finger tightened on the trigger.

Stone stood and his hand dropped to the Colt on his hip.

Years of practice in the army returned in an instant. His thumb flipped the flap open, and he palmed the butt.

In one smooth motion, the weapon slid from its holster and leveled at Charles.

Charles's gun went off—a gout of flame shot from the barrel.

Stone fired.

Blood bloomed from Charles's ear, and he collapsed.

If the screaming hadn't done it, the gunfire certainly did. The door burst open. Emmitt was the first into the courtroom. "What the hell?"

Price rushed the few steps to Charles and knelt beside him. He bent his ear to the big man's chest, then checked the pulse in his neck. He looked to Judge Thompson and shook his head. As Stone had done for Howard, Marshal Price ran his hand over Charles's eyes to close them.

Silence replaced noisy chaos as soon as the gallery realized the significance of the marshal's actions. Death was common on the frontier but shootings like this were not. Stone scanned the room. Not likely more than a handful of spectators had witnessed a killing like this—right in front of them. Shocked expressions, blank faces, and gaping mouths told the truth of that.

Instinct and training had pressed Stone into action. This wasn't how he had wanted it to end. He walked to the front and stared down at Charles's body. Twice he opened his mouth to speak but nothing came out. Price stood and clapped him on the shoulder.

"Nothing you could have done. You know if you hadn't shot him, he might've killed Judge Thompson."

Stone continued to stare at the body, saying nothing, his shoulders slumped. Had Howard been telling the truth? Sure seemed so, yet now they'd never know. He'd killed the one man who could confirm the truth.

The doctor arrived and Stone stepped back to give him room. As he did so, he caught sight of the soles of Charles's boots. Something niggled at him just then. Mulling on it didn't bring anything to mind, so he knelt to look closer at the bottom of the boots. And then it struck him. Confirmation of the truth of what Howard had spoken. Across the heel was a single slash, just like the bloody print he'd seen the day after Sally's murder.

CHAPTER 25

THE MORNING SUN warmed his back. Sweat trickled down his neck, and he twisted his shoulders to relieve the tickling sensation. His arm rose and fell in even rhythmic strokes as he drove another stake into the ground. Sally had always tended the vegetable garden. The memory brought a tear to his eye, but he scrubbed it away. The tears came less often, but they still came on occasion.

Flater was hard at work with his head down and missed the display of emotion. The lanky German had readily agreed to hire on. Flater had rented a place in town after Willis had evicted them, but work was scarce, and he had a wife and four children.

The bullet Charles intended for Judge Thompson killed a perfectly good framed photo of the territorial governor instead. A thankful judge realized that the homestead hadn't been abandoned. And with Willis dead, there was no one to pursue a claim. He dismissed the case with the court's gratitude and a warning against vigilantism.

With the late planting, harvest was still a few months away. Thanks to Flater's hard work and skill, it shaped up to be a good year. Stone wiped his brow and went back to work. When the stake was secure, he scooped the tomato vines up and twisted a length of twine around them. He tied it off loose enough to allow the plant to continue to grow.

"Almost as good with that vine as cow pokes down Texas way

are with a piggin' string." The click of a gun's hammer accompanied the comment.

Stone froze. His heart thumped in his chest—he had allowed himself to believe Clinton was no longer a danger. He glanced in the direction of Flater.

"Lookin' for your man? Took the mule team over yonder." Clinton paused. "Waited a long time for him to leave."

Stone shifted to face the gunman.

"No, I prefer you facin' that-a-way."

Stone stopped. "So now what, Cyrus? Shoot me in the back?"

"Not above it. Gonna have us a chat first. Then might be we'll get down to the killin'. Hope for his sake your man stays away that long."

"Me too. So why are you here? Railroad can't get my land if I'm dead. I've seen to that."

"Funny you ask. My boss, this lil' runt of a man, requested I offer you a cash deal. Sign over your deed, and he'll let you cash out your livestock and equipment. Refuse, and, well, thet's why I'm here."

"Doesn't seem to be much to discuss, then."

"Nope, not really."

Stone's mind raced. He was sure Clinton did not intend to leave any witnesses. Yet, what choice did he have with a gun in his back? Nodding toward the house he'd built for Sally, he said, "Deeds up there."

"You first."

The two men walked to the steps. Stone used the thighs of his trousers to dry the sweat from his hands. His Henry—loaded and ready—was right inside the door where it always hung whenever he was home. His boots thudding on the wooden stairs was followed by the sound of Clinton's boots and the jingle of the Texan's spurs. They crossed the porch and Stone pushed open the door. His hand twitched as he prepared to make his move.

"Don't try it." The barrel of Clinton's weapon poked hard into Stone's back. "Won't be needin' that rifle."

Stone sighed. Cyrus chuckled.

The door banged shut behind him, and he led the gunman across the room to the narrow staircase. They climbed together, Clinton a few steps below.

Stone had re-arranged the loft. He gave Sally's sewing machine to Sven Larson's wife—she'd admired the piece several times and could sew almost as well as Sally. The bed was at the top of the stairs now. His trunk was underneath it on the stairs side. The arrangement prevented Clinton from sliding around Stone so instead was forced to stand on the stairs behind Stone, his head even with the middle of Stone's back.

"Nothing funny, now. Just get the deed and close 'er up."

Stone nodded as he tugged the trunk from under the bed. The bed rail prevented the lid from lifting more than a few inches, but it was sufficient for Stone to slide his hand in. He felt around inside the trunk with both hands until he touched the object of his search.

He steadied the holster with his left hand and yanked the Colt out from within the trunk, jabbed the barrel in the space between his chest and arm, cocked the gun, and then fired the weapon. He prayed he had the angle right.

The roar of the weapon in close quarters deafened him, and the flame from the powder explosion burned his shirt and flesh. As Stone turned to his attacker, another roar, loud despite the ringing in his ears, preceded white hot knives stabbing into his back. He jerked and tumbled down the stairs. Something soft broke his fall, and then the world went black.

CHAPTER 26

ORGAN MUSIC RANG throughout the sanctuary, but Stone barely heard it. He stared down the aisle of St. Paul's Episcopal Church. None of the impressive architecture caught his attention, though only yesterday he had been awestruck by it.

Strawberry-blonde curls cascaded over her lace-covered shoulders. Each deliberate stride carried Sally closer to him, and she smiled as their eyes locked on each other. An eternity later she stood before him.

Stone repeated by rote what the minister told him to say, oblivious to everything save her smile.

> *Do you, Judiah Stone*
> *Take this woman to be your*
> *Lawfully wedded wife?*
> *To have and to hold,*
> *From this day forward,*
> *For better, for worse,*
> *For richer, for poorer,*
> *In sickness and in health,*
> *Until death do us part.*

He had repeated his lines but still couldn't believe that this angel had agreed to marry him. It didn't matter to him that none of their family could come to the wedding. The owner of the dress shop came as witness and Stone grabbed his roommate from the boarding house, an Irishman named Homer, to serve as his. For now, all that mattered was that she was here with him. They would have a lifetime together—a lifetime to make their own family.

A sharp elbow poked him in the ribs. Stone whipped his head around.

"A'boot time ye turned around, ye fool." Homer thrust his hand out. "Here's the ring. Now be puttin' it on the lass's finger."

Stone was too happy to be embarrassed. He smiled and took the gold circle and gently slid it onto Sally's hand, repeating whatever words the minister told him to say. He couldn't say what they were—he was too busy remembering the day he first saw her. Joy filled his heart—the first real joy he'd experienced in five years. A tear threatened to form, but he forced it back.

Sally's warm breath broke his reverie and tickled his ear as she whispered into it. "Judd Stone. Don't you think it's high time you kissed me?"

Not the last suggestion of hers he would gladly follow, but it was the first as husband and wife.

CHAPTER 27

THE HUM OF conversation broke through the wall of consciousness.

"He gonna be okay?"

"When can we see him?"

"He needs his rest. Not even awake yet. Let him be."

Stone recognized the voices. He popped his eyes open and blinked back the intrusion of the bright daylight. Scanning the room, he realized he was at Doc Brady's again. "I'm awake, Doc."

Friends flooded the room despite the protestations of the wizened doctor. Flater and his wife were there, as were Larson and Jackson. Others too. Doc Brady shuffled through the press to his bedside, as hunched over as ever.

"How do you feel, son?"

"Fine, I think. How long have I been here?"

"Since yesterday." He turned and pointed to one of the men behind him. "Flater brought you in. Lucky for you he was close enough to hear the gun play."

"Where's Clinton?"

"Dead. Your bullet took him in the gut and would have killed him eventually, but he broke his neck falling down your stairs. Probably saved your life, since he cushioned your fall." He chuckled. "Ironic."

"How long are you planning to make me stay here?"

"Does it matter? You just go do what you want regardless of what I say."

Stone laughed and then winced as he grabbed at his ribs. "Guess I earned that."

Several men laughed with him.

"You should be fine in a few days. In the meantime, when your guests are finished, someone else needs to chat with you." Doc Brady waved to the corner of the room.

The crowd parted. Marshal Price sat in the oak rocker in the corner, a grim expression on his face. He nodded in greeting.

CHAPTER 28

AT THE TOP of the courthouse steps, Stone looked to the sky and took a deep breath. Letting it out slowly, he gazed at the bustling streets of Yankton. Tension drained from his face and body—he felt like a new man. He brushed his hands down the front of the new leather vest and black canvas shirt. "Seems kind of strange. Haven't worn brand-spanking new store-bought clothes since the army."

Marshal Price eyed him. "You wear them well."

Stone nodded but said nothing. After a quick trot down the few steps, he mounted Cordelia.

"Your business concluded?"

"Yup." He reached into the new vest's front pocket and pulled out a silver dollar. Flipping the circle into the air, he continued, "Sold the homestead to Flater." He caught the coin.

"Well, then you're buying drinks. If you don't mind me asking, how much he pay ya?"

"My full asking price." Stone flipped it again. "A whole dollar." Grabbing the coin, he smiled and slipped it back in his pocket.

"Then you're buying the first round. Spend all those profits. While we're discussing such things, here's some more silver for you." Marshal Price tossed something toward him. The sun glinted off the circle as it spun.

Stone snatched the object from the air. Palming it, he gazed down and admired the piece. Then he pinned the star to his chest.

"Come on, Deputy U.S. Marshal Stone. We have warrants to serve." Price nudged Zeus to a trot.

Stone pulled alongside. Ulysses trailed behind, loaded with packs. "Don't suppose our business will take us to the reservation, do you?"

"Likely. Why?"

Stone stared at the marshal with a sly grin. "Might be there's a woman I'd like you to meet."

BURIED IN THE family lore is the story about D.N. Sample's paternal great grandfather many times removed who was captured by a native raiding party during the French and Indian War. Though D.N. was never able to confirm it while his maternal grandfather lived, but the story is that he, for the love of a woman, passed on the opportunity to travel with a Wild West show as a trick shot artist.

Born near Buffalo—Buffalo, New York rather than Buffalo, Wyoming or actual buffalo herds—D.N. yearned for western adventure, so he dragged his wife and son west as far as Missouri, where he has resided since 1993.

D.N.'s lifelong obsession with the western genre began at a young age watching *Gunsmoke* every Saturday night with his father. Later, his grandfather's collection of Zane Gray novels—a collection he inherited—sucked him in. During college, D.N. discovered Louis L'Amour, whose novels were far more exciting than Systematic Theology. Forty years later, he's turned to writing stories about the old west and hopes to do justice to his heroes, both in real life, and on the pages of his favorite paperbacks.